THE
ANSWER IS
DAWN KIMBERLY JOHNSON

Published by
DREAMSPINNER PRESS

5032 Capital Circle SW, Suite 2, PMB# 279, Tallahassee, FL 32305-7886 USA
http://www.dreamspinnerpress.com/

The Answer Is
© 2015 Dawn Kimberly Johnson.

Cover Art
© 2015 Paul Richmond.
http://paulrichmondstudio.com
© 2015 Cover Photo
DWS Photography.
cerberuspic@gmail.com
Cover content is for illustrative purposes only and any person depicted on the cover is a model.

ISBN: 978-1-63476-229-8
Digital ISBN: 978-1-63476-230-4
Library of Congress Control Number: 2015905062
First Edition June 2015

Printed in the United States of America

This paper meets the requirements of
ANSI/NISO Z39.48-1992 (Permanence of Paper).

Chapter 1

"I WAS rushing across campus one afternoon, my head just spinning with everything I had to do, and spotted her sitting alone beneath that oak near the science building." Lonnie Bellerose shrugged and managed a smile as he explained to a group of art patrons how he'd come up with the idea for his thesis show. He shook the hair out of his eyes, but it fell right back.

"She looked so quiet and peaceful, so different from how I felt at the time, and that caught my eye. I began to notice her more frequently, always in the same spot, so one day I approached her and we talked." Lonnie gestured at the portrait. "Malloy plans to become a trial lawyer. The scar is from a childhood car accident, so she's had it for as long as she can remember."

The group stood silently and stared for a few moments. Then one of them muttered, "She's beautiful."

Lonnie smiled and turned toward the voice. "Yes, I agree. Malloy was my first subject. After that I began taking notice of other students who were often ignored, not part of the university brochure, or not looked at twice. And this is what's come of it," he said, sweeping his arm past the portraits lining the wall.

Members of the group smiled, nodded, and thanked Lonnie for his time before wandering away to corner the next graduate. One of the last, a vaguely familiar professor, shook his hand and congratulated him for his "intriguing work." Lonnie couldn't decide if that was a compliment, but he managed to pleasantly send the man on his way. His attention immediately went to the entrance as another person, who wasn't his boyfriend, joined the festivities.

Absently greeting someone else who crossed his path, he noticed the other graduate students each had family, in one form or another, attending the show, but he was on his own tonight, at least until his date arrived. He smiled. *My date.* Lonnie's twin sister was home with her newborn, her husband, and her in-laws. The elder Belleroses were still in France, collecting Lonnie's grandmother.

They had all sent their good wishes and expressions of pride for a job well done, and they promised a group celebration when they finally gathered in one room. Though disappointed, Lonnie understood and was fine with it. Each student had received a number of invitations for family and friends to attend on opening night, but he'd only needed one for Jamison. The rest he gave to other students who could use the extras.

A burst of laughter sounded to his right, and Lonnie jerked in that direction to see a father congratulating his daughter on her sculpture as the mother stood by snapping pictures of everything. Across the room he witnessed another artist explaining a photograph to his parents and younger brother. They appeared enthralled… well, his parents seemed to be. The brother looked as though he'd rather be anywhere else. The kid—about thirteen or fourteen—eyed the champagne flutes on the trays the waiters carried. *I see trouble ahead for that one.*

Lonnie sighed and hugged himself, trying to appear at ease as the crowd moved around the room. After all, he was an artist standing in a gallery that displayed some of his best work to date. He should be all smiles and charm and wit. Instead, he felt as though he stood out like a two-headed goat, afraid to move, all hooves and confusion, bleating above the conversations.

On top of that, Lonnie had the distinct impression of being watched. He couldn't shake it. He looked to his right and his left, then settled again on examining the campus beyond the wall of windows at the gallery's entrance. He searched the mist-shrouded grounds for any sign of Jamison, but he was nowhere to be seen.

"Here, have a drink, Mr. Bellerose." Professor Eloise Bink smiled and sipped her champagne, urging him to do the same from the flute she'd provided. She taught several art history classes, and Lonnie had been her assistant while earning his master's.

He took a sip, then said, "Just call me Lonnie, please. I'm not your TA anymore."

She smiled and tossed her short and sassy new haircut out of her eyes, the silver-gray strands catching the light. "I'll call you Lonnie when you call me Eloise."

He frowned in thought. "I think I can handle Bink but nothing more casual. Will that do?"

"Acceptable."

They sipped in unison, the bubbles nearly making him sneeze.

"You appear agitated. Waiting for someone?"

"Jamison's coming, though he should be here by now."

"No family?"

He shook his head. "Parents in France, Amber birthed a new human being, and brother-in-law is hovering, so... no. No family tonight." A chill ran through him, so he took another sip of his champagne. It didn't warm him, and this time he did sneeze, loudly, causing a few heads to turn in fright. His face heated, and he nodded his apologies before depositing the flute on a passing tray.

He turned to the entrance again and gasped softly. Through the floor-to-ceiling windows, he caught a glimpse of a tall, broad-shouldered silhouette hurrying toward the building. The campus lights along the path reflected off what little fog lingered above the lawn, giving the approaching figure a mysterious, superhero-like quality. To Lonnie, he seemed to be moving in slow motion and to his own soundtrack. Lonnie's heart soared, and he excused himself from Bink to cut through the crowd and meet his man at the door.

"Hi," he said, beaming up at Jamison as he walked in looking all kinds of gorgeous.

The worried frown on Jamison's face vanished as he smiled down at Lonnie. "Hi, yourself."

"You look fantastic." He stood on tiptoes to give Jamison a peck on the lips, but Jamison pulled back, the frown returning, his gaze darting around the gallery. Lonnie sighed, took his hand, and tugged him deeper into the room. "I have someone I want you to meet." He paused to look over the faces surrounding them, and when he spotted Bink again, he resumed his tugging.

Glancing around as he followed Lonnie, Jamison asked, "Isn't your fam—?"

"No," Lonnie said, "but they sent their congratulations."

"Ah, Lonnie, back so soon?" Bink said, turning to face the two of them as they reached her. She blinked up at Jamison, her expression remaining warm and friendly. "Whom do we have here?"

"This is Jamison Coburn. Jamison, this is Professor Eloise Bink. I've mentioned her before. I was her teaching assistant." His words rushed out as he gripped Jamison's big left hand tightly. *Mine.*

"Yes," Bink said. "I'm certainly going to miss you in that capacity. Perhaps I'll find something else for you." Lonnie laughed at that.

Jamison's hand swallowed hers. "Good to meet you, ma'am."

"And you, Mr. Coburn." She grinned at Lonnie before continuing. "Anyone who can make him daydream at his desk is definitely someone I want to get to know."

Lonnie gazed up at Jamison and caught the embarrassment as it crossed his handsome features. His chest filled with joy and pride that Jamison was here for him.

"Oh... I don't know about that, ma'am," Jamison said.

"Bink, Mr. Coburn. Please call me Bink."

"If you'll call me Jamison."

She grinned. "Agreed. Champagne?" she asked, grabbing fresh flutes from a passing waiter. She handed them each a glass, and they clinked them in a toast to Lonnie's accomplishment.

JAMISON SIPPED his drink, then turned to hide his grimace. Champagne was not going to be a favorite, which was good since he probably couldn't afford it. After several minutes of polite interrogation from Bink, she left to circulate while he watched the other fancy, educated folk meander about, gazing at the artwork, smiling, laughing, oohing, and aahing. He fought down the urge to loosen his tie and focused on Lonnie instead—the familiar, the miraculous.

I'm here with him.

It had been a simple statement on the face of it. A month ago, standing in a house he had helped renovate, he took the hand of the man he loved and uttered those four little words, outing himself to virtual strangers. It had rolled off his tongue, just as sweet as you please, but it meant so much. For Jamison, it was like stepping off a cliff. The moment it was out of his mouth, he had felt chilled, had braced himself for the sky to fall on his head, but that hadn't happened. Not yet, anyway.

One of the strangers was a longtime friend of Jamison's boss, Lincoln Frye. And surely the man would mention it to Lincoln— something along the lines of "I didn't know your boy Jamison was a faggot." To which Lincoln would undoubtedly say, "Neither did I!" and promptly fire him. But no, that word wouldn't be used. The stranger was related to Lonnie by marriage and knew Lonnie was gay... maybe not as gay as Christmas, but definitely gay as... *what? Easter?* Which was gayer? *How gay am I?*

A waiter approached him with a tray of tiny food. He knew he was supposed to take only one or two, but he was so hungry he wondered if the guy could be convinced to simply upend the tray into his mouth. With one hand captured by Lonnie and the other holding his nasty-ass drink, Jamison watched the food glide out of reach before he could even catch a whiff. He sighed and went back to watching Lonnie be delightful.

Since he came out, very little had changed for Jamison. He could count the number of people who knew about him on two hands. Aside from Lonnie—who knew better than anyone just how gay he was—there was his best friend, Torpedo, Jamison's mother, and his aunt Jo. They loved him and knew him best, especially now. *Finally.* They had various reactions: his mother was devastated and probably still in shock, Torp was unnerved but remained his friend and brother, and his aunt Jo seemed fine with it, had possibly seen it years ago. Who knew?

Cackling laughter broke out across the room, startling him, and he sipped his champagne, remembering too late that he hated the taste. *Gah!* He set the glass on a passing tray to make sure that didn't happen again and wiped a sweaty palm on his pants. His gaze found Lonnie again. He was animatedly telling some story to a couple of stodgy professor types. Jamison grinned.

Whatever happened down the line, the look in Lonnie's beautiful green eyes on the day Jamison claimed him had been worth it. He watched him now as he greeted and chatted with anyone and everyone who approached him. Lonnie appeared relaxed, but Jamison knew he was probably a wreck inside, uncomfortable with all the attention and fuss. He would need some comforting later.

Jamison grinned as wicked, lustful thoughts floated through his mind. He was going to peel his man out of that suit and—

"What are you thinking about?" Lonnie asked suddenly, staring up at him.

"Oh… uh," Jamison said, glancing around. "This is nice, this show…."

"Okay…." Lonnie smirked. "It shouldn't be much longer. Then we can head out."

"You can tell, huh?"

"That you're uncomfortable? Yes, but I'm right there with you, babe."

"You deserve to celebrate, Lon. You worked so hard for this."

Lonnie leaned against him and stroked Jamison's lapels. "There are things I'd much rather be doing with you right now."

The two of them had fallen into a comfortable routine of movies, meals, and spending hours in bed at one apartment or the other. Jamison smiled, recalling those hot, sweaty moments with Lonnie in his arms, followed by ice cream and cuddling. It was heaven.

This thesis show, however, was their first big-deal date in public as a couple. Lonnie had earned his master's, and Jamison had been determined to celebrate the event with him. He'd showered and dressed up, getting ready as he'd done in the past when taking out a woman. Tonight the people surrounding them might assume he was just a good friend of one of the artists—if not for the hand-holding, kissing, and possessive affection from Lonnie. It's not like they could look at him and know he was gay. Could they?

Jamison recalled how he had worriedly rushed around as he got ready earlier that night. Checking himself in the mirror, turning to see how the jacket he'd purchased fit across the shoulders, smiling widely to check for all-white teeth, then tilting his head to locate any errant nose hairs or… *other* things. He'd blown into his palm to sniff his breath, then checked the time. He'd patted his breast pocket for the invitation, his jacket pocket for breath mints, and his pants pocket for his keys. Then he'd headed for the gallery and Lonnie, trying not to think about all the college types he'd be mingling with, those educated, worldly people, people like Lonnie but so unlike him.

"And who's this?" an elderly lady with faintly lavender hair asked Lonnie, both of them gazing up at Jamison.

Lonnie smiled and touched his arm. "Oh, this is my—"

"Jamison Coburn, ma'am," he said quickly, smiling at her and taking her veiny hand gently in his. "Good to meet you." He thought he saw a bit of color reach her cheeks as she smiled and giggled like a little girl.

Jamison wished he'd been able to convince Torp to attend so he'd have someone to talk to while Lonnie was busy schmoozing, but his best friend hadn't wanted to be surrounded by the smarty-arty crowd any more than he had. However, for Lonnie? To support the most magical, wondrous man he'd ever met? Jamison would don "business casual" and do his best not to embarrass them both.

Chapter 2

JP LEANED forward and fingered the miniature snow globe on the desk because focusing on the pretty piece allowed him to avoid his new boss's assessing gaze. The globe held a gilded village caught in a snowstorm, a land where magic was possible, where love and miracles could happen. He picked it up and shook it hard, wreaking havoc upon the immobile, captive inhabitants.

"Let me get this straight," Stewart Dimple, his boss and former colleague, said. "You don't want a byline on this piece?"

"It's not a 'piece,'" he said. "It's a few lame paragraphs about a university art show. No one cares." *I certainly don't… or I* didn't.

"It's your job to make them care."

JP had nothing to say to that, nothing that would help him keep his job, anyway, such as it was.

"You may have been a big shot in Baltimore, able to write about whatever you wanted, but you fucked that up—"

"I know what I did—"

"—so now you write what you're told."

"Yeah, yeah, Stew." JP pointed at the computer on the big desk. "It's written, isn't it?"

He'd reluctantly attended the first fifteen or twenty minutes of the art show, talked to a couple of the artists and guests, asking questions to get enough color and details to fill a couple of column inches as quickly as possible. He had better things to do, men to do, but then… he'd seen Lonnie Bellerose walk out of a back room.

His Lonnie, the man he'd fucked over and mistreated before landing in rehab. JP had lingered out of sight, watching Lonnie chat with professors and art lovers. His hair was the same, wild. His light brown skin flawless. Same tight, lean-muscled body. He wasn't surprised by his cock growing hard, but the ache in his heart had caught him off guard.

Lonnie was apparently on his own for the gathering, and JP had considered approaching him, but changed his mind at the last second. He wasn't sure how he'd be received. Despite Lonnie's open, warm smile as he listened to attendees blow smoke up his ass, there was a sadness in his eyes, a sadness JP suspected he had caused. He felt a momentary twinge of guilt but dismissed it, heading out to find a bar and a fresh fuck to distract him.

Spotting Lonnie at the show was the main reason he didn't want a byline. The artist was sure to read the account of the evening, and JP wasn't ready for him to know he was back in town. "What's next?" he asked Stewart.

The man huffed and tapped a few keys on his computer. "There. No byline, as you requested." He shuffled a few papers on his desk. "Now this next assignment *will* require a byline. It's your typical 'local folks make good' series. Your profiles will anchor the Community page each week."

"Not really my purview, though, is it?" JP affected his most disinterested expression as he ignored the frown that clouded his boss's face.

"Given your history, not much is your purview anymore." Stewart slid a folder toward him and leaned back in his chair, hands clasped confidently over his abundant belly. "Your penchant for nose candy blew everything out of the water, so the crime beat or the mayor's office—one and the same lately—will need to be earned, regardless of your experience."

JP hesitated a moment before snatching up the folder. He didn't have a choice in the matter, and Stewart knew it, judging by the abundance of smug on his ruddy face. JP was aware he only had this job because Stewart and he had worked together for a few years in Baltimore before the guy had taken over the tiny *Overbrook Times*.

With his court-appointed rehab completed, the conditions of JP's probation were to stay sober, attend regular NA meetings, and stay employed. He'd just come from a morning meeting, his last for a few days. He did the minimum of two a week and now had an entire weekend free from listening to seemingly endless horror stories of loserdom. He'd never shared his own. His story was no one else's business, and of course, *he* wasn't a loser.

Speaking of losers, he thought as he opened the folder. It held his assignments, several lame human-interest pieces: some unwed mother had finally secured her college education, and her rug rats were oh so proud; an ex-con had opened an auto body shop; a grandmother and her grandson had won a national contest with a spectacular baked potato recipe. *Really?*

Spectacular? It's a potato. And some dude had lost his father as a boy—*boo-fuckin'-hoo*—but was now making his mark in Overbrook. *Oh my God, shoot me now.*

JP knew not to express his feelings out loud. After all, these stories would be the next step on the road back to his previous life. To his respected job, his luxury apartment in Baltimore, his friends. Though he'd been warned about the dangers of hooking up with former pals, people he used to get high with, he had plenty of other people who cared about him, people he had never partied with. At least he used to.

There was Carole—*Karen?*—from *The Baltimore Sun* front desk, a sensible mother of three who always asked how he was doing when he showed up for work; Stewart, currently sitting across from him, wheezing through his cigar-damaged lungs and watching him with beady black eyes; Lonnie, of course; his… his building maintenance man, whose name escaped him at the moment. They were, or had been, his friends. They had cared at one time… before he let it all go to hell.

He flipped through the files, giving them a quick scan and looking at the bare bones of data on each subject—age, story angle, contact information, photo. The pictures had come from various places: a graduation, a gym membership, community functions, the DMV, etc.

"Damn. That's one big dude," he said, pausing on one photo. He glanced at Stewart, who nodded. "He got a record?"

"Nope. By all accounts a good kid."

"How many baby mommas?"

"None that we know of." Stewart frowned. "His father was killed in a robbery of the family store when he was just ten. Raised by his mother. Been working at Lincoln Frye Home Improvement for years." Stewart sighed, leaned forward, and clasped his hands on the desk. "I think Frye is some sorta surrogate daddy."

"What's his deal? I get that he overcame adversity and blah, blah, blah, but—"

"Check the catalog."

JP turned another page and found a glossy sheet showing handmade furniture. "Damn," he whispered.

"Yup."

"He made these?" He met his boss's eyes in disbelief, then examined the catalog and photo of his subject again. The man looked like a destroyer of worlds, not a woodworking artist.

"Contact info's all there. Good luck."

Summarily dismissed, he replaced the snow globe and left the office, carrying the file with him. He made his way to his new cubicle. *Banished to live among the peons. Fabulous.* Well, he figured being arrested for cocaine possession, public intoxication, and destruction of property would do that for you.

He removed the photographs of his subjects from the file and stared at them for a moment before setting the furniture maker aside. "I'll save the best for last," he mumbled as he fingered the picture. The subject was a good-looking man. Unblemished dark skin, shaved head, and kind eyes, if you got past your initial fear. "So, Mr. Jamison Coburn," JP whispered, "what's your story?"

Chapter 3

THE IDEA formed in an instant. Like the afterimage of a lightning strike, it lingered behind his eyelids. As it continued to blossom, Lonnie lay in the dark, silent and still, pondering last night's festivities. *I'm done*, he thought. He'd earned his master's. *Now what?*

On his right Jamison slumbered, a warm wall of muscle. The man had seemed ill at ease throughout the show, not having much to say to anyone, not even to Lonnie, and basically grunting at the art. Jamison hadn't relaxed until they'd gotten back to Lonnie's, locked the door, and collapsed into each other. Jamison had deftly removed Lonnie's suit while nibbling at his neck and each inch of skin as he exposed it. Then Jamison had made love to him, carefully, slowly until Lonnie thought he might expire in bliss.

When the sky began to lighten and his boyfriend shuffled into the bathroom to get ready for his day, Lonnie immediately flicked on the bedside lamp, grabbed the pencil and sketchpad he kept under his bed, and began drawing. For half an hour, he worked, erasing here, smudging there, until he produced a skeletal black-and-white representation of what had appeared to him.

Lonnie quickly tucked it all away as Jamison reappeared in the doorway, wide-awake now—his large, powerful body shiny and fresh—and smiling at Lonnie with love and heat in his dark eyes. About an hour later, after sucking each other off and then gobbling their breakfast, they enjoyed a lingering good-bye kiss at Lonnie's front door. The perfect start to a great day.

Once Jamison drove around the corner, Lonnie hopped in his noisy Beetle and headed for the university. There he unlocked one of the art department's smaller studios, grabbed one of the larger canvases he'd purchased, and faintly recreated his sketch on it. From his art supply stash, he selected his palette, paints, and brushes and began mixing the colors before gradually adding them to the canvas. As he slowly breathed life and detail into the scene, his thoughts shut down, and the room around him faded and blurred.

A man possessed, he didn't let up, and several hours later, he added the final strokes, put down his palette, and stretched, popping his shoulders and back. He let his gaze travel over the painting, taking in every aspect of it, but instead of feeling satisfied and pleased, he felt a wriggle of doubt coil in his belly. Well, doubt or the result of skipping lunch.

At first glance the painting seemed fairly straightforward: two figures standing hand in hand on a rain-washed street and preparing to cross in traffic. One of the men was much bigger than the other, powerful-looking with a shaved head and dark brown skin. The other man had lighter but still decidedly brown skin and a mess of spongy curls on his head. They spilled into his face as he leaned forward a bit to watch for their opening, a safe place for them to dash across the street.

"Very nice, Mr. Bellerose."

"I thought we agreed last night you'd call me Lonnie?" Smiling, he turned slowly to face Bink, who stood in the doorway of the studio. "And thank you."

She approached, and nerves gathered in his chest. Bink didn't say anything more for several moments as she examined the piece. Then she frowned.

"What?" Lonnie asked.

"Calm down, son. I'm simply taking in your narrative."

He settled and waited, watching her. She would get to it eventually. Working as her teaching assistant as long as he had, he'd learned a while ago he couldn't rush her contemplations.

"There's hope in this image, feelings of possibility and excitement, but there's also trepidation, uncertainty even… danger?"

Lonnie turned to search his painting for what she was seeing. "Excuse me?"

She gave a throaty chuckle. "Oh, I think it's adorable the way you create without any awareness of your motivations. A lot of artists today create to make a statement, be it political or some social commentary, similar to what you accomplished with your thesis show—putting the spotlight on people who are in the shadows, avoided." She continued to stare at his painting, tapping her chin. "But usually, Lonnie, when you're deeply in the zone, so to speak, you create from your gut, putting on canvas your very insides and heart for the world to see... *and* interpret."

He examined the painting again for a few seconds, then turned to her and asked, "Why don't you lay it out for me?"

She smiled gently and stepped forward, taking a deep breath before beginning. "The two figures are holding hands. They support each other. The larger man, who I'm guessing is your Jamison, watches the smaller man—has to be you, considering that hair—but you're too busy searching for threats to see where his focus is."

Lonnie's face heated, but he said nothing.

"Are the finer details of their expressions missing because you don't yet know what he sees when he looks at you, or because you believe there's nothing there to express?"

Lonnie shrugged.

"The street is wet from a recent rain. A fresh start. The sun has broken through the clouds, signaling hope and joy. Look at how the pavement, normally grimy and worn, seems to twinkle like diamonds in the sunlight. Delightful. But," she said, pointing to the upper right corner, "there's heavy use of indigo here, alluding to storms headed their way." She faced him. "The question is, are these threats imagined"—she blinked at him slowly a couple of times, like a very smart cat—"or likely?"

Lonnie stared at the image, giving her words several moments to sink in.

"You want to talk about it, son?"

Not looking away from the painting, he said, "We said we love each other."

"That's a bad thing?"

"We've known each other for less than—"

"Irrelevant."

Lonnie gaped, ripping off his glasses, then his scarf to free his hair, which he felt explode over his head like a magician's trick bouquet. "It's hardly irrelevant, professor. What do we actually know about each other?"

She lifted an eyebrow, and it was her turn to shrug. "You made a handsome couple at the show last night, though he did seem a bit nervous, almost more so than you. But when in doubt, I find it usually helps to take stock."

He thought about that, his expression relaxing into a smile as his head filled with images and emotions wrapped up in Jamison. Then he sighed deeply and explained, "Well, he's strong, silent, and gorgeous, but he believes most people fear him on sight."

"Did you?"

He smirked. "No, but I'm not telling you my first thoughts upon meeting him. They are… inappropriate in mixed company."

She pouted. "Fair enough. Go on."

"He never went to college. He lost his father when he was a boy. He's recently come out to his mother—"

"Did she shun him or something?"

"No… I mean she's *not thrilled*, but I think she's got his back. I haven't met her yet."

"What else?"

"He's a gifted artist. Works with wood, furniture building." Lonnie's gaze settled in the farthest corner of the room.

"I see," she said, smirking. "What does he know of you?"

"You'd have to ask him."

"Oh, come now," she insisted. "You must have some idea, must have told him something about yourself."

"He likes to watch me work. In fact, he sort of hovered while I did the mural for Amber, seemed fascinated by it." Lonnie considered that. "I told him a bit about France, about my parents, and about my grandfather, the way he… the way he felt about me."

"Does he know about your ex, um…? What was his name?"

"Jerry. Jerry Pool, and no. He doesn't know about him."

"I see." She went silent and focused on the painting again, obviously waiting for—

"Say it," Lonnie urged.

"I think a man you're so interested in should know about an abusive relationship."

Lonnie scoffed. "It wasn't abu—"

"We've been through this, Lonnie," she said, stepping closer, her reliable outer calm unraveling somewhat. "They don't have to strike you to *hurt* you. A black eye or broken bone isn't necessary to undermine you, to tear you down, make you doubt yourself, make you feel... worthless." She glanced away and ran her fingers through her hair. When she turned back to face him, she was collected. "That's exactly what he did. I watched you change over the course of that relationship, and it was not pretty."

Lonnie stared at her in silence for several moments, then looked away. "I don't like thinking about JP."

"We never like to think of them, of that time, but it becomes part of you, whatever scars they managed to inflict," she pointed out quietly. "Besides, you told Jamison about your grandfather."

"Well, I'd had a nightmare, and he was... comforting me." Lonnie pulled at his hair. "It just came out!"

"No need to raise your voice."

"Sorry, but it's... difficult not to doubt. We spent a weekend together, we declared our love, and he gave my sister a rocking chair he'd made...." Lonnie brightened. Now that they were off JP, he hit his stride. "He's really quite talented. I'm thinking of taking him to the museum in Baltimore...." He sighed wistfully. "I just think at this point it should all be light and fun and 'look how delightful I am. Love me.'"

"According to you, he's already said he loves you."

Lonnie tugged on another strand of hair and ignored her observation. "Why lay all my strange at his feet so soon?"

She pointed to the painting. "You clearly have concerns about your future with him. But think of it this way. Since, as you say, you haven't known each other that long, most of what you have between you *is* future. It's unwritten. There's a lot of possibility there. Just take your time, feel your way, and be honest... with him and with yourself."

Lonnie nodded meekly.

"Now," she said, glancing at her watch, "I'm meeting my nephew for a late lunch." She turned and headed for the door but shouted over her shoulder, "Sign your piece, son. I suspect it will be in a gallery sooner than you think." Then she was gone, cutting off any chance for Lonnie to sputter and protest in false modesty.

He turned back to the painting and stared at it for a while. Hearing and saying "I love you" so soon wasn't his only worry. Jamison was also newly out. He'd told his mother and his best friend, but coming out was a process that never really ended. Meeting anyone new or running into a long-lost friend who only knew you as straight would mean doing it all over again. He wasn't sure Jamison realized that quite yet. And after enjoying years of passing, he faced giving that up… *for me*. Lonnie squirmed a bit, his skin tingling.

He put his glasses back on and, using the thin, hard end of a brush, scratched *Alonzo Bellerose* across the bottom of the painting.

Chapter 4

JAMISON CARESSED the wood, searching for any rough spots or imperfections with his bare, calloused fingers. His gaze followed behind his hand, gliding along the bench edge, the raised back, down the right foot and then the left. He felt a jagged area inside the Shaker arch of the left foot and paused to grab a small square of sandpaper to smooth it out. When done he rose and stepped back from the bench. He'd used maple and planned to finish and seal it with a mixture that would protect but also show off the beauty of the grain. The bench would turn heads on Lincoln's showroom floor.

After a long day of demolition and carting debris to the bigass dumpster onsite, he'd decided to pay his mother a visit. He hadn't had clean clothes at Lonnie's that morning and didn't want to walk into his mother's house stinking of labor and sex. So he'd rushed back to his garage apartment for a quick shower and change.

The place was only big enough for one, but it allowed him to live in a nice area at a rent he could afford. The odd jobs he did for the owners of the main house, Edgar and Cora Standlea, didn't hurt. Edgar had aged beyond cleaning gutters and trimming trees, so Jamison handled anything Edgar couldn't any longer, and they thanked him with lower rent, homemade baked goods, and the occasional invitation to dinner.

The drive back to his old neighborhood had been as uneventful as ever. He no longer noticed the homes growing more and more haggard as he went, though the closer he got to his mother's place, the better maintained the homes and lawns became again. Perhaps they weren't as grand as where he lived now, but the people he'd grown up around clearly took pride in ownership.

After arriving at his childhood home, he'd headed straight for the garage in back and opened up his workshop. He'd planned only to work for an hour or so, but he quickly lost himself and vaguely remembered his mother coming out with a glass of lemonade, a hug, and a kiss, then disappearing again. Now, several hours later, she appeared again.

"You gonna eat with me, baby?"

Jamison turned toward his mother, Alanna, who stood in the back door of her house watching him. He wondered how long she'd been standing there, and he suddenly felt guilty. The original reason for stopping by was to see her, catch up with whatever was going on in her life, but instead he'd ended up working on his latest piece in her garage. He'd heard it calling to him, urging him: *finish me, make me pretty, show me off.*

His living arrangement didn't leave any space to store his equipment, let alone use it. Jamison supposed a decluttering of the Standleas' garage—a family's furniture and keepsakes collected over the decades—could make room. But deep down he knew keeping his equipment where it was would please his mother. It meant he would always come back. Tonight she probably thought he was avoiding her, but that wasn't his intention. Unfortunately, now he had to leave.

"No, ma'am. Thank you, but I'm taking dinner over to Lonnie. He's babysitting tonight."

He saw disappointment play over her beautiful features, but she quickly brightened.

"How is that new baby?" she asked as he shut down and secured any tools he'd used.

"He's fine, but Remmy's just a month or so old, Mama. He doesn't do much." *He just sort of lies there… and leaks.*

He turned off the light and locked up before joining her at the back door. After following her inside, he turned on the security light and bolted the door behind them.

"Everything a baby does, no matter how tiny they are, is precious. It's hard to believe you were ever that small. And Remmy? What sort of name is that?"

"Short for Rembrandt. Some famous painter."

"Lordy, what will these people think of next?" she asked as she opened the refrigerator and removed a pie dish.

Jamison's mouth began to water at the thought of homemade peach pie.

"Does he… does your friend babysit his nephew a lot?"

Jamison shrugged. "Uh… so far the baby's been passed back and forth between his parents and grandparents. This is Claude and Amber's first night out in weeks, and since Claude's parents finally left, Lonnie's jumping at the chance to have Remmy all to himself tonight before the next pair of grands arrives in a couple of days."

"Well... do you think you should intrude?" she asked as she cut two pieces of pie and placed them on a sturdy paper plate.

"Intrude?" Jamison frowned as she secured a sheet of plastic wrap over the pie and plate. "I'm surprising him with dinner. I...." He hesitated as he thought it over. "I don't think he'll see it as intruding, Mama."

She nodded without looking at him, then sighed. "Where are the other grandparents?"

"In France. There's a family farm there."

She nodded. "I see."

"They were supposed to be here right after the little guy arrived, but since the paternal grands were already here, they decided to take their time, get Great-Grandma Bellerose ready to travel."

She nodded and held out the pie-filled plate. "Take this with you for dessert, baby."

Jamison smiled. "Thanks, Mama. I appreciate it." He leaned in and kissed her still-smooth cheek. "Lonnie will appreciate it too." He held the plate in one hand and bent over to hug her tiny frame with the other arm. "You know, if you'd like to meet—"

She pulled away suddenly and held up a hand to silence his suggestion. "No... no, baby. This is fine. Just fine," she said, not looking at him. "You have a good night with your friend."

Jamison deflated a bit and allowed her to usher him to the door. "Good night, Mama. I promise to spend more time with you next time." As always, she watched until he climbed in his truck, then shut her door. He stared out his windshield at the neighborhood, the streetlights creating puddles of illumination every few yards, and wondered at her comment. *What does "I see" mean? Does it mean anything?* No. He was reading shit into it, feeding it with his own doubts about him and Lonnie. They enjoyed each other. What else mattered?

Before starting the truck, he glanced at the house again and caught his mother peeking at him through a curtain. As he pulled away from the curb, he tapped out a quick good-night on his horn, then turned onto Little Avenue and headed for Ming Empire to pick up dinner. On the way he allowed his mind to fill with memories of the first day he'd met Lonnie.

He remembered Lonnie pulling up in that noisy VW Bug of his, while he and Torp unloaded cabinets for the Palmers' kitchen. What had sealed the deal for him? Was it the way those shorts had hugged Lonnie's ass? His green eyes? That smile? His clumsiness? The insecurity he tried and failed to hide? That ridiculous hair, just made for tangling your fingers in?

Or was it Lonnie's artistic ability?

Jamison smiled to himself as he recalled sneaking up to the nursery at the Palmers' to get a peek at the mural Lonnie was working on, at the time little more than a faint pencil sketch on the wall. Then, weeks later, it had blossomed into a striking landscape of the Bellerose family's farm in Cognac, complete with an image of young Lonnie drawing alone in the courtyard while his twin sister Amber dangled upside down from a tree she'd climbed.

Whatever the attraction was, Jamison found Lonnie Bellerose mesmerizing, a balm to his otherwise chaotic thoughts and worries. The man had driven into his life and upended it, quieting the internal conflict he'd felt for so long over being closeted and trying to live up to his father's example. Lonnie was home and peace, and the last thing Jamison wanted was distance from him. But he could sense Lonnie holding back. *Why? Have I done something wrong?* He sighed. All he seemed to have were questions. Maybe he should put them to the man himself.

Earlier that day similar thoughts had nearly caused him to injure his best friend. If Torp hadn't ducked, Jamison would have knocked him in the head with a load of paneling he was carting to the dumpster. There would have been blood to clean up or possibly a trip to the hospital.

Jamison tried to apologize while Torp shouted at him, and their boss, Lincoln, came out of the house demanding to know what the hell was going on. Embarrassed, Jamison had dutifully repeated Lincoln's site safety rule: "Rushing on the worksite leads to rushing to the ER."

When he went on to explain he was simply hoping to carve out time to visit his mother, Lincoln's expression had softened. "Oh, how is Alanna, son?"

"Uh… fine, sir."

Lincoln nodded, wiping sweat from his dark face, and his tone became brisk once again. "Well, tell her hi for me, and"—he paused at the back door—"you might want to think about getting yourself a girlfriend. You're nearly thirty, aren't you?"

"Next month, sir." Jamison frowned in confusion.

Lincoln had continued into the house, grumbling, "You should be rushing off to meet your *lady* instead of your mama."

Smiling and shaking his head at the memory, Jamison pulled in at the drive-through and placed his order. After he collected his meal and pointed his truck in Lonnie's direction, his mind once again turned to earlier in the day.

His best friend had had some questions of his own for him.

"So...," Torp had shouted above their demolition efforts, "how are things?"

Jamison wiped his face, chugged some water, and then asked, "What things?"

"Between you and Lonnie? Don't think I didn't notice you didn't correct the boss's romantic advice."

Jamison shrugged. "No need to." It was only a matter of time before his boss found out. Lincoln was fairly friendly with Jamison's mother, attending the same church and all. And although she wasn't exactly shouting from the rooftops about her son dating a man, it was possible she might confide in Lincoln at some point, or ask his advice on how to *fix* him. He continued to worry about how his boss might react when the inevitable happened—maybe even feared it a little.

"Right." Torp had grinned knowingly. "You think he'd have a problem with you likin' dudes?"

"Don't know. Don't care."

"*Right.*" Torp nodded, gazing at him through narrowed eyes.

"Stop sayin' that, will ya?"

"Why?"

"Because it sounds like you think I'm full of shit."

"Your words, not mine, bro," Torp said. "And for the record, I don't. Look, you told me. You told your mama. You can tell Lincoln. He's known you almost as long as I have, Jam."

Jamison had frowned. "Maybe I'm telling people as I need to." It's not something he'd announce. He didn't even know how to begin that conversation. "There's no need to introduce Lonnie to my boss."

Torp's eyes widened at that. "You mean you introduced him to your mama?"

"No! I mean, not yet. She ain't ready for that. Lonnie's not ready for that. Hell, *I'm* not ready for that. Besides I haven't met his parents yet. They're still out of the country."

Torp nodded. "Fair enough, but you should know Kimmy wants to meet him. We could double date or somethin'. Maybe a movie?"

That brought Jamison up short, and he nearly lost his balance with the latest load of debris he was carrying. "Really?" He couldn't stop a smile from breaking through as he imagined the four of them going out together. That had sounded safe, just friends gathering for dinner. "Great! We'll set it up… soon."

Now, as he headed for the Palmers' place, Jamison wondered about not correcting Lincoln. A simple "I'm good, boss. I have a boyfriend" would have done the trick, but he hadn't said anything. His throat had seemed to seize up. The urge to speak was there, but he couldn't vocalize it.

Torp would soon be a married man, with priorities other than getting drunk every weekend. But truth be told, that behavior had already been curtailed with Kimmy in his life. The noose, or leash, was tightening, and Torp had never been happier… much like Jamison had never been happier now that he and Lonnie were together. But being a married man, a husband, and a father were things Jamison had seen around him every year of his life. He had examples. He had community.

Not so on the gay front. After being on the down low for years, snatching whatever anonymous release he could with strangers, being in a relationship with a man, being out and proud or whatever? That wasn't something he felt comfortable navigating publicly. He was terrified Lonnie might mistake his inexperience and hesitancy for doubt about the two of them. The last thing he wanted to do was add to the insecurity Lonnie thought he was hiding so well.

He had to figure out how to walk through the world as a gay man, holding Lonnie's hand, kissing him, making him feel special. *I am a gay man*, he said to himself. *I'll just keep walking, I guess. See where it takes me.* As long as Lonnie was there beside him, he knew everything would be all right.

Chapter 5

"WHERE'S MY little man?" Lonnie cooed as he entered the nursery. Remmy stirred, kicking his feet at the sound. He stuffed a pudgy fist in his mouth and began to gum it in earnest as his uncle neared the crib. Lonnie liked to believe Remmy would soon recognize his voice or, if not that, the shape of his hair. After all, he had grabbed any moments he could—which weren't many with Claude's parents hovering—to feed his nephew, maybe change a diaper, or just sing to him.

He leaned over the crib and checked Remmy's diaper before gathering up the newest Palmer in his arms. He patted the baby's back and stroked his curls while humming a soothing tune as he crossed to the changing station.

He was thrilled to have this one-on-one time with the little guy. Remmy's paternal grandparents had left just yesterday, and Lonnie had a small window of a few days before his own parents blew into town, back from their extended stay in France. They had planned to arrive only days after Remmy's birth, but there was some legal business to take care of at the family farm, which took weeks longer than expected. Now Grandma Bellerose would be tagging along too—well, she was a great-grandmother now.

"Would you like that? Would you like to meet your great-grandmother?" he asked softly. "Let's get you changed, okay?" For a moment he fought the wiggly legs and feet to unsnap Remmy from his onesie. "Hold still." He laughed. "You're a feisty little pooter, aren't you?" He removed the fouled diaper, grabbed a wipe, cleaned Remmy's bottom, and added a dab of rash cream where needed. "A dash of powder, close the new diaper, snap snap snap, and you're all set. Hooray," he sang gently, waving his fingers beside his own face as he smiled down at the baby. "All dressed and"—Remmy sucked fiercely at his little fist—"clearly starving."

"There are two of my three favorite… oops, four favorite men," Amber said as she entered the nursery. "Nearly forgot Dad. How's my little one?"

After a quick squirt of hand sanitizer, Lonnie scooped up Remmy and cradled him. "He's clean and dry and hungry for Mommy's ta-tas."

"Lonnie!" Amber admonished. She softly cupped Remmy's round head as she gazed at him, and in a gentle singsong voice, she said, "Mommy's milk is in the back of the fridge, isn't it, baby? Yes, it is." She turned to Lonnie and took in his smiling face. "What?"

"You sound like an idiot."

"Oh, go fu—*forget* yourself."

Lonnie laughed. "Nice save."

Amber smirked as she looked Lonnie up and down, taking in his lemon-yellow sweat shorts and his black T-shirt bearing the image of red, high-top Converse dangling by their shoestrings. On his feet were old flip-flops, each with one large purple plastic daisy on the toes. "You *look* like an idiot," she declared.

He twisted and turned, trying to examine his clothing while holding the baby. "Why? I need to be comfortable while I watch after your spawn, sis." Lonnie preened, making Amber giggle. "Besides, I make this work," he declared as he continued to sway.

"Yeah, keep telling yourself that. There's no one who could make *that* work." She reached out and tenderly brushed some curls out of his eyes. "Anyway, thanks for doing this, little brother."

"Ten minutes younger does not make me your little—"

"Claude and I haven't had a moment to ourselves for weeks, and I'm eager to connect with *mah man*."

"Uh… you do that in the restaurant, and you'll be arrested."

Amber glared at him, but he caught the smile playing at her lips. "Ha. Ha. You know exactly what I mean, silly: dinner, adult conversation, gazing into each other's eyes over candlelight." She grabbed Remmy's foot and mouthed his toes for a moment before saying, "You know, all the things that led to this little fella right here."

Lonnie frowned. "Hmm, I thought Bruno Mars and tequila shots led to this little fella."

Amber snorted but remained mum on the subject.

"Seriously, how are you feeling?" he asked after watching her gaze at her son for a moment. "Are you really up for a night out?"

"We're having dinner, not going dancing." She sighed. "There's hardly any pain, but I run out of steam more quickly. That's no fun. We'll make an early evening of it. I want to get a good night's sleep."

Remmy squalled, and Lonnie bounced gently to settle him down.

"Hmm," Amber said, frowning, "maybe I should warm a bottle before I go?"

"I can warm the bottle just fine. You and Claude get going before you lose your reservation."

Lonnie's stomach growled loudly, and Amber's eyes widened in surprise before the two of them dissolved into laughter. "Have you eaten today?" she asked.

"A bit."

"A candy bar from a vending machine is not a meal, Lon."

He shrugged. "Got inspired early this morning and went straight to the studio to get it done."

She leveled an older-sister glare at him, then reached out and tried to pat down his hair. "How are you and your big handsome man doing?"

"We're good," he said, beaming so widely his jaw ached.

"I sort of hate to leave you here all alone."

"Only 'sort of'?"

"Well… I don't want you fainting from lack of nourishment. You know there are a couple extra bottles of breast milk in the fridge if you get desperate." Holding her tummy, tender from the C-section, Amber laughed heartily at Lonnie's revolted expression.

"I won't be alone. I've got Rembrandt C. Palmer to keep me company."

The doorbell rang, and then they heard Claude say, "Come on in!" but everything after that was too muffled to make out.

Amber and Lonnie shared puzzled looks, then both silently agreed—communicating in that way some twins do—to head downstairs. After taking it slowly for Amber's incision and the baby, they reached the bottom to find Jamison standing in the entryway next to Claude and holding a bag of carryout and a plastic-wrapped plate.

"Hi." Lonnie grinned uncertainly. "What are you doing here?"

Jamison's gaze flicked from Lonnie's head to the daisies at his toes, and his smile broadened. "I thought you could use some company while you babysit Remmy. Well, that and some dinner." He held up the bag.

Lonnie gasped. "God bless you!"

"He's not kidding," Amber said as Claude helped her on with her coat. "His stomach growled so loudly a moment ago, the windows rattled."

Ignoring her, Lonnie crossed to Jamison and leaned up to kiss him. Remmy, squashed between them, squawked in earnest, and Jamison jumped back.

"Oh, hey, little dude," he cooed, but the timbre of his voice apparently wasn't pleasing to Remmy's ear because he wailed louder. "Sorry about that." He looked to Lonnie and Amber for forgiveness.

"He's just hungry," Lonnie explained quickly, "like his uncle. Follow me." He turned his back on his sister and Claude and headed for the kitchen, shouting, "See ya later, guys. Have fun."

"They'll be fine, dear," Claude reassured as his wife hesitated.

Jamison unpacked their dinner, spreading the containers out on the kitchen island he had helped install last month, while Lonnie heated Remmy's milk, then settled on a stool to feed him. Munching on chicken, Jamison pointed at them with chopsticks and said, "I thought baby bottles were bigger than that."

"Nah. He drinks a few ounces at this stage," Lonnie explained. "He'll get a bigger bottle when he's a bigger boy." He cradled the infant in his arms, smiling and talking softly to him as Remmy drank hungrily, blinking up into his uncle's face and reaching for his hair with pudgy fingers.

Jamison stifled a snort too late, drawing Lonnie's attention from Remmy. "What?"

Pointing at them, Jamison said, "I was just thinking how much you and your sister look alike. Do you think he knows you're not her?"

Lonnie frowned and thought about it. He looked back down at Remmy and smiled widely. "Of course he knows. We may resemble each other, but we don't smell the same, we don't sound the same, and I'm not… uh, cushy up top like she is."

"Especially lately," Jamison muttered.

"Pardon me?" he asked, raising an eyebrow.

"No, wait," Jamison said, laughing and trying not to aspirate the sweet and sour sauce he'd just squirted in his mouth from an errant packet. "I'm sorry." He began hurriedly dishing out the rest of the food. "It's just that Torp had noticed Lincoln's office manager, Cartha. She's pregnant, and the 'titty fairy'—his words, not mine—has arrived. I didn't mean nothin' by it."

Lonnie looked past Jamison into the living room and noted the family photos on the shelves and walls, so it was likely Jamison detected the significant change in Amber's curves of late. "Well, I like that explanation a lot better than believing you checked out my sister's rack," he said.

"Your sweet rack is the only one I want, babe."

Lonnie tried not to smile at that but failed; then, as the aroma of the food filled the air, he licked his lips and eyed the steam rising from it. "Oh God, I'm starving," he said after he set the baby bottle down, carefully repositioned Remmy on his lap for burping, and began gently patting the baby's back while leaning him forward against his palm. "You can either feed me or burp this here baby while I eat."

Jamison's eyes went wide. "I'll feed you."

"Really?"

Jamison shook his head. "I can't hold the baby." He held up his hands, one of which could nearly hold Remmy in his entirety. "I might break him."

Lonnie chuckled. "Okay. If you say so."

"Which do you want? We got broccoli beef, sweet and sour chicken, spring rolls, or…. Mama sent homemade peach pie? You name it, it's yours."

"Oh, that was nice of her." He thought about it. "Spring roll, please, sir. I need something quick."

Jamison sprang into action and dug out a roll to hold to Lonnie's lips—waving it in front of him, letting him catch the scent, then pulling it back when he went to take a bite. The first time earned a grin, but the second time earned a glare, so Jamison stopped playing and let him capture the roll. The satisfying crunch and flavor burst in his mouth, and he moaned around the food. The arousal in Jamison's eyes did not escape his notice.

"Good?" Jamison asked as he watched Lonnie's mouth work.

"So good. You have no idea."

"You have a bit of shell… just… there," Jamison said, pointing to the corner of Lonnie's lips.

"Got napkins?" Lonnie asked, looking among the little white boxes littering the island.

"I got it," Jamison said.

He leaned closer, and Lonnie couldn't help grinning as he realized what was coming. They kissed, Jamison's tongue darting out to collect the errant crumb. Jamison hadn't lied about it, but Lonnie had no doubt he would have in order to steal a kiss. *Can you steal something that's already yours?* he wondered. He laughed softly and kissed Jamison back, but a gentle burp from Remmy pulled them apart.

"Oop, we have liftoff." Lonnie placed a cloth diaper over his shoulder and lifted Remmy to it. "Good boy," he cooed as he rubbed the baby's back. He glanced at Jamison. "How does he look?"

Jamison leaned over to look at Remmy. "Hmm, he looks sleepy and puke-free," he whispered.

Lonnie carefully got up to take the baby to the den, where his sister kept a bassinet for naps during the day. When Lonnie returned to the kitchen, Jamison was chowing down on some broccoli beef.

"Sorry. I didn't want it to get cold," Jamison said.

"It's fine, babe." He placed the baby monitor he'd grabbed from the den—its twin rested next to a slumbering Remmy—on the island between them and took his seat. "Gosh, this smells so good. I'd better dig in because the moment Remmy's wet or bored or hungry again, he'll be howling for attention."

They ate in silence for several moments, and Lonnie could feel Jamison's gaze on him as he enjoyed his meal. Then Jamison went all domestic and asked, "How was your day?"

Lonnie blinked at him a couple times while he chewed. "Uh, I spent most of it painting at the university. Bink stopped by and gave me her opinion."

"A new piece, huh? Can't wait to see it."

"You will," Lonnie said, squirming. "I promise." He popped a chunk of broccoli in his mouth. "What did you accomplish today?"

"Worked on a demo on East Avenue, then went by Mama's to work on a Shaker bench I'm building."

"I bet it's gorgeous," Lonnie said, his face lighting up. Jamison smiled shyly. "I'd love to watch you work sometime." He hoped his watching wouldn't be a distraction, but like Lonnie, Jamison could probably tune out the world while he worked, when he was in the zone.

The smile on Jamison's face faltered, but he said, "Sure. We'll pick a day to do it."

Chapter 6

AFTER EATING they moved to the living room sofa, where Jamison hoped to make a meal out of something else entirely. The peach pie could wait. He plopped down on the cushy piece of furniture and spread his legs, inviting Lonnie to stand between his knees, which he did with a knowing smirk. Jamison slid his calloused hands beneath Lonnie's T-shirt, lifting it, mapping the hard planes and contours of his abdomen. He grinned when Lonnie shivered beneath his touch and pulled him forward to kiss his faint treasure trail. Or course, Lonnie snorted and tried to squirm away from Jamison's insistent lips.

"Oh no, you're not going anywhere, mister."

"Jamison!"

"Shh.... Lon, the baby," he warned.

"The baby?" Lonnie whispered, caressing Jamison's head and tickling his ears. "The baby is sleeping."

Jamison stopped his nibbling long enough to look up into Lonnie's aroused gaze. "He won't be if you keep shouting like that."

Lonnie pulled his own shirt off over his head and straddled Jamison's lap, where he ground against him. Jamison pressed his hand against the tented front of Lonnie's sweat shorts, enjoying the heat and hardness, and making Lonnie moan and push back.

They kissed desperately, but then Lonnie gasped, "What if I promise to be quiet?", bit an earlobe, and deftly opened Jamison's belt and jeans. He reached inside, and Jamison threw his head back, praying for control and calm as Lonnie gripped him.

He loved it when Lonnie took charge. Even though he was much smaller in build, he wielded power with his green gaze. It kept Jamison riveted to the spot, shivering beneath Lonnie's touch and dazed by his smile.

"Not possible," Jamison said, panting softly.

They locked eyes, continuing to stroke each other, then kissed slowly, lingering, nipping and licking their way forward into a deeper lip-lock, drawing deeper and faster breaths, urging each other on. Lonnie stopped suddenly and removed his heavenly hand from Jamison, who bit off a curse. Grinning, Lonnie whispered, "If you don't want me shouting, then we'd better stop now."

Jamison's reaction was instantaneous. Retaking charge, he flipped Lonnie onto his back, pinning him to the sofa. A startled gasp escaped Lonnie, but then he laughed softly and gazed up into Jamison's eyes as he hovered above and tangled his fingers in Lonnie's hair, tugging gently.

The scent and heat pouring off Lonnie's skin made Jamison dizzy with need, his muscles jerking, convulsing as he fought to control himself, to take his time, a tug-of-war he'd surely lose in the face of the beautiful, tantalizing man in his arms.

Lonnie reached out and traced the contours of his chest through his shirt, pinching his nipples. "You with me?" he asked softly.

"Always," Jamison whispered.

Their gazes never left each other as Jamison drew his fingers down Lonnie's bare chest. He watched the muscles beneath the light brown skin jump and twitch as his hand neared Lonnie's lower abdomen. Lonnie's eyes were dark now, half-lidded with want, and he squirmed to be set free. Jamison brushed a hand over the firm heat within his shorts.

"H-hey, big guy, surely you've got better uses for that," Lonnie prodded. Jamison's smile grew, and he peeled Lonnie's sweats and briefs off him in one quick motion, drawing a whimper from him and revealing his beautiful cock. It rose from a thatch of soft, dark curls, heavy and hot, curving back to kiss Lonnie's abdomen, leaving a trail of sticky pearlescence behind.

Jamison lowered himself between Lonnie's legs, lifted one of them over his shoulder, and buried his face against Lonnie's crotch. He breathed deeply, and his exhalation sparked a sharp wriggle from Lonnie, but there was no escape. Jamison created a scent memory of him—knowing him, claiming him. He licked and nibbled both of Lonnie's balls before taking a swipe up the length of his cock. He chuckled softly when Lonnie cut off a cry, slapping his hand over his mouth in deference to Remmy.

He felt Lonnie's fingers trying to gain purchase on his shaved head and knew Lonnie wished there was a head of hair to latch on to—it had been mentioned more than once—something to anchor him, to keep him from flying apart. Jamison certainly understood. When their positions were reversed, he liked having those curls of Lonnie's at hand. All he had to offer for a grip were his smallish ears, and they were hardly adequate or capable of keeping someone from flying off the surface of the earth and scattering in a million different directions, never to be whole again. At least that's how Jamison felt when Lonnie set him off.

When he licked back to the top of Lonnie's cock and lingered, making eye contact before closing his lips over the head, Lonnie tried to lift off the sofa, tried to go deeper, but Jamison wouldn't allow it, holding his hips firmly against the cushion.

Lonnie moaned and whimpered, thrashed and bucked, prompting Jamison to release his cock with a noisy, slurpy *pop*. "Shhh, Lon," he warned.

"N-need…," Lonnie hissed.

Jamison claimed his cockhead again, but this time he kept going, swallowing Lonnie at a painfully slow glide. Jamison was too busy relishing the hard, hot weight of Lonnie against his swirling tongue to consider what a pretty picture he made; too busy listening to each blissful sound and utterance; too busy enjoying the tickle of Lonnie's dark curls against his nose; and too busy clocking every tremble and gasp. It wasn't long before the reliably vocal Lonnie shouted, "J-J-Jam!" and erupted, spilling down his lover's throat and quenching his thirst.

Ding-dong!

Startled, Jamison let Lonnie's cock fall from his mouth, rose up on the sofa, and stared at the entryway. "Lon…. Lonnie?" he whispered urgently, frantically shaking Lonnie's thigh to get his attention. He looked unconscious but happy, and for a second, Jamison smiled down at him. He knew the moment Lonnie heard the knocking, as his pliant body suddenly stiffened and his eyes widened.

Lonnie leaped up off the sofa and immediately pitched forward on unsteady legs, but Jamison was there to catch and right him. Lonnie smiled a thank-you before slipping his briefs and shorts back on and heading for the door. Remmy chose that moment to let out a demanding wail, and Lonnie stumbled to pause in the hallway, clearly torn about which direction to go in.

Jamison held up a hand. "I'll get the baby. You get the door," he directed, tossing Lonnie his shirt, which he scrambled back into. Lonnie gave him an apologetic glance, but Jamison's cock had long since calmed itself. Impatient knocking at the front door would kill the mood for anyone in such a compromising position.

Jamison hurried out of the room and into the kitchen, where he drained the last of a beer and stuffed one remaining spring roll in his mouth before ducking into the den. The baby quieted when he saw Jamison's face above him, illuminated by the desk light.

"Hey, little man." Jamison finished chewing and swallowed quickly. "I'm here, and I'll take you to your Uncle Lonnie, okay?" *Will I? Can I?* He'd promised to get the baby, but he'd never actually held Remmy, let alone picked him up. The baby gazed up at him in the dim light, waving his little fists and kicking his tiny feet.

Jamison heard multiple voices in the living room now, so he swallowed and steeled himself, giving Remmy a hard look. He wasn't gonna let such a tiny creature stump him. Remembering the times he'd seen Lonnie handle his nephew, Jamison grabbed one of the many tiny bottles of hand sanitizer sprinkled throughout the house and vigorously rubbed the goo all over his hands. Then he leaned over the bassinet and gently slid one massive palm beneath Remmy's head and shoulders, the other under his bottom. The blanket rose with the baby, dangling loosely, but Jamison only had eyes for Remmy, who continued to look up at him with eyes a lot like his mother's—and Lonnie's.

The baby didn't wriggle or flail too much as he cradled him into the crook of his arm. He smiled as he tucked the blanket around his little body, then gently tickled the baby's tummy with one finger.

"There ya go, little dude," he whispered as he ran a finger over Remmy's curls. "Safe and sound." Jamison swayed slowly back and forth—something else he'd seen Lonnie do—and tapped the baby's belly again. "I hope Uncle Lonnie and I didn't wake you with our sofa sex."

"Ahem!"

Jamison whirled around so quickly, Remmy went rigid in his arms. Lonnie stood in the doorway of the den, and behind him stood two people Jamison had never seen before.

"Jamison Coburn," Lonnie began as he flipped on the overhead light, "I'd like you to meet my parents, Arthur and Ginger Bellerose." Jamison gaped at the couple. Upon closer inspection he detected the similarities between them and Lonnie. The combination of the man and woman had clearly produced his gorgeous boyfriend. "They, uh... took an earlier flight," Lonnie explained, color rising to his cheeks.

Arthur, a tall, distinguished-looking white man with longish hair, more pepper than salt, had a hand resting against the small of his wife's back and an expression of surprise on his handsome face. Ginger, a beautiful woman with high cheekbones, flawless dark brown skin, and a short, tightly curled Afro, watched Jamison so closely he could practically hear her wheels turning.

He couldn't speak, and it was at that moment he felt a *rat-ta-tat-tat* vibration against his palm, the one cupping Remmy's bottom. He glanced down at the baby. His little face was scrunched in intense effort, as if he smelled something bad. *Not yet*, Jamison thought, but he knew it was coming and suddenly felt as though he was holding a fragile bomb.

"Jamison," Lonnie said, "are you okay?"

Before he could answer, a tiny elderly lady pushed her way between Arthur and Ginger to stand beside Lonnie. She had short white hair and glasses that made her green eyes look much larger than they were. She began speaking rapidly, but Jamison didn't understand anything coming out of her mouth, and then he watched in building horror as Lonnie started speaking the same way, both of them gesturing toward Jamison and the baby.

He caught his name once, before blurting "Remmy pooped" and holding the baby out to them, to someone, anyone. Smiling, Lonnie came forward and took the baby, and then he and his mother left the room, cooing but then tsking at the odor emanating from his diaper. Jamison stood there, alone, facing Mr. Bellerose and… Lonnie's *grandmother*?

"It's nice to meet you, Jamison," Mr. Bellerose said, his words heavily accented, stepping forward with one hand extended in greeting, the other cupping his mother's elbow as she slowly moved along with him. Jamison managed to shake the hand offered him. "This is my mother, Diane."

Jamison looked down at her, his mind a blank until a childhood memory came to him: an old, black-and-white movie he'd watched with his parents when he was seven. He had sat snuggled between them on the sofa, watching the "kissing" movie play out. He hadn't really minded. He was happy to sit there in the dark between the two people who loved him most. The movie had been set in Paris. He'd seen the Eiffel Tower in several scenes as his mother sighed at the beautiful couples onscreen— ladies in fancy dresses and gentlemen in suits and very shiny shoes.

His father had laughed at Jamison's reaction to the kissing. *"Isn't she pretty, Jam?"* he had asked, nudging his then-narrow shoulder. *"Wouldn't you like to kiss her?"* Every time, Jamison's response had been an adamant *"No!"*—he would never kiss a girl! Then his father would lean over him and kiss his mother, making her giggle. But even more puzzling was when the men in the movie kissed the ladies' hands. He didn't see the purpose of that either.

Lonnie's grandmother looked almost as fragile as Remmy, so he carefully took her tiny hand in his and bent to kiss her knuckles. She gasped, and for a moment, he feared he'd done the wrong thing. But when he straightened and looked into her eyes, he saw only delight there and color rising to her wrinkled cheeks.

"It's good to meet you, ma'am."

She smiled and patted his hand. "Un beau jeune homme," she said. Jamison looked to Mr. Bellerose, who winked at him and grinned.

Chapter 7

LONNIE GLANCED at the nursery doorway for a fifth time, earning his mother's exasperation.

"For goodness sake, dear, they'll be fine," she declared, then bent over Remmy at the changing table. "And you, yes, you are all clean and fresh again," she said as she scooped him up in her arms. "I'm your *grand-mère*, and it's probably time for a bottle, yes?" She looked at Lonnie imploringly.

"Uh… no, Mom. Sorry. He ate less than an hour ago."

Ginger pouted and looked down at her grandson. "Then why did you wake, little one?"

Heat rose to Lonnie's face, and he shrugged. "He was obviously gassy," he said, nodding to the diaper pail where they'd secured the Pamper bomb, "or too hot or—"

"Maybe someone's 'sofa sex' woke you, hmm, sweetie? Yes, they did, didn't they? Those randy boys." She turned a smirk on her son, and Lonnie wanted to flee in shame, again glancing at the doorway. But when he thought back to his little tryst on the sofa and how very good it had been, he had no regrets.

With no hair or adequate ears to grab, Lonnie had used one fist to block his mouth and the other hand to claw at the cushion beneath him as he watched Jamison deep-throat him, no portion of his cock visible, only Jamison's smooth, dark brown head facedown in his crotch and rocking gently back and forth between his legs. Oh but the sensations, the wet warmth, his busy tongue, gripping throat….

Lonnie sighed.

Ginger sighed too. "Your young man is quite… *something*."

Lonnie turned back to his mother. "Huh?"

She smiled, swaying with Remmy, who gazed contentedly up at her. "He's just not what I expected when you told me about him last month."

"How so? I told you he was kind and gorgeous and gentle and gorgeous and quiet and… gorgeous." Lonnie lifted an eyebrow in question. "He's all that."

"And a bag of chips, no?" She winked and Lonnie snorted. "Well, he looks nothing like that Jerry person." Ginger frowned, a hint of anger flashing in her eyes.

"True, and he's the opposite of JP in many other ways." He puffed up his chest and raised his chin. "Jamison thinks I'm miraculous."

"Your Mr. Coburn is observant too, I see." They laughed together, and Lonnie stepped closer to let Remmy grip his finger. "Your face lights up when you speak of him. Lonnie, you sound like you're in love."

His smile faltered. "We've said that to each other, but...." Looking down, he absently fingered the shiny edge of a baby blanket folded near the changing station.

"Yes?"

He glanced up through his lashes at her. "Now I'm worried maybe we... jumped the gun?"

"Why? Have your feelings changed?"

"No. If anything, they feel... deeper, like I can't imagine my days without him."

"And nights, no doubt."

"Mother." She winked at him again, and he relaxed. "At least I don't want to imagine it." He stared into her eyes. "But love, it takes time." He smirked. "You don't fall in love with someone over a weekend. This isn't a movie, for goodness sake."

"Oh, I don't know," his mother said, her tone thoughtful. "I *knew* the moment I saw your father."

"So you've told us. I know you met in Paris, two strangers on the street."

She smiled. "Well... *yes*, but...."

"But what? You liked the looks of him, didn't you?"

"I should let him tell you the whole story. It might surprise you." She sighed, apparently lost in thought for a moment. "We talked and talked that afternoon for hours." She smiled at him. "But, given Jamison's comments earlier, I suspect you two have done more than talk."

"Mom!" She laughed heartily at her son's shock. "Let's join the others. I don't want to overwhelm him with the Bellerose clan just yet."

Ginger gave her son a stern look. "He's a big boy. I'm sure he can carry on a conversation without you holding his hand."

"Actually, he's not much of a talker, not with strangers." Lonnie inched toward the door.

Ginger giggled. "Let's go before your head explodes." They left the room and descended the stairs, Lonnie leading the way.

"What's with Gran's hair?" he asked.

"Oh, you like it? She hasn't been to the States in so long, and she wanted to look more… *hip*, I think is the word she used. Her long hair was a chore to care for, especially at her age and with that bursitis in her shoulder. Anyway, she was quite fond of Judi Dench's hair in the last Bond film she saw, so we went with that once we got her in the chair in Paris."

They headed for the den. "I bet she feels a few pounds lighter, right?" Lonnie said, and they both chuckled as they entered the den.

Diane asked what was so funny as she sat in a leather club chair, looking eager and ready to hold her great-grandson.

"It's nothing, Grand-mère," Lonnie said, immediately noticing Jamison was missing. Absently, he reassured Diane, "Le bébé a fait une drôle de tête." It was a harmless lie. After all, babies made funny faces all the time, so of course they were laughing. Hoping Jamison hadn't fled the house, he said to his father, "How are things in here?"

"Fine, fine," Arthur said. "Maman seems a bit taken with your young man."

Jamison reappeared, carrying a small glass of orange juice. He presented it to Diane.

"Merci."

"You're welcome," Jamison said, then went directly to Lonnie's side and clasped his hand. He thrilled at Jamison's touch as they faced his family. They each needed reassurance and eagerly gave it to each other. Ginger knelt by Diane with Remmy in her arms, and they murmured in French to the baby while he and Jamison looked on.

Lonnie leaned up and whispered in Jamison's ear, "How about we take the luggage to their rooms?"

"I'm in."

They stepped toward the door in unison.

"We'll take care of your bags," Lonnie announced, and the two of them hurried out, still holding hands. He grabbed his grandmother's bag and carried it to the first-floor guest room she'd be using while in town. Then he and Jamison picked up the rest of the luggage and ran up the stairs with it. Well, Jamison ran up the stairs with his two bags, but Lonnie struggled a bit with the one he carried. It was one of his mother's, and his haste coupled with the unwieldy weight and shape of it nearly sent him sprawling over the banister. When Lonnie finally reached the second floor, Jamison was standing in the hall waiting for directions.

"There at the end on the left," he instructed as he lugged the bag along with both hands. He feared he might dislocate a shoulder. Once he and Jamison were in the room, they set the bags on the suitcase stands, and Lonnie gently closed the door. He latched on to Jamison's large frame, seeking comfort. Those big, strong arms encircled him, and the tension fled his body.

His parents' early arrival had thrown him. He expected Amber and Claude would be settling them in, not him. He squeezed Jamison around the waist, praying he hadn't been as overwhelmed meeting the Belleroses as Lonnie felt at the moment.

"I like your gran," Jamison said, a smile in his voice. "I don't understand a word she's saying, but I like her."

Lonnie smiled, pressed his face into Jamison's chest, and held on tighter.

"They all seem nice, Lon," Jamison said as he rubbed his back soothingly.

"Oh… well, they are," Lonnie mumbled before pulling free and hugging himself instead.

"Then what's the matter?"

"Nothing…." He glanced at Jamison, then away again. "I've missed them. I just…." He sighed and shook himself, then slid back into the embrace. He felt hollowed out, and Jamison's touch seemed to fill him up. It *was* great to see his parents, but it brought up memories, not all of which were pleasant. "Remember when I told you how my grandfather didn't really… *care* for me?"

"Yeah."

"Having them here just reminds me of that time, and I start to feel… wrong." He wriggled against Jamison. "Like my skin doesn't fit or something." He paused, could practically hear Jamison's confused frown. Lonnie stepped back and looked up into his eyes. "Sounds nuts, right?"

Jamison was silent for several moments as he gazed down at Lonnie. Then he said, "Do they know that?"

Lonnie laughed. "Of course not. What would I say? 'Papa, tell me you love me. I need to hear it. I need to know I'm okay in your eyes.'"

Jamison shrugged. "Why not?"

"We don't talk like that. Amber's more like Dad, and I'm—"

"—a mama's boy," Jamison finished, smiling.

Lonnie frowned, one eyebrow rising in challenge. "I wouldn't put it like that, exactly."

"They love you, Lon."

He snorted and rolled his eyes. "Of course they do, silly."

"Alonzo!" Arthur Bellerose shouted from downstairs. Lonnie's body went rigid.

He freed himself from Jamison again, hating the chill that settled about him. He leaned out the bedroom door. "Yes, Papa?"

"I have examined the contents of the kitchen, and I would like to visit the market before your sister returns."

"Okay. We'll be right down."

"Want me to tag along?" Jamison asked, rubbing up and down Lonnie's arms.

"Nah. I got this," he said and took a steadying breath. "Come on. You can walk us out." He grabbed Jamison by the hand, and they hurried down the stairs together. He collected their jackets while Jamison said his good-byes to the ladies, with a dainty farewell belly tickle for Remmy. Then the three men left the house.

"I found this partial list on the freezer," Arthur said. "A good starting point."

Lonnie nodded and held up a finger asking his father to hang on a second. He walked Jamison to his truck, where they lingered and kissed. "Thank you for everything tonight," Lonnie whispered, even though there was no way his father could hear them from where he stood by his rental car. "I hope they didn't put you on the spot."

"Anytime… and nope. I mostly kept busy cleaning up the kitchen while you were upstairs." They kissed again, and Jamison bid him good night.

He lingered there by the curb and watched Jamison drive away. Once his taillights were out of sight, Lonnie joined his father in the rental car. The drive to the store was mostly silent. Lonnie spent the time reading the list and adding to it as items came to him. Arthur navigated the dark streets fairly easily, only needing one nudge in the right direction to the all-night grocery store. His parents resided in Manhattan, and each time they visited, they needed a couple of days to readjust to the quiet of little Overbrook, Maryland.

They had parked, entered the store, and checked six items off their list before Arthur said, "Thank you for the announcement and photographs of your show, Alonzo," startling Lonnie a bit.

"Oh, uh… you're welcome, Papa." Lonnie grabbed a bag of soft chocolate chip cookies, and chastised himself silently for his next question. "What did you think?"

"I found your choice of subjects intriguing, effectively giving exposure to those most often invisible around you. Very nice."

"But still not something I could make a living with?"

Arthur sighed. "Son, I do not wish to argue with you. It is obvious you love what you are doing. I am confident you will find your way eventually." They were all the way to the frozen food section before Arthur spoke again. "Your friend seems nice."

Lonnie, who had been walking ahead of their shopping cart as he compared the list to the items they'd already collected, looked up and tried to figure out if what he thought he'd heard was, in fact, what his father had said.

"Pardon?"

"Your boyfriend? Jamison?" Arthur repeated. "He seems nice."

Lonnie stood and stared.

"Why do you look at me like this?"

"You've… well, Papa, you've never talked to me about… who I date. I'm… frankly, I'm stunned."

Arthur smiled. "I have learned, through your sister, of your affection for Mr. Coburn, and…."

"And…?"

Arthur combed a hand back through his thick, wavy hair. "And we would like to know more about him, if we may. I know you have discussed him with your mother… as you did your last relationship…."

Lonnie stared for a few more seconds, blinking at his father—or the man pretending to be his father. He'd spoken in depth about JP to his mother and only mentioned him in passing to Amber. Apparently she'd learned the gory details from their mother as they discussed the new man in his life. *I really should have seen that coming.* The fewer people who knew how stupid he'd been, the better. Then he thought of Jamison and how he still didn't know the whole story.

"Sorry. I just didn't think you'd care to hear about those things."

"Alonzo, I want to know you are happy and, if not, why."

Lonnie slowly relaxed, processing, and they continued on with their shopping while he talked up Jamison. He told his father about the handmade furniture, how they'd met, and Jamison's quiet nature.

"I noticed he is not much of a talker," Arthur admitted. "But I can appreciate a man who does not speak until he has something to say."

A lot like you, Papa. "True, but sometimes, even if he has something to say, he holds it back."

"Pourquoi?"

"He's afraid I won't like it or I'll judge him or I'll end things… who knows?" Lonnie opened one of the glass freezer doors and rooted around for a moment, then pulled out two boxes of Tater Tots. His grandmother loved those.

"Do you not think you should know?"

Lonnie shrugged. "We haven't been dating all that long. There's still a lot to figure out."

Arthur nodded. "I am still figuring your mother." He sighed and began searching the ice cream selection through the glass doors. "Alonzo, do you see…? Where is the…? Erm…." He turned and blinked at Lonnie. "La crème glacée Rocky Road?"

"Rocky Road?" He stepped up to the case and spotted a gallon on the top shelf. "Here," he said, opening the door. "Should we get two?"

Arthur chuckled. "Knowing your mother and sister as I do… yes."

Lonnie added the gallons to the cart, and they continued to the next aisle. "Now, about your young man," Arthur said, appearing thoughtful. "I believe communication is most important. If you have questions and doubts, ask for answers, no?"

"Yes, Papa." Lonnie looked away and sighed but then turned to face him once again. "Speaking of communication," he said, grinning, "what were you doing to catch Mother's eye the day you met?"

This brought his father up short, and Lonnie was amused by the color rising to his cheeks.

Chapter 8

"BOSS, YOUR lunch is gettin' cold," Torp called across the backyard of their renovation site.

Jamison glanced over his shoulder at Lincoln. The man was on his phone, pacing inside the house. They could see him passing back and forth beyond the big, new arched window of the dining room. The conversation looked intense, which piqued Jamison's curiosity. He caught Torp's eye, but his friend shrugged, so they went back to eating.

"Kimmy says the four of us could meet for drinks and dinner this Friday? Maybe Blaketon's? How's that for you?"

Jamison nodded and chewed quickly. "I'll check with Lonnie after work, but it sounds good."

"How's your mama?"

"Fine." He sighed. "I brought up meeting Lonnie to her, but she shot me down."

"That's too bad, dude, but she'll come around."

"She did cut him a piece of pie, so at least she's not pretending he doesn't exist anymore."

They laughed softly.

"So, you was sayin' you met his parents…. What are they like?"

"Nice. Pretty. Even his daddy. He's a white man, but you probably figured that out. Lonnie's mama looks like some sort of African princess or somethin'. So beautiful. I mean… wow!" Jamison lit up. "Oh, and his gran is a tiny little thing, but she seemed to like me."

"What you mean 'seemed to'?"

"Well, she doesn't speak English. They're French—well, not his mother. She's from here."

"Snooty?"

Jamison thought about that. "No, not snooty. Just… different. Classy. Educated. Refined."

Torp snorted. "Yeah! Everything you ain't, huh, Jam?"

He grimaced, though he knew Torp was teasing.

"Jamison!" Lincoln shouted from the back doorway.

"Yeah, boss?"

"Come here a minute, will ya?"

"Be right back."

He hopped up and jogged over to Lincoln, who stood at the top of the back stairs looking down at him. "Just had a phone call from a guy at the *Overbrook Times*. They'd like to do a feature on you for their Community page."

What Jamison had eaten of his lunch threatened to reappear as he tried to grasp what Lincoln had just told him. He gulped. "Me?"

"Yep."

"There has to be a mistake, boss. Why would anyone want to write about me?"

Lincoln came down the few steps and sat in front of him. "Your story might interest people, son. Think about it. You lost your daddy so young, you stayed out of trouble, and you grew into a damn good man, a man with skill and an impressive talent."

"But—"

"They'd showcase your furniture, and it might get some attention for my business as well. After all, I'm a tiny part of your story, right?" he asked, gently punching Jamison's arm.

Jamison nodded as his thoughts raced, but when he didn't say anything else, Lincoln went on, lowering his voice. "Listen, there aren't a lot of stories like this written about *our* men, ya know? You didn't go to college—"

"I wanted to—"

"—and you've had a lot of obstacles in your life, but you overcame them with good hard work."

All that was true, but he wasn't one to share. This stank of trouble to him, though he didn't exactly know why.

"Didn't you tell me once that a local dealer tried to recruit you to be a runner for him when you was just a little thing? Right after your daddy died? Promised you money to help out your momma, didn't he?"

I've never been a little thing. "Yeah, but—"

"But what?"

"What kinda questions they gonna ask?"

Lincoln shrugged. "I guess they want your story, how you resisted easy money—"

"There was nothing *easy* about it."

"—your feelings about your life, how you got where you are, maybe what you want for your future, wife, family… that kinda stuff." Jamison once again couldn't find his voice, and Lincoln got to his feet. "It's your decision, but I thought I should give you my opinion. Your story could inspire someone else. Let me know what you decide, okay?" he said as he walked back into the house.

He stared after Lincoln for several moments, then returned to Torp's side and picked up his cola for a few gulps. After a hefty belch, he began eating again.

"What'd the boss want?" Torp asked.

"Newspaper wants to do a story on me," Jamison mumbled around his food as he stared off across the yard. The sky was a bright blue, sprinkled with the occasional wispy cloud. And though the sun dominated, its heat didn't quite cut through the chill of the day… or the chill of the nerves gathering in his chest.

Torp, however, looked thrilled. "You. Are. Shittin'. Me. That's wicked, Jam! You gonna be a celebrity. Wait 'til I tell Kimmy." He laughed, then took a bite of his hoagie, smiling and chewing as he shook his head in disbelief.

"I haven't decided if I'm gonna do it yet," Jamison said, glancing sharply at his best friend.

Torp's eyes bugged. "You gotta, Jam. I can see it now," he said, raising his arm and swiping his hand across the sky as though he was reading a marquee. "Local boy does good for…." Torp frowned, and Jamison laughed. Torp glanced at him from beneath a knitted brow, a bit of color rising to his cheeks. "Yeah, well… you know what I was goin' for."

"Yeah, I know. Thanks."

He tapped Torp upside the head, and they laughed together, but Jamison felt uneasy. He wondered if he could get the questions ahead of time. *They do that, don't they?* He looked at the house. Normally he'd go to Lincoln for advice, but his boss clearly wanted him to do the interview.

He could be worrying for nothing, but he couldn't stop thinking this article could out him… to everyone. *If I was honest.* He froze for a second, considering what lying might accomplish, but he couldn't actually deny his feelings for Lonnie, could he? On the other hand, he couldn't help imagining the folks in his old neighborhood grabbing their morning newspapers off the stoop, sitting down to breakfast, and learning that Alanna Coburn's little boy liked dick.

DURING THE rest of the week, he and Lonnie had spent every day together—sometimes breakfast, always lunch and dinner, sex, movies, the occasional ice cream in bed—but Jamison had yet to bring up his potential interview and how unnerved he was by it. Shoving those thoughts aside, he decided to focus on their double date with Torp and Kimmy. Now that he and Lonnie had their first date—the thesis show—behind them, Jamison felt more comfortable with the idea of it and had gone through much the same fussy procedure in preparation. But this time he wasn't worried about embarrassing Lonnie in front of his smart, classy university friends and colleagues. Tonight they were meeting up with people Jamison had known most of his life, and he was actually looking forward to the evening.

Rushing down the driveway to his truck, he heard, "Jam? Jam Coburn! What the fuck you all dressed up fo'?" He slowed at first, peering into the dark street and wondering who would call him that on this end of town. When he saw who it was, he continued on to unlock his driver's side door before turning reluctantly to face Delroy Pritchard, a resident of his former neighborhood.

"Got somewhere to be," he explained. *Meeting my boyfriend for dinner. Just say it.* His eyes narrowed as he considered his old buddy. "What you doin' on this end of town?"

"My old lady and I just closed on a house over here." Delroy jerked a thumb back over his shoulder at a woman sitting in a shiny new car, glaring at them. Apparently it had been a long day for her. "She wanted something classier, and I wanted somethin' further away from her mama." Delroy laughed heartily, slapping his thigh.

Short, loud, and built like a fireplug, Delroy had always been a hard worker with a good head for business. He'd started young, making downtown deliveries for Phil Bloom, a local baker, who, having no children of his own, had taught the young Pritchard all he could about baking, eventually hiring him at his shop—a shop Delroy now owned.

"How's the baking business?"

"Great! Just opened my second shop over here, but…."

"What?"

"Well, it's nothin' really. Might have to go to court is all."

Jamison frowned. "Someone get sick?"

"Nah, nothing like that. Last month a couple dykes came in for cupcakes."

"What?"

"Dykes… lesbians?"

Jamison grinned. "Yes, Del, I know what lesbians are. What's the problem? You sell cupcakes, don't you? And if I remember right, they're delicious."

Delroy puffed up. "Hell yeah, they are. I tweaked old Bloom's recipe. Now they're perfect."

"But what? You don't serve lesbians?"

"Of course we do, but they wanted birthday cupcakes for their son."

Jamison waited, but Delroy seemed to think that was sufficient. He glanced at his watch and saw he had plenty of time to kill before picking up Lonnie, but the last thing he wanted to do was shoot the shit with Delroy. He climbed behind the wheel. "Sorry. I'm still waiting to hear the problem, Del."

Delroy lowered his voice and stepped closer to the truck. "People like that shouldn't be raising kids, dude."

Before he could stop himself, Jamison burst out laughing. Delroy stepped back from the truck, insulted. "What the fuck is so funny?"

"Sorry… sorry, man," Jamison said, trying to catch his breath, "but refusing to sell them cupcakes isn't going to stop them from raising their son. It's just going to get you sued."

Delroy frowned, staring down and kicking at the pavement. "Yeah. That's what's happening, all right." He looked up. "But Pastor Jackson says we need to push back at the gays taking over the country. It ain't right!"

"I hope Pastor Jackson is paying your legal bills, Del, 'cause that's a load of bullshit." Jamison turned the key, and the truck roared to life.

"Hang on, Jam." Delroy grabbed the door and looked over his shoulder at his wife. "I ran into Torp last week, and he said you was seeing someone. That right?" Jamison nodded slowly. "My Vinnia was hopin' you and her baby sister Pearl might—"

"Uh… yeah, I went out with Pearl, and she's great, but I'm seein' someone else now."

"Yup, so is she, but Vinnia don't like the guy. She'd rather it be you, but I guess it wasn't meant to be, huh?"

"Guess so. Well, I gotta go, man."

"Ooh, you rushing off to meet the lucky lady now, right? Cool. Cool." Delroy smiled and winked. "Maybe we can all double-date sometime. I mean now that we're in practically the same neighborhood. What do you say?"

Jamison winced. "Uh… maybe. You two have a good night, okay? And congrats on the house." Delroy barely had time to step away before Jamison slammed the door and drove off.

Ten minutes later Lonnie unlocked his apartment door to let Jamison in and vanished. Before he could even enter, Jamison heard bare feet padding on the hardwood floor as Lonnie scurried into the bedroom, probably buck naked—at least that's how he imagined him—and shouting over his shoulder, "Almost ready! Almost ready!"

"No hurry, babe," Jamison called. "We got time." They weren't due at the restaurant for another thirty or so minutes. Lonnie's place was a tiny bit bigger than his, better decorated and more welcoming. The only visitors Jamison had ever had at his apartment were Torp, Lonnie, and his mother—one to drink beer and watch football, one to love on, and one to give her opinions.

Jamison lingered by the bookcase in the main room, looking over the titles, searching for a certain yellow one. *There it is.* He snatched the volume from the shelf and glanced at the bedroom door before plopping down on the sofa to look through it. He'd discovered the book about rural French farm life two weeks ago and had started leafing through it whenever they were at Lonnie's. He wanted to better understand where the Bellerose family came from.

Just outside Baltimore, Overbrook had offered Jamison mostly concrete grayness, hard-edged bricks, and honking horns. He traced a finger over the peaceful photographs of French farms and marveled at all the green and wide-open spaces beneath a deep blue sky. Where he'd grown up, back in his old neighborhood, there was no vast expanse of green. The weeds pushing through the sidewalks, while hardy, weren't a match for the images he gazed at.

One picture showed a couple having a picnic on a blanket in a rolling field that seemed to go on forever. He smiled, realizing nothing was stopping him from taking Lonnie on a picnic in Overbrook Park. *We could do that. We could get a blanket, maybe Mama could pack a lunch, maybe we could all go— Yeah, that's not happening. Not any time soon, anyway.*

"Maybe we can go there someday," Lonnie whispered in his ear.

Startled, Jamison slammed the book shut.

"Oh! Sorry, babe. I didn't mean to scare you." Lonnie laughed and came around the sofa to curl up next to him. He opened the book again and smoothed the pages down. "Would you like that? Visiting France?"

"I'd like to… with you. I want to see your family farm."

"Okay. It's a date." Lonnie gave him a peck on the cheek and got to his feet. "I'm sure Amber and Claude will want to take Remmy too, at some point. Of course, you'll have to get a passport."

"Got one." Jamison continued turning the pages.

"You do?"

He looked up and smiled. "Yeah. When we were in high school, Torp and I had all these plans to travel the world, working our way through each country, so we applied for passports at the same time." He shrugged. "Had to renew mine last year. Don't know if Torp did, though."

"Ah, so you'd be good to go."

He looked Lonnie over and smiled at the dashing figure he made. His outfit was a lot snazzier than the simple suit he'd worn to the thesis show—dark jeans, thick white belt, fitted gray suit jacket and vest over a black silk shirt, open at the collar. And on his feet? A pair of shiny, dark purple dress shoes. He looked like a runway model.

Jamison got to his feet, forgetting all about the book. He held Lonnie's arms out to take him in.

"Sorry I was running behind," Lonnie said, looking down at himself as if he'd come up short. "I was helping Bink with an installation at the university gallery. She's interim director but still carrying a full class load, so if they don't hire someone permanent soon, she's gonna scream boogity."

"You look amazing," Jamison whispered.

Lonnie grinned as he relaxed and stepped closer to smooth Jamison's collar. "You look pretty good yourself, Mr. Coburn." Lonnie stood on his tiptoes and kissed him, and for several seconds, as their tongues played against each other, the flavor of minty freshness filling his mouth, Jamison's thoughts fled south, and he considered canceling dinner. But Lonnie pulled back suddenly. "Uh-uh. We're going to dinner, so"—he gestured to Jamison's crotch—"just tell Jam Junior to stand down."

Jamison was still chuckling over that comment when he started his truck and headed for the restaurant.

Chapter 9

AFTER ABSORBING the tableau for thirty seconds, Lonnie found he liked Blaketon's. The smiling faces equaled positive energy, while the pleasant music, soft lighting, and waitstaff—moving gracefully and silently through the dining room taking care of their charges for the evening—came together to create a welcoming atmosphere. And finally, the tiny lights strung like a canopy over the room, the dark furnishings, faux-painted walls, and high windows looking out on surrounding structures equaled a stylish décor.

The four of them sat tucked away in a corner at a table that had black bench seating paired with chairs. They placed their orders quickly, each selecting something different, and moments after their dishes arrived, Lonnie paused to look out across the room. He admired how the bare bulbs strung above them made the patrons look as if they were dining beneath the night sky. He sighed and gave Jamison's hand a squeeze, perplexing his boyfriend but drawing a smile from him nonetheless.

"I've wanted to eat here for months now," Kimmy said, interrupting the moment. "I've heard raves about their food, and they weren't wrong." She sliced into her pepper-roasted chicken and moaned as she chewed. Then she quickly cut another piece to offer Lonnie, who mirrored her with his crab cakes. It wasn't until they had fed each other, smiled, and licked their lips that they noticed Jamison and Torp watching them intently, eyes wide.

They'd hit it off immediately, largely because Kimmy was fascinated by Lonnie and his heritage. She was one of the few teens in her high school who had chosen French over a more practical foreign language, like Spanish. Her teacher, Mrs. Oleander, had been thrilled to have such an enthusiastic student in her class and even expanded the usual course work—vocabulary, culture, and some history—to include cooking a traditional French meal for extra credit.

On his end, Lonnie found Kimmy bright, fun, and hilarious, especially when telling stories of Torp and Jamison as younger men, something he couldn't get enough of. He still had much to learn about

Jamison, and Kimmy and Torp were great resources. Not as good as Mama Coburn would've been, but he had no control over when or if she'd deign to meet him. They laughed and drank and shared stories and food for two hours.

Then, after several glasses of wine, Kimmy said something that caught Lonnie off guard. He blinked at her. "What interview?" he asked, staring. She frowned and looked to Torp and Jamison. Lonnie did too. Both men were frozen and silent where they sat. He turned to Jamison. "Babe? What interview?" Jamison squirmed a bit and looked away, but Lonnie kept his gaze locked on him, until Jamison finally replied.

"A reporter at the *Overbook Times* asked to do a feature on me... about my life so far. You know, my success in the face of hardship and such."

"That's fantastic!" Smiling, Lonnie looked at each of their faces. Kimmy and Torp clearly agreed with his assessment, though they were more subdued about it. But Jamison looked as though he'd just made an appointment for a root canal—without anesthesia. Lonnie's expression faltered. "Isn't it?"

"I don't want to do it, Lon."

"Why?"

"I don't know what to say, and I don't wanna sound stupid... embarrass myself."

He placed his hand on Jamison's arm. "You're not stupid. You should be proud of who you are and what you've accomplished." Lonnie glanced at their dinner companions, who nodded but kept quiet. Turning back to Jamison, he said, "You're a talented artist. Your work is beautiful, and people should know about it."

After several moments of silence, Jamison patted Lonnie's hand and said, "I'll think about it, okay?"

Lonnie frowned slightly and nodded. "Okay." He didn't get it, but it was Jamison's decision.

"I'm gonna drain the snake," Torp announced, drawing a frown from Kimmy.

"I'll join you," Jamison said, rising to his feet.

Lonnie watched him go, then turned to Kimmy. "I don't get his reluctance. If someone wanted to feature me in an article, I'd be all over that!"

"Would you?"

He blinked at her. "Why wouldn't I?"

She grinned as she peered at him. "No deep dark secrets, huh?" His mind immediately went to JP. When he didn't say anything, she sighed. "Jam's a pretty private guy, Lonnie. And until he met you...."

Okay, he got it, and he turned to stare at the entrance to the restrooms. "He was in the closet, on the down low," he mumbled, "and we're asking him to talk about one of the most painful moments of his life." He felt Kimmy watching him, but he shook it off, grinned at her, and changed the subject. "I should definitely bring my parents and grandmother here before they leave town," he said before cutting a bit off Jamison's steak and popping it in his mouth.

"How much longer are they going to be here?"

"No idea," he said before following the steak with a swig of his wine. He leaned back against the bench with a sigh and patted his nonexistent belly.

"So, will it be a movie or dancing?" she asked.

"Huh?"

"If we linger with coffee and dessert here, then we can go dancing at a club instead of rushing out to see a movie. There's nothing downtown I really want to see anyway."

"Where'd you have in mind?"

"Skulduggery. It's a new place," she said. "I hear it's killer."

"I think I've heard the name." He glanced toward the restrooms again, wondering how to support but not push Jamison. "Mixed club, right?" he asked absently.

"Uh-huh. Should be a blast. Jamison can *move*."

"What?" He blinked at her, eyes wide.

"Jam. He's a great dancer."

"He is?"

"You've never danced with him?"

He shook his head slowly. "Never really came up, and I'm... I'm not so good."

Kimmy narrowed her eyes, looking him up and down. "I find that hard to believe."

"It's true. I've been told I look like I'm having a seizure. My sister told me once I looked like I was fighting off a swarm of bees."

She laughed before she could stop herself and snorted a little wine, then coughed a bit before saying, "Sorry."

He chuckled and passed her a napkin.

After she dabbed at her face, Kimmy said, "So you don't dance at all?"

"Oh no, I *dance*. I love it, but… it's just… well, nobody else loves it."

They were still laughing when their dates returned to the table.

Jamison dropped into his seat, glanced at each of them, then eyed his slightly smaller steak. "What did we miss?"

Lonnie squeezed Jamison's hand and smirked, fluttering his eyelashes. "What do you say, handsome? Wanna dance with me?" The flicker of uncertainty that replaced the fondness in Jamison's eyes did not escape Lonnie.

SKULDUGGERY WAS loud and crowded, with flashing lights, sweaty, wildly dancing bodies, and laughing, drunken faces. Very different from Blaketon's. Lonnie doubted anyone could hold a decent conversation within its walls, but they weren't there to talk. Jamison didn't appear to know where to look first. Then he spotted the bar and headed straight for it, Lonnie followed, and Torp called for them to wait up.

"Bourbon!" Jamison demanded, slapping cash on the bar.

The bartender produced his drink, and Jamison gulped it down, then turned to look around the room.

"What can I get you?" the bartender asked Lonnie, but Lonnie's focus was on Jamison, his sweating face, his darting eyes, his fidgeting hands.

"Uh… let me have a Stoli, rocks," he finally answered. His drink appeared, but before taking a sip, he nudged closer to Jamison. "You okay?"

"Huh?" Startled, he looked down into Lonnie's concerned eyes. "Oh, babe, I'm fine. Just…." Lonnie followed Jamison's gaze to several male couples grinding to the beat on the dance floor and turned his attention back to Jamison, who looked… terrified.

He stretched up to Jamison's ear. "You know, we don't have to dance if you don't want to."

"Of course, I want to," Jamison said a bit too forcefully.

Lonnie eyed him. "You just seem sort of—"

Jamison grabbed his hand and dragged him to the dance floor, where he proceeded to dance like his life depended on it. Lonnie felt caught in a whirlwind and struggled to keep up. Torp and Kimmy joined them, but they weren't smiling. They watched the two of them, uncertainty filling their eyes. Lonnie stopped dancing and stared at Jamison until he stopped as well.

"What's wrong, baby?" Jamison shouted.

Lonnie gazed into his warm, and currently panicked, dark brown eyes. "You tell me. You're acting like a maniac, and that's something people usually say about me when I'm out here."

"Lon—"

"No," he said stubbornly. "What's up with you?"

Jamison smiled his most charming smile and slid up close to him, wrapping an arm around Lonnie's waist. "This is what you do, isn't it? Dance with the man you love?"

Lonnie pulled free and stood there, arms folded over his chest.

"What?" Jamison asked, the picture of innocence.

"You look...." Lonnie glanced around them at the other dancers. "You look frightened," he shouted above the music.

Jamison shrugged as though he didn't know what Lonnie was talking about, and he kept dancing. Lonnie watched him for a moment, then turned to his right and smacked the ass of the nearest gyrating young man to get his attention.

"Is there a patio?"

The guy pointed, and Lonnie took hold of Jamison's arm and pulled him from the dance floor to the back of the room. He'd be damned if he'd stand there and let himself be lied to, not after everything he'd shared with Jamison. *Everything but JP*, he thought, immediately pushing the realization away. They reached a lavender door marked Patio, and Lonnie shoved it open.

The silence that enveloped them the moment the door slammed shut was acute. Lonnie's ears continued to buzz from the onslaught in the club. The air was cooler outside, and he kept Jamison close at hand as he steered them to a table next to a vine-covered fence. They sat together without speaking for several moments, and gradually the sounds of a typical night in downtown Overbrook became discernible: distant traffic, streetlights buzzing, the odd cricket, and other intimate conversations and murmurs coming from the darkness along the narrow, graveled area.

"What's going on?" Lonnie finally asked.

"Nothin'. I'm just worried about the interview."

"So you've decided to do it?"

Jamison shrugged and looked away.

Okay. Lonnie drummed the tabletop with his fingers, waiting and staring at the side of Jamison's head hard enough to be felt, he hoped.

Finally, Jamison turned to face him again and sighed before saying, "I don't know what I'm doing, Lon."

"What?" His insides felt as though they'd turned to water, and he clasped Jamison's hand, as if that would hold them together. Lonnie was taken aback by how terrified he suddenly felt.

"I'm sorry about being weird in there, but I've never... *danced* with a man. I was trying to be okay with it, comfortable, but it's still so new to me. All my... all the stuff before... they were hookups, anonymous, meaningless. But you," Jamison said, grinning sheepishly at him, "you mean everything, and I don't want to fuck this up. I want to be the best I can for you. Don't want to hide anymore. I want to be able to show you how I feel, show everyone."

Relief washed over him, making him light-headed. "You do, Jamison. Every day. The way you look at me, say my name, hold me, touch me, kiss me.... All that shows me how you feel." Lonnie looked away, toward the other couples around them. "I should probably remember that more often," he said softly.

"But you're so easy with it all." Jamison sighed.

Lonnie snorted. "Easy? Don't get me wrong. I'm a lot better than I used to be, but do I strike you as someone 'at ease' in this world?"

"Yes. To me, yes."

Lonnie grinned. "It takes time. You're looking at the product of seventeen years of knowing who I am, of navigating the world as a gay man. You've been on the down low all these years, so I get that this relationship road we're on is new to you. Just know I'm here for you. You'll get there... someday."

"Someday? I don't want to lose you in the meantime. I'm afraid I won't be strong enough, good enough, and I'll disappoint you."

"You can't, babe."

"Promise?"

"I promise." Lonnie smirked. "Now before we go back inside and dance, I want you to remember that there are lesbian couples, straight couples, folks in transition, even groups of friends dancing together in there. Everyone is welcome. That includes us." They stood. "And I'll try my best not to put your eye out."

He led a chuckling Jamison back inside and onto the dance floor. Once they found the beat and matched it, Lonnie felt the tension and awkwardness slowly leave Jamison. He saw it in his face, in his smile, and suddenly all the people and noise around them faded. This was just right. They fit. *Remember that*, Lonnie told himself.

The music and lights and people swirled around them, and he couldn't stop the smile that appeared on his face or the joy and warmth filling his chest. Maybe it was the alcohol he finally got to drink, but Lonnie didn't really care. He wanted to hold on to Jamison and the joy he saw in his man's eyes for as long as he would have him.

Chapter 10

HE HADN'T imagined it. He hadn't been *that* high. JP rolled over, disengaging himself from the sweaty, panting young man he'd brought back to his hovel. His guest had springy dark brown curls all over his head and creamy light brown skin, smooth and unblemished like his ex's. Earlier in the evening, after snorting two lines in the men's room, JP and his guest had spent some quality—if rushed—time in a stall together, tugging at each other's clothes, among other things, and then making out in a dark corner of Skulduggery.

And who should walk in but his Lonnie? The real thing, not some twitchy substitute, who currently warmed the other side of the bed, his own spunk cooling on his chest. JP had already lost interest. Of course he had. They'd gotten off. It was time for the kid to leave. Thankfully, the young man realized that without being told.

"Thanks, man," Twitchy said as he rolled out of bed and began hunting for his clothes. "It was fun."

JP watched him walk into the bathroom, that perfect ass tempting him once again. He listened to Twitchy running water to clean up, flushing the toilet, and getting dressed. From his nest among his mangled sheets, JP asked, "You're not expecting me to call, are you?"

The kid grinned knowingly at him as he exited the bathroom. In the dim room, JP could still see the wealth of experience in the guy's brown eyes—the only flaw in his fantasy. "Nah, I don't do repeats, dude."

JP nodded curtly. "Lock the door behind you." He rolled over on his stomach, hugged his pillow, and waited to hear the front door slam. When it did, he jumped out of bed and put the security chain on the door, then headed into the bathroom for a shower… and to think. There was a lot to think about, because if he wasn't mistaken, the subject of his upcoming interview was the man who'd had his hands all over Lonnie. The two of them ground together—when Lonnie wasn't spastically dancing all over the floor, that is—and looked at each other as though they were in love.

He used to look at me like that, he thought as he spread lather over his heated skin. He stood beneath the spray, letting the water beat the tension out of his shoulders, a tension that shouldn't have been there after his romp with Twitchy.

As he dried off, he considered the little he'd read about Jamison Coburn. He never would have pegged him as gay, but you couldn't always tell from appearance. JP stepped from the shower, swiped the fog from the mirror, and smiled at his image. *What does Lonnie see in that guy?* They couldn't have been more different. JP was bigger and stronger than Lonnie, but nowhere near the size of Tall, Dark, and Scary. *He could probably break me in half.* Also, where Jamison was dark-skinned with a shaved head, JP was white and had more of a scruffy-Brad-Pitt thing going on. He couldn't take Coburn down face-to-face, so he'd have to *gradually* work his way back into Lonnie's good graces.

Despite his drug use back then, he remembered how hard he'd been on Lonnie. But he could… *would* do better this time. Do things right. Not be so critical of Lonnie's goofy behavior and clumsiness, of his snorting laughter, or the way he cooked or cleaned. *I can be better.*

He left the bathroom and set about changing his sheets and tidying the bed, trying to make the room as if Twitchy had never happened. The scent of sex still hung in the air, but the linen-fresh bite of his shower gel nearly masked it.

Before falling asleep, he grabbed his phone off the nightstand and found two messages: one from his boss, asking if he'd heard from his remaining interview subjects, and one from…. *Coburn.* JP listened to it, and a smile slowly spread across his face as Coburn agreed to the profile and asked him to call and set it up. He could hear a muffled version of the club's driving beat from earlier that evening in the background.

Perfect.

IT WAS somewhere around 2:00 a.m. when Jamison parked outside Lonnie's building and slid out of his truck. He made it around to the passenger's side in time to steady Lonnie as he hopped down and stumbled a bit, but Lonnie shook him off and straightened up to fish his keys from the back pocket of his jeans.

"I got this," he mumbled.

From the front seat Jamison retrieved the jacket and vest Lonnie had shed after only a few minutes of dancing. He secured the truck and set the alarm. The neighborhood was a safe one, but it was a habit he'd formed years ago and saw no need to break. He followed behind Lonnie, watching his sweet ass weave its way up the walk, moving with him, arms out and ready for assistance should Lonnie need it. Lonnie took two stuttering steps to his left as he sorted through his keys, but he quickly corrected his trajectory all by himself.

"Not much of a drinker, huh, babe?"

Lonnie glanced over his shoulder. "Doesn't take much. I'm the first to admit I'm a lightweight, but—" He whirled and pointed at Jamison. "—I don't get hangovers, so… good for me!" he shouted to the sky, punctuating it with a thrust of his fist to the heavens. He turned back to the apartment building and unlocked the door. "Follow me, studly." Lonnie crooked his finger at him.

Jamison couldn't help grinning, but at this rate, he'd never get Lonnie in bed tonight. He followed him into the vestibule and scooped Lonnie into his arms to carry him up the stairs. Lonnie giggled the whole way and was still giggling when Jamison set him back on his feet at his door.

After locking the door behind them, Jamison hurried into the bedroom, where Lonnie had headed, and tossed the vest and jacket in a chair by the door. He approached Lonnie, who was trying to unbutton his shirt and kick off his shoes at the same time. Jamison got ahold of him just before he teetered too far to the left, and he took over, reaching around and impatiently tugging the shirt free of his jeans. Lonnie sighed and relaxed back against him, allowing it. They slowly swayed together, a slower dance than when they were at Skulduggery. Lonnie's moves at the club had been enthusiastic, sometimes frightening, but Jamison had loved watching him lose himself to the beat. It was a beautiful thing to witness.

"So what did you think?" he whispered against Lonnie's ear.

"I enjoyed myself. I think Kimmy's fantastic, and Torp's a lucky man…."

Jamison nibbled at him. "We should do it again."

"That depends."

He stopped nibbling. "On what?"

"How Torp handled our kissing."

Jamison snorted. "Didn't notice, don't care." He pressed against Lonnie, eager to get at him. "We didn't make out any more than the two of them, so he should be fine with it."

"Ooh, listen to you," Lonnie cooed, turning to face him and wrapping his arms around Jamison's neck, "all 'full steam ahead and damn the Torpedo!'"

Jamison's laughter burst out of him as he cupped Lonnie's behind. When he quieted, he said, "We'll go dancing again soon. You were quite... um...."

"Yes?" Lonnie lifted an eyebrow above his heavy-lidded green eyes, a smirk on his lips.

"Captivating."

Lonnie nodded sleepily. "Good answer." He closed his eyes and nuzzled against Jamison, tickling his face with his hair and causing him to shiver with want.

"Ready to enjoy yourself some more?" Jamison asked.

Without waiting for an answer, he captured Lonnie's mouth with his own and welcomed Lonnie's tongue, letting it slide between his lips. As they kissed, he undid Lonnie's belt, unbuttoned his jeans, and tried to work loose the tiny, slippery buttons of his silk shirt. But his fingers were too big to manage them, so Lonnie took over and stepped away from him, a playful smirk on his face.

"I'm going to be bare-assed any second now," Lonnie said, finally managing to kick off his shoes, "so you'd better get busy, mister."

Jamison did as he was told, and thus a laughing, clumsy race began, but somehow he ended up bare-assed while Lonnie ended with a sock hanging off the end of his foot and one leg in, one out of his shorts as the two of them fell together onto the bed.

"J-Jamison... c-condoms," Lonnie gasped, rutting against him. "Y-you know w-where...."

Oh, he knew exactly where. He leaned back, stretching with his left arm and fumbling with the drawer. Lonnie rolled with him, continuing to kiss and nibble at his mouth, continuing their skin-to-skin contact and delicious friction. Jamison blindly slapped his hand around inside the drawer and captured a strip of condoms, which he tossed on the bed, followed closely by a small tube of lube.

He rolled Lonnie onto his back and quickly freed him from his shorts. His beautiful cock sprang free, and Jamison was momentarily mesmerized by the picture before him: Lonnie prone beneath him, an expanse of hot, light brown skin, a slender but muscled body, his chest rising and falling quickly in anticipation. Then his gaze reached Lonnie's eyes and found their usual green dark and heated with want.

"I think you're a bit drunk, Lon." He opened the lube and spread some on his fingers.

"So what if I am…. Jam?" Jamison smiled at the use of his nickname. Lonnie rarely did that. "Are you complaining?"

"Never," he whispered, leaning in to taste Lonnie again and pressing a lubed thumb into him, working him open, loosening him up. He almost lost control of himself when Lonnie moaned deeply, so Jamison pulled back, donned and slicked the condom before slowly pushing into Lonnie's tight heat.

He froze for a moment, trying to discover a calm he did not feel.

"No," Lonnie whispered, and Jamison opened his eyes.

"No?"

Biting his lip, Lonnie reached out to lightly scratch down Jamison's chest. "Hard, Jamison. Give it to me hard and fast."

"But Lon—"

"I'm ready, babe." Lonnie closed his eyes, squirmed beneath him, and pleaded, "Now."

Jamison gripped the firm globes of Lonnie's ass and drove into him. Lonnie gasped, but a blissful grin appeared on his face, and Jamison fought to maintain control as he increased the pace. He plunged in again and again, until their skin glistened with sweat, until their moaning and grunting melded with the rhythmic squeak of the strained bed. Lonnie clung to him, wrapping Jamison up with his arms and legs, panting, whispering encouragement in his ear but at the same time hindering his movements.

Unable to get the angle he wanted, Jamison pulled away and out, sparking an outraged howl from Lonnie. "Turn over," he commanded, and Lonnie did without hesitation. Jamison entered him again, steadying him with a bruising grip on his hips. *Ah, that's better*, he thought as his mind fogged over and he pounded into his lover repeatedly. Suddenly Lonnie keened into his pillow, inner muscles clamping down on Jamison and drawing a shout from him. They froze in place for many exquisite seconds, then collapsed on the bed together, panting and giggling as the bouncing of the mattress ebbed.

WET SPOT be damned, Lonnie thought as he lay beneath Jamison, tangled in damp sheets and waiting for the tremors to finish their final lap around his body. Eventually, Jamison lifted off and pulled free of him, causing Lonnie to gasp and shudder slightly. He rolled over while Jamison disposed of the condom and then began wiping Lonnie clean with a discarded undershirt. He watched Jamison work, matching the lazy smile on his lips, and remembered the way Jamison had looked at him earlier, almost worshipping him—much as he looked now. Lonnie's breathing slowly returned to normal, and Jamison's attentiveness made his skin tingle from toes to scalp. Speaking of toes, he wiggled them and was surprised to find that lone sock still clinging to his right foot. He lifted his leg slightly. *Man, that's one tenacious sock. I should buy some more of those.*

Finished tidying up, Jamison snuggled behind him, wrapping Lonnie in his arms, pulling him back against his chest, and burying his nose in his hair. "I love you, Lonnie."

I love you too, he thought.

"You okay?" Jamison asked as he found Lonnie's hand and tangled their fingers.

"Yeah. I'm good… I'm great."

"You seem… somewhere else."

"No, just thinking."

"About?"

How you could possibly love me so soon. "How much I love you." He felt Jamison smile against the back of his neck.

"Good to hear, babe."

He could have left it at that, end of conversation, but then he wouldn't be *Loonie* Bellerose—forever shooting himself in the foot. "My father told me an interesting story the other night."

"Yeah?"

"He said Mom fell for him the moment she saw him attack a guy twice his size."

Jamison snorted. "Doesn't seem like something your dad would do."

"Tell me about it."

"What set him off?"

"Some jackass hassled Uncle Benoit outside a bar over some woman, and Dad jumped on the dude's back. Started whaling on him." Lonnie turned in Jamison's arms to face him. "I should point out this was thirty or so years ago." He lifted a leg over Jamison's lap and grinned when he began to harden. "Mom'd been in Paris studying for about a year and had found many of the French a bit reserved for her taste. Then she spotted Dad tearing into a behemoth to defend a brother who definitely didn't need it."

"Love at first punch, huh?"

"Something like that." Lonnie reached between Jamison's legs and began stroking him, smiling as Jamison's eyes fluttered shut for a moment, his breath quickening. He thought about the day they had met, how he'd forgotten his own name while standing before such a big, beautiful man. And when Jamison gently reminded him, "You're Lonnie Bellerose," staring with those deep-set, dark eyes, Lonnie had promptly walked into a door. He'd come undone. *Love at first stumble?* "Have you decided about the interview?" he asked.

"Yeah. I called while you were dancing," Jamison said. "Left a message but haven't heard back yet."

"Should be fun…."

"It still worries me a bit."

"Don't. I used to know someone who wrote for a newspaper. They'll probably want to visit your old neighborhood. They'll definitely want to see your furniture." Lonnie hesitated. "And they'll probably ask you about your father… maybe even that night—shit. Now *I'm* worried."

Jamison laughed and gently kissed him for a while before they drifted off to sleep.

Chapter 11

HE FRAMED his subject in the photo so the name on the grocery store was visible and in focus at the same time as the man—the massive man; the massive, gorgeous man. Though not exactly a wizard with a digital camera, JP was adequate, at least good enough for the Community page of the *Overbrook Times*.

"Good one. Now give me a smile." *Okay, almost a smile.* "Listen, try to relax, Mr. Coburn."

"You can call me Jamison, but this ain't exactly relaxing for me. I'm not used to being...."

"The focus of attention?" JP prodded.

Coburn nodded, then shrugged.

"Then why agree to the interview?" JP asked, trying not to let his frustration show. He quickly snapped another picture, and Jamison tossed an annoyed glance his way. "All this could have easily been avoided."

"Folks thought it was a good idea."

"Which folks?"

"My boss, best friend... others."

"Your mother?"

"Haven't told her yet."

JP paused and straightened from behind the camera. "Oh? I was hoping to get a quote from her about you."

Coburn stared at him for several seconds. "I guess I could call her," he said slowly.

"Great! Now, you worked here as a boy?" He indicated the store. It wasn't quite a hole-in-the-wall, but it wasn't a store that would have everything a person could need, either. It sat on a street corner, a dark green awning reading "fresh vegetables" shading the entrance, and the name Coburn Grocery on a bright yellow sign above that.

Coburn nodded. "During the summers, I did the odd job, stocking shelves, some sweeping, stuff like that. After... Dad died, I gave it up and started cutting lawns, doing jobs around the neighborhood for spending money."

He turned abruptly and walked into the store, JP on his heels.

"Hey, Uncle Ray." A lanky, balding middle-aged man stood by a shelf to the right of the entrance. He appeared to be conducting an inventory of household goods: garbage bags, buckets, rakes, mulch. His eyes lit up when he spotted his nephew.

"Jam! How are ya, boy?"

"Good, I'm good." They embraced.

"Who's your friend?"

"Uh…."

JP rushed forward, extending his hand. "I'm Jerry Pool, from the *Overbrook Times*. Most folks just call me JP." They shook hands.

"A reporter?" Ray frowned.

"Yeah… I get that reaction a lot. You'd think I was a lawyer." He laughed heartily. "I'm doing a feature on Mr. Coburn for the Community page."

Ray narrowed his eyes for a moment, then pointed at JP and nodded. "Yeah, yeah. I liked the one about the young mother getting her degree."

"Thank you."

"Inspiring."

"Exactly. That's what I told Jamison, but he's not so excited about it."

Coburn stood off to the side, apparently lost in memories as he gazed around the small store. There were two registers, only one of them being operated at the moment by a young man ringing up an elderly woman's purchases. He gave her the total and waited for the woman to figure out how to pay with some type of card—maybe debit or credit. *Probably food stamps.* Exasperated, she dug into her purse and produced cash.

"Oh, Jam's always been a quiet boy," Ray explained, "but around the right people, he just lights up."

"Really. Like who?"

Ray was about to answer, but Coburn said something, something they couldn't quite catch. "What was that, boy?" he said.

"He died right there." Coburn said softly, pointing to his left. JP met his eyes. The pain in them took him aback for a moment. "The layout's changed since then, been updated a bit." Coburn's gaze moved on, appearing to take in the contents on the shelves, but JP doubted he actually saw much of it.

Ray remained silent.

"Surely you've been back before today," JP said. Coburn shook his head and continued to stare into space. *Holy shit.* JP had no response to that.

"My brother James and me owned the store," Ray explained, "but he handled the day-to-day running of it. Always tried to do everything himself. When he passed I moved back to town and took over and made some changes." Ray pointed to the clerk at the register. "That's Timothy Ferguson there"—the kid waved to JP—"I hired his sister Christine too. They help me run the place."

"Can we go?" Coburn asked suddenly.

"Uh… sure," JP said. "Don't you need to call your mother?"

"Yep, but"—he held up his cell phone and shrugged—"forgot to charge it last night."

Ray pointed to the back of the store. "You can use the office phone, boy."

"Thanks, Uncle Ray." Coburn moved off, and JP turned back to Ray.

"He's a good boy," Ray said. "Always been a hard worker, polite, never loses his temper."

"I've only heard good things." JP fiddled with his camera.

"And that's all you'll hear."

"I will say his furniture is impressive."

"Oh yeah." Ray laughed and slapped the clipboard he held. "Jam surprised all of us with that." He quieted and his gaze dropped to the floor. "I sure wish his daddy could have seen it."

JP tapped his foot. His first interview subject had been forthcoming, eager to talk about his burgeoning car repair empire. The graduating single mom had been as well. Not so with Jamison, nor apparently with his friends and coworkers. While photographing the furniture at Lincoln Frye's showroom yesterday, JP had asked Frye if there was anyone special in Jamison's life, but he claimed he didn't know of anyone. Now facing his subject's uncle, he said, "So, he's talented, handsome, hardworking…."

"Yeah?"

"He'll be, what? Thirty this year?"

"Yep, it's comin' up, I think."

JP sighed. "No girlfriend? It would really add to the story. You know how readers like a happy ending. I'm starting with his past, his beginnings. I'll work up to his now, and I'll finish with his hopes for the future. You know—handmade furniture business, maybe a wife and kids?"

"Oh, well…." Ray looked up at the ceiling, pondering. "I don't know of anyone special to speak of, but maybe Alanna will. She's my sister-in-law, Jam's mama. They're damn close. He had to be the man of the house after… you know." Ray and JP stared at each other for a moment. "I guess you hafta include that?"

"Yes, sir. It's tragic, but those details will show how far he's come from such a painful place. It's inspirational."

"Mama's ready for us," Jamison said, walking back to the front of the store. He glanced suddenly through the front doors, said, "Thanks, Uncle Ray," and rushed outside. JP thanked Ray and followed on Jamison's heels. "Hey, Mrs. Rappaport!" Jamison shouted, catching up to the elderly customer from moments ago.

JP stood by and watched Jamison take the woman's bag of groceries and walk her across the street to her home four houses down the block. *The man's a fucking Boy Scout.*

JP PEERED at each of the many photos of a young Coburn that lined the mantel in front of him: kindergarten graduation day, standing between his parents wearing a tiny paper cap and gown and smiling proudly despite two missing front teeth; in his father's arms, a weak smile on Jamison's tear-stained face as they stood over a blue bicycle lying on its side; in a much-too-big apron, standing on a chair at the kitchen counter next to his mother, "helping" her mix batter for something. He was smiling or laughing in all of them.

Then he was older, and the smile was gone.

At least you knew your father. Not everyone can say that.

Alanna Coburn entered the room, carrying a tray. "Oh, let me help you with that, ma'am," JP said, rushing over and relieving her of it. Shortly after introductions were made, Alanna had enlisted her son to examine a leak in the bathroom sink upstairs, thus leaving JP alone with her, which was exactly what he wanted. They sat, and she poured them each a cup of coffee.

"Tell me, young man, what other stories are you working on? I can name some folks you might like to write about. We have some colorful characters in this neighborhood, let me tell you." She laughed softly and sipped from her cup.

I wonder if you know just how colorful your son is. "Thank you. I might take you up on that. Coming up, I have a story about a grandmother and her grandson winning a baking contest."

"I believe I read a nice piece about a woman getting her degree."

"Yes, ma'am. These stories are designed to showcase the good news in our community, to inspire people, and your son's story certainly qualifies."

Alanna eyed his camera. "You won't be needin' my picture, will you?" She patted her hair, making sure nothing was out of place. She needn't have bothered. She looked lovely, though JP did note Mrs. Coburn had seemed a bit out of breath when she answered the door.

"No, ma'am." JP grinned as the ghost of disappointment clouded her face briefly. "Though... now that I think of it, a shot of the two of you together would be a nice touch." She brightened, quickly hiding a smile behind her coffee cup. "I'd also like to get a couple of shots of Jamison in his workshop."

"Oh, that shouldn't be a problem. All his equipment is out in the garage. He comes here to make his furniture."

"Did his father teach him?"

"James? Oh Lordy no. It was his shop teacher, Mr. Dunlop. Said Jamison took to woodworking like a mosquito to blood." She laughed again, and JP joined her.

He glanced down at his notes. "Well, ma'am, I did my research about... that night. My condolences, by the way. In spending the day with your son, we spoke with his best friend... uh, *Torpedo*...? Yeah. Okay." He tried to shake the disbelief out of his head. "I chatted with his boss, and we just came from the grocery where I talked briefly with Uncle Ray. I've collected all their impressions of Jamison, from the child he was to the man he's become." Through all this, Alanna nodded, smiling sweetly. "Now here we are."

"Yes?"

"Is there anything you can tell me about your son that the others couldn't?"

Alanna appeared to ponder that for several moments. "No, Mr. Pool. He is what he seems to be. A good man, just like his father."

JP laughed. "No doubt, ma'am, but your brother Ray said you might know if Jamison has anyone special in his life."

Her expression crumbled, and her pleasant smile went brittle. "I don't see what that has to do with anything."

Bingo.

"Our readers enjoy a good love story," he continued, smiling.

"Well… no, I'm sorry, but Jamison just hasn't met the right young lady yet."

JP jotted that down. "Well, that's a shame, but perhaps this profile will catch their attention."

Alanna smiled weakly just as Coburn thundered down the stairs.

"All fixed, Mama," he said, wiping his hands on an old, worn towel.

"Th-thank you, baby."

JP hopped up from his seat. "Jamison, I just need to get some shots of you in your workshop. Your mother tells me it's in her garage?"

"Uh… yeah. Okay." Coburn glanced at his mother, but she wouldn't meet his eyes. "Follow me."

HE SHOWED JP his completed Shaker bench and the next project he had planned—a simple swinging crib for Lincoln's office manager Cartha, which he made JP promise not to mention in the article. It was a surprise.

"How long does something like that take?" JP asked.

"It depends how much time I have to spare. If I'm busy on a renovation job for Lincoln, I can only work on this stuff when I carve out the time, but I get here at least once a week."

JP made some notes. "Where do you see yourself in five years?"

Coburn thought about it. He thought of Lonnie, the two of them living together in a home of their own, maybe one Jamison had renovated. He could get a good price if he did the upgrades himself.

He glanced back at JP and saw him draw his fingers back through his blond hair, pulling it out of his bright blue eyes. The hair fell right back into place, and JP smiled at him, waiting. *Fuck.* Jamison slid his gaze over the man from head to toe and back again. He was fit, muscled. There were lines at the corners of his eyes, but they seemed more from laughter than a lot of years. He guessed JP wasn't much older than he was, if not the same age.

"I'd like to make a living with my furniture, maybe have a small renovation business of my own someday."

"That's gonna take a lot of hard work."

"I'm not afraid of hard work."

"A degree would help with running your own business."

"Didn't have the money or the grades for college, and not everyone goes, ya know. Did you?"

JP smiled. "I did, yes. Got a bachelor's in journalism."

"But it wasn't something you *had* to have to do what you do, right?"

JP nodded. "That's true, but college isn't just about the academics. You gain critical thinking skills, but more importantly, higher education introduces you to the world beyond your ratty little neighborhood— different people, ideas, ways of living. It opens your eyes and mind to the possibilities." JP shrugged. "That's what it did for me, anyway."

"A mind is a terrible thing to waste, right?" Jamison said.

"Sorry." JP scuffed his shoe against the concrete. "Didn't mean to get carried away, but I shudder to think where I'd be if I hadn't gotten that degree."

Jamison watched him squirm for several moments, then said, "Anything else?"

"Oh, uh… what about a family? Right now it doesn't sound like you have much time for a social life."

There it was again. All day the reporter had been *almost* asking about his personal life, his romantic life but not quite going all the way. Jamison had stood by Torp's side as JP asked him a few questions about any shenanigans they got into as kids. But with Lincoln, Uncle Ray, and then Mama, Jamison had been out of the room. He wondered what they'd discussed.

"I try to make time when I can."

"So you do have someone special in your life?"

"I do… but I'm not gonna talk about it."

JP nodded and made a note in his pad. "Do you have any enemies?"

He frowned. "That's a weird question."

"I only ask because everyone I spoke with today had only fantastic things to say about you."

"That's good, isn't it?"

The reporter stared at him a moment, then smiled. "It's a miracle."

"So, is that it?" JP nodded, and Jamison began shutting down the garage and locking everything away. "When do you think this will run?"

"The week after next, for sure. I have the grandma-and-grandson bakers next week. They're quite the duo." He laughed, and Jamison smiled, the knot of suspicion in his stomach loosening. "Can I contact you if I have any follow-up questions or need clarification?"

"Sure."

"Thank you for your time, Mr. Coburn."

"Jamison, remember?"

"Of course… Jamison."

Chapter 12

LONNIE'S NOISY purple Beetle came to a stop, and after a familiar screech of his parking brake, he hopped out. Swinging his keys a couple times before stuffing them in the front pocket of his knee-length khaki shorts, he headed for the Overbrook University School of Art and Design. Bink had news to share but wouldn't do so over the phone, so here he was, running up the front steps of the rather unappealing brick building. It had seen better days, but the modern gallery addition constructed three years ago brought in a lot of business from Baltimore, DC, even Dover.

It was late in the day, so the student traffic in the hall was light. Most were probably in studio rooms painting or sculpting or designing some great piece that would change the world. He grinned at the thought. Lonnie knew how solitary his existence could be when he was painting, which was one reason stepping into Jamison's arms could be so transforming, his focus exploding outward again, sights, sounds, and sensations rushing at him after hours of experiencing only the rhythm of his breathing and his brush against the canvas.

He rapped on Bink's third-floor office door.

"Come in!"

He had visited countless times, but now Lonnie stepped into unfamiliar territory. The bookshelves along the right wall were practically bare. The thick curtains normally covering the large window at the back of the narrow space were gone, flooding the room with light that revealed bare walls, now empty of the numerous student paintings and photographs she'd collected over the years, leaving only the afterimages of their frames.

"Uh...."

"Ah, Lonnie! Glad you could make it." She looked him up and down. "Why are you dressed like a first grader in Catholic school?"

He looked down at his outfit, smoothing out the navy cardigan and tugging at the buttoned collar of his pale blue shirt underneath. "What? I took Gran and Mom to lunch."

She waved a dismissive hand. "Never mind. Please have a seat." Bink moved from behind her desk to clear away a pile of files from a pink tweed Queen Anne chair in front of it. Lonnie sat and continued to gaze around him. Not only had the room changed from its normally clogged condition, but Bink herself was dressed in jeans, T-shirt, and a ball cap. Even when they'd worked together on the gallery's most recent installation, Bink had been dressed as the professor she was: pencil skirt, sensible heels, and suit jacket. This… this was floorboard-scrubbing Bink.

"What's happening?"

She paused in her packing. That's what it was. Packing. "Oh, how very mid-to-late '70s of you," she said with a smirk.

"Bink," he said, gesturing to the shelves, walls, and piles of books on her desk. "What's with all this? You look like you're leaving." His heart pounded more forcefully for a moment, and he sat forward in his seat. "You're not *leaving*, are you?"

Bink took a seat behind her desk and contemplated him. She appeared to be carefully selecting her words, which he knew was not a good sign.

"Are *you* leaving, Lonnie?"

"Pardon me?"

"We've discussed this."

Lonnie frowned. "Have we?"

"You've secured your master's." She spread her hands out toward him as if showing him the world at his feet. "What's next for you?"

"Uh…." Lonnie's first instinct was to share his plans to putter around Overbrook, play with Remmy, love on Jamison, paint some murals to pay the bills, maybe… hell, he didn't know. For so long his drive had been to get the degree. He hadn't thought seriously beyond that to possible office work, ditch digging, house painting… what? He realized she was asking what he was going to do with his future.

She was right; they had discussed the topic periodically over their years together, but never seriously. At one time Lonnie had mentioned going to France for a few years to hone his craft, create a larger body of work unique to him. Maybe secure a show and then explode on the international art scene to much applause. Those were his idealistic expectations as he entered Overbrook University for the first time, right before he became involved with JP. They were on-again, off-again during

Lonnie's undergraduate years, and it ended for good as he launched into the master's degree program.

He'd also once toyed with the idea of opening a gallery of his own in Baltimore or perhaps San Francisco or New York, but then he'd stepped that back to apprenticing at a big-city gallery before tackling one of his own.

There was still a lot to learn no matter which direction he chose. Being able to paint did not give you the skills to manage a business.

He blinked at her. "Why do you ask?"

She leaned forward and grinned at him. "If you're planning to stay in Overbrook instead of flying off to France to hole up on the family farm and paint until you drop, I am now in a position to offer you a full-time position as my assistant in managing the campus's Michelle Gallery."

The original panic faded only to be replaced by an entirely new panic. "What? How? *What?*"

"I'm no longer interim director. I've got the job and have the green light to hire my staff." She sat back in her chair and sighed. "Signed the contract this morning." She steepled her hands. "Of course, I'll be cutting my course load. Professor Harland will be picking up that slack." She shook her head sadly. "Those poor young minds."

Lonnie snorted before he could cover.

"So, are you interested? It comes with full benefits and a"—she seesawed a hand slightly—"liveable wage. It's good practical experience."

"Bink, I don't know what to say. It's very generous of you, but I'll need to think about this."

"Of course, I understand." She returned to her packing, putting books in a box. "I won't actually take over for another two weeks, but I thought I should make the move to my new office downstairs go as smoothly as possible by decluttering in here." She folded the lid shut and secured it with a tape gun. "I don't know what I'll do with central air and heat and windows that actually open and close." She winked at him.

"Why me?"

She didn't look at him as she grabbed an empty box nearby, set it on her desk, and placed several books in it. "Several reasons. First, in all the time I've known you, not once did you declare a plan for your professional life after getting your master's. Second, I like you. And third, Overbrook is your home, Lonnie. You're not a graduating student itching to flee the state for more exciting locales." Bink paused and peered into his eyes, an intensity sparking in them. "I want this gallery to grow, to pull in professionals and visiting artists from DC and beyond. I want it to rival any big-city gallery while still maintaining its small-town comforts and atmosphere."

"That's a tough balance to strike."

"Yes, but with your help and dedication, we'll get there. You and I, Lonnie, make a good team."

He stood and gestured at the chaos before him, looking around the room. "Is there anything I can help you with here? Right now?"

"That's kind of you, son. Um…." She glanced at her possessions. "Could you clear off the rest of those tomes for me so I can pack them? Those, just there on the lower shelf."

He did as she asked, also grabbing two more boxes on his way back to the desk. They worked together for another forty minutes, packing, sealing, and labeling until the contents of Bink's office were whittled down to knickknacks, coffee mugs, and office supplies. They fell into their respective seats and smiled at each other. Lonnie propped his feet up on one of the boxes he'd packed and folded his blue summer cardigan in his lap. His activity had him sweating in the now-stuffy room.

Bink tossed him a bottle of water and sipped her own. "How is Jamison?"

"He's—oh!" Lonnie sat forward suddenly, dropping his feet flat on the floor again. "I forgot to tell you. He's being interviewed for a community profile by the *Overbrook Times*."

"Indeed… that's interesting."

"Yep. He wasn't too excited about it at first, being so private and all, but we managed to talk him into it. He should be proud of his accomplishments." Bink smiled at him, and Lonnie calmed himself. "What?"

"You appear proud enough for the both of you."

He laughed and got to his feet. For a moment he was perplexed about how to navigate his way through the boxes littering the floor to the door. "Do you need help with these, ma'am?" He glanced up at her. "We can stack them against that wall until you're ready to move."

"Thank you, but I've hired a couple of burly athletes to carry everything to my storage unit in the basement. They were short on beer, pot, or hooker money." She waved a dismissive hand. "I didn't ask for specifics."

"Oh, well, then… thank you, for considering me," he said, extending his hand to her. "I'll give you my answer soon."

She shook his hand. "You're welcome, son. Take care."

Barely able to contain his excitement, Lonnie fled the arts building and ran to his car. He knew exactly whom he wanted to share his news with first.

Ten minutes later he screeched to a halt in front of the Standlea residence. Lonnie was out of his car and halfway up the drive leading to Jamison's garage apartment in the back before he realized the familiar big blue truck wasn't there and stopped in his tracks, disappointed. He turned to leave.

"Can I help you?" a voice called out from the deep shadows of the front porch of the big brick house on his right.

"Hi! Is that Mrs. Standlea?" He shaded his eyes with his hand to see better. "It's Lonnie, Lonnie Bellerose…. Jamison's—"

"Oh yes! The artist. Good to see you, my boy." She walked to the top of the steps, the sunlight finally illuminating her. She was a tiny, pretty Asian woman with white hair turned up neat and tight on her head. Her full makeup was in place, and she wore a lavender sundress and sandals. But Lonnie was surprised to see her with a cane. She'd always seemed so spry when he'd seen her before.

"Ma'am, are you all right?" He pointed to the cane.

She glanced at it, then shook it at him. "Oh this thing is just for my hip replacement. Still building strength in it. Nothing to worry about. My doctor says I'm on track. Now, about your fella." She thought for a moment, tapping her chin. "He's been gone most of the day, but I did ask him to pick up a few things at the grocery store for dinner. Were you supposed to meet up with him? I can… I can…." She fumbled for a moment in one of the big pockets on the front of her dress. "I can give him a call, if you like," she said, brandishing a cell phone with keypad numbers on it big enough that Lonnie could almost read them from where he stood.

"Oh no, ma'am, thank you. We didn't have plans. I just had some good news I wanted to share. I'll catch him later."

"All right. If I see him before you, I'll tell him you stopped by."

"Thank you, Mrs. Standlea. Take care." She went back into the house, the screen door screeching as she opened it and slapping shut behind her. Lonnie headed for his car. On the way he noticed a stocky, well-dressed black man leaning on the hood of a shiny silver sedan. He didn't think it had been parked there when he'd pulled up. Then again, he hadn't exactly been paying attention.

"Hey there," the guy said, and Lonnie paused at the end of the drive. "Looks like you and me are looking for the same dude, huh?" The man shoved off the hood and approached him. "Name's Delroy Pritchard. I'm an old friend of Jam's."

"Oh." Lonnie shook Delroy's hand, noting a faint aroma of sugar and baking bread. "Good to meet you. I'm Lonnie Bellerose. I'm Jamison's—"

Three quick taps on a truck horn filled the air, and Jamison pulled up so fast Lonnie and Delroy had to scurry out of the way. He continued on to the back of the driveway and parked right below his apartment.

"Nearly ran me over the same way Friday night," Delroy mumbled.

"Friday?" Lonnie asked.

"Yeah, me and the wife were over here looking at the house we just closed on."

"Congratulations."

"Thanks. Anyway, I caught Jam all dressed up and headed out to meet his lady, but he was in such a rush, I had to jump out of the way." Delroy grew thoughtful. "Hmm, now that I say that out loud—" He chuckled. "—I get why he was in such a hurry. She must be a real looker."

Lonnie glared at the "old friend of Jamison's."

The horn on Jamison's truck blared sharply as he struggled out of the cab with grocery bags. "Hey, Lon," he said breathlessly, frown lines on his forehead and a strained smile on his face. "Delroy, didn't expect to see you again so soon."

"Yeah, well I told you our new place is in the area. I just came over to find out what church you go to on this end of town." Jamison opened his mouth to answer, but Delroy kept right on talking. "Also wanted to get your digits so Vinnia and I might set up that double date with you and your girlfriend sometime. The wife is eager to make friends over here. Ya know... *couple* friends."

"Oh...."

Lonnie looked between the two of them and opened his mouth to inquire about Jamison's new lady friend, but Mrs. Standlea came out on her porch again.

"Jamison, can you bring those in so I can get dinner started before Edgar's bingo night is over?"

"Yes… yes, ma'am, coming." Jamison hustled away. "Be right back. Don't… don't go anywhere!" He disappeared into the house just as Delroy yelled after him to wait.

"Damn! He always was an odd duck," Delroy said, glancing at his watch.

"Huh?"

"Listen, Larry—"

"It's Lonnie."

"—my Vinnia's waitin' on me." He fished a business card out of his jacket pocket. "This has my info on it. Ask Jam to give me a call, won't ya?" He headed back to his shiny car, waving good-bye over his shoulder. "Good ta meet ya. Thanks!"

Lonnie watched him go, then examined the card. It read:

Bloom's Bakery
Delroy Pritchard, Proprietor

Chapter 13

JAMISON HURRIEDLY put away Mrs. Standlea's groceries, wondering for the four minutes it took what Lonnie and Delroy were talking about.

"I can handle it from here, son," she said, watching him with confusion in her eyes as he dashed around the kitchen to the cabinets, the counter, and the refrigerator.

"Uh… okay, ma'am. Here's… here's your change." He dug in his front pocket for the fifteen or so dollars (she always gave him too much) he had left over, but when he held it out to her, she closed his hand around the bills.

"You keep that for gasoline, dear."

"Mrs. Stand—"

"Don't argue with me," she said, shaking a vegetable knife at him. She took her seat at the kitchen table and resumed chopping cucumbers. "You and your friends are welcome to have dinner with me and Edgar tonight, if you like."

"Thank you, but I think Lonnie and me have some things to talk about."

"Oh yes, he did say he had good news to share."

"He did?" Jamison blinked at her.

She nodded, and he peered out the kitchen window and saw Lonnie standing alone behind his truck, staring at something in his hand. "I'll… uh, see you later, ma'am." He went outside, and Lonnie smiled at him, which eased the tension in his chest.

"Hello again, babe."

Lonnie kissed him, and Jamison tried not to pull back and glance at the street.

"I hear you have good news?"

"Yes, but let's go inside."

"What's that in your hand?" he asked as he led the way up the stairs on the outside of the garage.

"Oh, your friend left his business card. Said to give him a call—" Jamison entered the dim apartment first. "—so you and your 'lady friend' can set up a date with him and his Vinnia." Jamison grimaced and turned to face Lonnie, who chucked the card at his face, nicking him on the cheek.

"Lonnie, it's just a misunderstanding," he said, rubbing just below his left eye.

"Uh-huh."

"I thought you had good news." He went to the refrigerator to grab a beer. "Want one?" Lonnie nodded curtly and snatched the bottle from his hand when he offered it. "Come on, babe." Jamison wrapped him up in his arms and squeezed as Lonnie struggled. Then inspiration struck, and he slowly lifted Lonnie's shirttail and pressed the cold bottle against his bare skin. Lonnie yelped and tried harder to squirm free. "Now tell me your good news," Jamison demanded.

"Bink offered me a job," Lonnie squealed. Jamison finally released him, and Lonnie quickly moved out of reach, giving a little shiver.

"Yeah? Doing what?" Jamison collapsed on the sofa and put his feet up on his milk-crate coffee table. He gulped the beer, hoping beyond hope Lonnie would let Delroy's comments go.

Lonnie dropped down next to him with a sigh. "Assistant director of the campus gallery."

"Babe! That's fantastic!" He examined Lonnie's expression, reaching out to brush a few curls out of his eyes. "Isn't it?"

"Yeah... sure, but it bothers me that I haven't given things more thought." Lonnie glanced at him from the corner of his eye, put his feet up on the table next to Jamison's, and began knocking his navy-blue-sneakered feet together. "Is there something more I should be shooting for? Have I waited too long to work all this out? Should I take what's being handed to me?"

Jamison considered those questions. He'd been without direction once, but he'd been a child at the time. By age thirteen he'd known what he wanted for himself. Well, most of what he wanted. His love of working with wood filled him up. His work with Lincoln paid the bills. He stayed on track, learned valuable skills, and saved his money. But it was his step off the track he'd laid for himself that brought him the greatest reward—Lonnie. Speaking of... when Lonnie snuggled down closer to him, seeking comfort, it made Jamison's life.

"My father never thought much of my pursuing art," Lonnie mumbled.

"He seemed okay with it."

"He was never as bad as my grandfather, but I could tell." Lonnie looked up at him, and Jamison smiled down into his green eyes. "He paid for it, but he'd rather I studied business, something practical, something with 'measurable value.'" Lonnie stroked Jamison's thigh with his beer bottle, and Jamison shivered. "He'll be thrilled if I take the gallery position." Lonnie chugged from his beer and followed it up with a loud, sustained belch. Then he covered his mouth and laughed.

Jamison grinned but gave no other sign he'd even heard it, keeping his *Good one!* to himself. "What else would you do?"

Lonnie shrugged. "Most people in my position end up teaching. I'd be good at it too. Or I could freelance—murals, portraits. I could wander the family vineyard. Hell, I don't know." Lonnie dropped his head on Jamison's shoulder and sighed. "Can't we just roll around in bed with each other for a few days until I figure things out?"

Jamison snorted and cupped Lonnie's face to bring their lips together. "Sorry, babe, but I have to work."

"Speaking of work, how did that interview go?"

"You were right," he said. "It wasn't as bad as I expected, but I still don't see how anyone could find me interesting."

"Aw…," Lonnie purred, rolling over and straddling him. "You, Mr. Coburn, are absolutely riveting."

He smiled and accepted Lonnie's sweet kiss.

JP SAT in his car across the street, staring up at the garage apartment Lonnie had disappeared into with Coburn. He knew what they were doing up there. It was funny. He hadn't thought of Lonnie once during his treatment, and not for a long time before that, if he was honest with himself. But after seeing him smiling at Coburn on that dance floor Friday, the way the big man had touched him, JP wanted nothing more than another chance with Lonnie. He wanted Lonnie to look into his eyes the way he used to… the way he now looked at that handsome behemoth of a man. When Lonnie traded back up to him, then JP would know he was back to being the person he should be. Lonnie was his Reset button. His fresh start.

He gripped the steering wheel until his knuckles paled, but whatever he felt now, he was glad he'd decided to follow Coburn home. He'd witnessed the awkward exchange between the three men near the truck. The stranger had looked like an old friend popping by to say hi. The guy clearly had no idea who Lonnie was. JP smiled and started his car. It was time to get to work on his article.

"I NEED the shower," Lonnie said, trying to shove Jamison off him.

"No." Jamison snuffled against Lonnie's neck, making him giggle. "I thought we were staying in bed for days."

"You remember pointing out how impractical that is?"

"Oh yeah." He rolled off Lonnie and stared at the ceiling, playfully tangling his left hand in Lonnie's hair. "We don't have anywhere else to be, though."

Lonnie's cell rang.

Dammit!

The bed dipped, and Lonnie elbowed him in the chest and kicked him in the shin as he twisted to reach the phone. "Hello?"

Jamison lay there, his eyes getting heavy and Lonnie's conversation a distant buzz. His mind and spirit still circled above the garage, above the neighborhood on a cloud of bliss. He could see the quiet, tree-lined street the Standleas had lived on for thirty years or more. Maybe he should start looking for properties to renovate for himself. Lonnie would need a studio with plenty of natural light. He'd probably want to be close to his sister and her family. *We'll need a guestroom in case his parents want to visit... someday, or maybe Remmy, when he's older.* An office would be nice.

"Jamison!"

He opened his eyes. "Huh? What is it?"

"We're having dinner at Amber's tonight with the family. That was her on the phone."

"Lon...."

"No. We're going. Mom's cooking, and she's a gourmet." He hopped out of the bed and headed for the bathroom. Jamison couldn't look away from that delicious body. "It'll taste great!" Lonnie declared before slamming the bathroom door behind him, and Jamison soon heard the shower running.

Yes, Lon, you do.

REMMY WAS in Arthur's arms screaming his head off when they arrived. Jamison found the sound terrifying, and he looked from one person to the next, wondering if they were as disturbed as he was. Amber, Ginger, and Diane were in the kitchen and appeared too busy to care.

"Is he okay?" he whispered to Lonnie.

"Yeah. Probably hungry or wet or something."

Sure enough, once Arthur plugged Remmy's squalling mouth with a small bottle of milk, Jamison actually thought he heard a sigh from the baby. Arthur sat in the leather Queen Anne in the living room, cooing to Remmy in French.

Lonnie's brother-in-law, Claude, ushered Lonnie and Jamison into the living room after greeting them at the door.

"Glad you could make it, gentlemen," he said. "This dinner has been in the works all day." He leaned close to Jamison's ear and whispered, "Should be spectacular."

Whatever was cooking certainly smelled great. Jamison had high hopes, but he also had some nerves, fearing some strange, exotic food he wouldn't be able to hide his feelings about. Hadn't he heard once that French people ate snails?

"There won't be any escargot," Lonnie said.

"What's that?"

Lonnie smiled up at him and said, "Snails."

"How did you—?"

Lonnie kissed him, and Claude said, "Aperitif?" holding out two glasses of wine.

Jamison took one and sniffed it. "What's—?"

"Wine before dinner," Lonnie supplied.

Jamison hid his frown behind sipping his wine, which he didn't care for, and there was no place to hide that grimace. Diane, in an apron and house shoes, appeared from the kitchen. She held her flour-dusted hands out, making grabbing motions, encouraging him into an embrace, and the smile on her face prompted Jamison to return it.

"Ravie de te revoir, Jamison."

Yep, he could figure that one out. "Nice to see you again too, ma'am."

She reached up, and he bent down to hug her. Then Diane patted his cheek, leaving a handprint of flour there. "Oh, excuse-moi. Alonzo, donne-moi quelque chose pour—" She opened and closed her fingers, as if seeking rescue and remedy.

Laughing, Lonnie skipped into the kitchen and grabbed a hand towel. "Grand-mère, permets-moi." As Lonnie wiped the flour from

Jamison's face, Jamison watched him—sighing at the long dark lashes framing his eyes, the pout of his bottom lip, his flawless skin. Lonnie looked into his eyes. *Sorry*, he mouthed. "Turn, let me check your jacket." Jamison did, and Lonnie gave it a swipe. "I'll hang this up. Go have a seat with Claude and Papa."

"Yes, Jamison," Claude called from the sofa. "Come in."

He did and settled his bulk in an easy chair facing toward the hallway. He glanced at Arthur, Remmy, and Claude, listened to the activity in the kitchen, then watched the hall for any sign of Lonnie.

"Busy day?" Claude asked and sipped his wine

"No renovation work, but I spent the day with a reporter from the *Overbrook Times*." He rested his wineglass on his thigh, never intending to drink another drop, but he was momentarily mesmerized by the rich color. "He's doing a profile on me and my furniture."

"That's great! When's it coming out?"

"A couple of weeks, I think."

"Very nice," Arthur said softly. He placed a cloth diaper on his shoulder, transferred Remmy to it, then gently patted his back. Jamison imagined him doing the same for Lonnie and Amber. "If they feature your furniture, it may bring in business, yes?"

Jamison shrugged. "I hadn't really thought about that."

Diane appeared in the entry, her apron now gone. "Le dîner est prêt."

Claude hopped up, as did Jamison, while Arthur slowly rose to carry Remmy to the den.

As they headed to the dining room, Jamison asked, "What are we having?"

All Claude said was, "Smells good, doesn't it?"

True, but that did little to ease Jamison's mind.

JAMISON SAT back and sighed. "That. Was. Delicious."

Ginger beamed at him, and Lonnie chuckled. "You sound surprised, babe."

The chicken cooked in cream would stick to him for months, but it was totally worth it.

Diane stood. "Aide-moi avec le dessert, s'il te plaît, Lonnie."

"Oui, Grand-mère." Lonnie disappeared into the kitchen.

"Diane made baked pears for dessert, Jamison," Ginger explained. "I think you'll like them." She winked.

He smiled back. He'd loved everything else.

Diane and Lonnie returned with dessert and coffee, and everyone sat around the table and chatted about their day as they enjoyed the treat.

Earlier, while Diane napped, Arthur and Ginger had gone for a walk in Overbrook Park, pushing Remmy in his stroller, and Amber and Claude had stepped out for a movie. Once everyone had congregated back at the house, Diane, Ginger, and Amber went to work on preparing dinner, though Amber wasn't allowed to help much.

"Claude's a much better cook than I am," Amber said, and her husband nodded before kissing her cheek. The baby monitor on the table squawked, and Claude hopped up to check on Remmy, allowing his wife to relax.

Ginger stood, as did Lonnie. "I'll help clear, Mom," he said as he began collecting utensils and empty plates.

Jamison pushed his chair back. "I can—"

"No, young man," Ginger commanded. "You sit and finish your coffee. We have this."

"Yes, ma'am."

"Jamison, how was this reporter who interviewed you?" Arthur asked. "Some in the media can be so rude."

"He was fine. Asked just about every question under the sun and took a lot of pictures."

"Did he talk to your friends?" Amber asked as Claude reappeared with Remmy in his arms and retook his seat.

"He spoke to my best friend, my boss, my uncle, and my mother."

"Not Lonnie?" Claude asked.

"Uh...." Jamison glanced into the kitchen. Lonnie and his mother were at the sink rinsing dishes and loading the dishwasher. "Lonnie wasn't around. We visited my old neighborhood, the family store, and Frye Home Improvement."

"You know...," Arthur began thoughtfully, "I believe I saw a profile like yours, Jamison, in the paper the other day."

He nodded. "Yes, sir, they're doing a series."

Arthur continued to stare into space, as though trying to retrieve an elusive memory. "I enjoyed the writing. Is it the same writer for all? A Mr. Pool?"

"Yeah, that's him," Jamison said. "Jerry Pool."

A crash from the kitchen startled everyone, set Remmy squalling, but Amber stared at Jamison in shock.

Chapter 14

LONNIE STOOD in the doorway to the dining room, shards of broken dinnerware in his hand. "Did you… did you say Jerry Pool?"

"Yeah." Jamison glanced at the faces around the table, then back to Lonnie. "Why?"

Lonnie said nothing, his mind spinning too quickly for him to speak. He turned from the doorway and went back into the kitchen to dump the dish he'd just broken at the sound of his ex's name. *He's back? What's he doing in Overbrook?* Suddenly Ginger was there, and shortly after, Amber, their hands on his shoulders, squeezing, supporting. He breathed deeply and tried to shake off the fog of self-doubt filling his head.

Then Jamison arrived, his scent, his steady presence and weight at his back. "Lon?" The hands of his sister and mother vanished and were replaced by Jamison's much larger, stronger ones. "Lon, tell me what's the matter. Please."

He turned into Jamison and embraced him, burying his face against his chest. God, he smelled good, but he hated that he needed this now, needed it to keep from flying apart. It was just the shock, he thought. *I'm not afraid of JP. I don't need protection from him. I'm still strong. Just need a moment….*

In the background, he could hear muttering in French and chairs moving as the family attempted to leave them alone… to talk. *Fuck.* Lonnie pulled back from Jamison and looked up into his dark, worried eyes.

"Let's have a seat out back, babe. I need to tell you something."

He led Jamison through the french doors, and they took a seat on the deck steps, side by side. Lonnie looked around, at everything except Jamison. This was where they'd first met. Jamison kept hold of Lonnie's hand. *How do I—?*

"Jerry Pool is my ex."

"From your reaction," Jamison said, glancing over his shoulder to the house, "from everyone's reaction, he's a bad guy, treated you bad. He hurt you?" Jamison's eyes darkened even more—if that were possible—and his expression clouded. Lonnie knew then he should never let the two of them meet again.

"Not like you're thinking, no." He sighed. "Everything was great at first. JP was smart and quick and made me laugh. And he was *so* gor—anyway. We were together for about three years, but it ended two years ago, and by then he was a mess, snorting all his money, and some of mine."

"He hurt you." Jamison couldn't seem to get past that statement.

"He broke my heart, criticized every move I made, to the point...." He sighed.

"What?"

Lonnie stared out at the yard. "I didn't know who I was anymore." Jamison squeezed his hand tighter, and Lonnie looked at him and smiled. "I was rushing in every direction to get him to love me like he did in the beginning, to still want me, treat me like I was special to him. But nothing worked. Finally, at a party one night he tried to get me to do a line of coke with him, but when I refused he...."

"What?"

"He beat him up," Amber said from the doorway.

"Amber!"

"He did, Lonnie! Mother told me. Don't you defend him!"

"He smacked me once," he said, doing exactly that.

"Once? And managed to black your eye *and* break a rib? That's one magic white man!" Her hands were on her hips, her expression thunderous.

Lonnie ignored his sister and faced Jamison. "Afterward he was mortified. He went into treatment."

"And left it after a week," Amber supplied.

Lonnie whirled on her. "Will you *please* leave us alone?"

"Dear, Remmy needs you," Claude called from the depths of the house, and Amber reluctantly went inside.

Lonnie turned to Jamison. "We need to hurry because Mom's going to take her place."

"Did you go back to him?"

"What?"

"Did you forgive him?"

Lonnie felt sick. "Y-yeah, for a b-bit."

Jamison nodded but said nothing. Lonnie rubbed his arm, gazed at his face, trying to read his thoughts. He eventually fell back on the familiar.

"I'm... I'm sorry, Jamis—"

"You don't have nothin' to be sorry for, Lon." He leaned over and kissed him. "I've seen it before."

"Seen what?"

"In my neighborhood, growing up. There was a family a couple houses down from us. The police came at least once a week, until...."

"It was never that bad."

"Lon." They stared into each other's eyes for several seconds, and then Lonnie *could* read Jamison's mind. *It would have gotten there.* "People go back. They don't think...." Jamison cupped his cheek, and Lonnie leaned into it, welcoming the warmth. "They don't think they deserve any better, and they go back." He wrapped Lonnie up in his arms, anchoring him, stopping the shakes that had begun. "You deserve so much better."

He squeezed Jamison hard around the waist, telling him silently he would happily hold him like that forever if he wanted. "I *have* so much better, babe," Lonnie whispered.

LONNIE TRIED to yank open the big glass door, but it was heavier than it looked and nearly threw him off-balance. Once he made it into the airy lobby of the building that housed the *Overbrook Times*, he approached the front desk, where a receptionist waited, watching him. She'd probably seen his bumbling. There was always someone watching.

"May I help you?" she asked.

"Yes," Lonnie said, smiling his sweetest. "I'm here to see Jerry Pool."

"Do you have an appointment?"

"Of course," he lied.

The receptionist got on her phone and spoke to someone, then looked back up at him. "I'm so sorry, but Mr. Pool is out on assignment. Apparently he's forgotten your appointment." She smiled widely, and Lonnie's grew brittle because he knew *she* knew he was lying. "May I take a message?"

"Please have him call Lonnie Bellerose." He gave her his cell number, then turned and fled. As he shoved through the doors to the outside, the sun hit him like a spotlight, illuminating his self-doubt. He had planned to what? Lay into Jerry? Trash his desk? Demand he stay away from him and Jamison?

But JP hadn't done anything but an interview. He didn't know who Jamison was to Lonnie. He unsteadily and slowly went down the front steps of the building but stopped at the bottom. Why open up communication again? *I doubt I even cross his mind anymore.* He turned to retrieve his number, cursing himself for getting worked up in the first place. JP was his past. He never had to see him again.

"Lonnie?"

Fuck!

He turned and faced Jerry Pool, a man he hadn't seen in two years. He looked good, if older. The drug abuse had left its mark on him, but he was still stunning.

"Hello, JP."

"What are you doing here?" JP glanced at the building, then to Lonnie.

"I was going to ask you the same thing."

A blond eyebrow went up. *Just like it used to.* "Well, I'm just coming back from an assignment—"

"No. What are you doing back in Overbrook?"

"Oh... uh, well, I finished my rehab, knocked around for a bit, and then Stew Dimple gave me a job. We used to work together in Balti— never mind." He stepped closer, and Lonnie managed to hold his ground. "I'm doing fluffy stuff for the paper, profiles and community pieces. Nothing to brag about."

"Maybe you'll be back on the police beat sooner rather than later."

"God, I hope so." JP chuckled, then slid his gaze appreciatively up and down Lonnie's body. "You look really good, Lonnie."

"Thank you." He put as much chill in his voice as possible.

"Listen, I know it's been a while, but I want to apologize for—"

"It's okay, JP. Old news. All in the past."

"Really?" His lovely blue eyes lit up with hope.

"Sure."

JP smiled broadly, then frowned after a moment. "Why are you here again?"

Lonnie laughed and glanced out at Overbrook's typical light traffic, his Beetle waiting in the shade of a big white oak across the street, and he wanted nothing more than to get away, to find Jamison. "It's a bit embarrassing actually."

"What?"

"I came by to cancel my subscription." *Stupid lie, stupid lie!*

"Oh."

Lonnie winced. "Sorry."

"No worries." JP stepped closer. "Hey, did you finish your degree?"

"Yep. Got my master's."

"Congratulations."

"Thank you, but I should really get go—"

"Lonnie, would you like to get a drink some—?"

"No…. Thank you, but no," he said firmly, looking steadily into those eyes. There was no criticism in them now, only an eagerness Lonnie didn't want to think about. "It's all in the past, but I haven't forgotten."

JP nodded, stared at the ground. "I guess you're seeing someone?"

"I am, yes, but my answer would still have been no."

"I understand. Take care of yourself, Lonnie."

"You too."

JP TURNED after entering the building and stared out the doors as Lonnie drove off in that hideous car of his.

"Mr. Pool," the receptionist called, "I have a message for you."

Once Lonnie was out of sight, he collected Lonnie's number and pocketed it. He wouldn't contact him just yet. But later? After the story hit? Lonnie would need someone to talk to, someone familiar.

He took the elevator to the second floor and entered the newsroom, heading straight for his desk. A couple of other reporters were working on whatever passed for news in Overbrook as he sat down to pound out his profile on the baking grandmother and her grandson. *Lord, help me.*

"Pool," Stewart said, strolling up to his desk, "which community profile you got for me this Friday? We need to promo it tomorrow." He took a deep sip of bourbon from his coffee mug and sighed. Stewart was rather proud of that mug because it read *Fuck You!* instead of *World's Best Boss.*

JP paged through his computer files and selected a photo of the octogenarian baked-potato ninja and her plump, greasy-faced grand-spawn. "Typing it up right now. I'll send this photo to the copy desk."

"You do that, and send them a blurb for the banner at the top."

"I'm on it, Stew."

His boss walked away, and JP smiled. Sadly, the story about Granny the baker was going to have a little accident between its midweek promo and its Friday debut. Luckily, he had a completed article ready to plug in its place, an article he'd crafted very carefully.

LONNIE STUMBLED over the bag by the front door. He recognized it as his father's.

"Where's Papa going?" he asked his mother, who came rushing forward with a baggie of snacks and stuffed them into a side pocket of the carry-on.

"He has business to take care of in New York." She clearly noticed the frown Lonnie didn't attempt to hide. "What is it?"

"I had some news I didn't get to share at dinner last night."

"Don't pout, son. You're too old for that."

"I'm not pouting, Mother."

"Drive us to the airport?" she suggested as she slipped on a sweater. "You can tell us on the way. Or you can wait. He'll be back in two days."

Lonnie held up his hand and caught the car keys she tossed to him.

"Shotgun!" Arthur called as he rushed down the stairs toward them. Ginger laughed musically and kissed him while Lonnie snorted, picked up his father's bag, and led them out the door.

On the drive he filled them in and, as predicted, Arthur was thrilled. "Will you take the job?" he asked, the enthusiasm clear in his voice.

Biting his lip, Lonnie glanced sideways. "I don't know, Papa."

Arthur sighed, and Ginger reached forward and squeezed his shoulder. Arthur grinned and patted her hand there. "Well, your Bink has given you time to think it over. You should take that time."

His father gave him a pat on the back and, overcome, Lonnie said, "Thank you, Papa."

On the drive they discussed what Arthur would be working on while away, the latest adorable thing Remmy had done, and Diane's obsessive interest in the American *Bachelor*. Lonnie and Ginger followed closely behind Arthur as they rushed through the terminal, but soon reached a point the two of them could not go beyond. So they said their good-byes with hugs and kisses and wishes for safe travel. He promised to call, then eventually vanished on the other side of security. Ginger didn't want to leave before the flight did, so Lonnie flipped through a magazine rack while she picked out a few postcards at a bookstore. Then they had coffee at a café while she filled them out. After the flight was airborne, they headed back to the car.

On the drive home, Lonnie shared his less-happy news. "I saw Jerry today."

His mother sat quietly next to him for several seconds. "Why?"

"I was angry, furious really, that he'd interviewed Jamison—"

"But—"

"Yes, I know. He has no idea we're together, and he was just doing his job."

"So?"

"I came to that conclusion a tad too late."

"What did he have to say for himself?"

"He apologized… for everything."

"Really? He apologized? As your mother, there is no forgiveness for that, just so you know."

Lonnie smiled. "Yes, I know."

"Did you tell him about Jamison?"

Spotting the exit he needed, Lonnie signaled. "I told him I was seeing someone, yes." They drove in silence for several moments. "He looked good."

"No, Lonnie!"

"Just an observation, Mother!"

From the exit to the driveway of Amber's home, they yelled at each other in French.

Chapter 15

JAMISON WORKED the paint roller in the typical *W* fashion, smoothing on the blue-gray—or something called Aqua Smoke—the homeowner had selected for the dining room. Sweat stung his eyes, and he carefully selected the cloth at his belt that wasn't covered in paint smears to wipe it away. He and Torp would be working all day Saturday to meet the Wednesday deadline, but he couldn't help smiling at how nice the place was looking. The white trim would set the room off nicely, but his smile wasn't just for that. After work he and Lonnie were going to dinner and a movie, and he planned to cap the night off with some lovin'. He sighed.

"Son?" Lincoln said, walking into the dining room.

"Yes, sir." He continued to paint, even more carefully now that his boss was hovering.

"This article on you is gonna get you a lot of attention."

"Huh?" He turned quickly to face Lincoln and found him reading the *Overbrook Times*.

"Son, you're drippin'! You know better than that."

"Oh… sorry, sir." He put the roller back in the pan and, dabbing at the now-abundant amount of sweat pouring off him, turned back to Lincoln. "What article?"

"You know what article. You were there for the interview." His boss rattled the paper out in front of Jamison. "This here profile on the community page." Lincoln met his gaze, smiling. "You'll have your pick."

My pick of what? "Th-that wasn't supposed to come out until next Friday." Jamison stepped closer, wiping his palms on his overalls, to stare over Lincoln's shoulder. The spread was great, the photos impressive, and his furniture came off amazing. He grinned. *I look pretty good too.* "Wow," he whispered.

"Yeah, yeah! I see that smile," Torp said, entering the room and reading his own copy.

Though he was on the spot, Jamison began to feel a bit like a celebrity. "I wanna read it." He reached for the paper, but Torp yanked it away.

"You can," he promised, "after I'm done. Nearly there."

"Lordy!" Lincoln exclaimed, pushing between them. "Cut out that foolishness." He chuckled softly and said, "You boys can break for lunch now if you like. Have a sit-down, enjoy the fame." He gave Jamison a hearty pat on the back. "Congratulations, boy!" Then he walked out front to eat in his truck as usual.

"I'll grab our grub," Jamison said. "Let's go out back."

Torp nodded, still reading, and followed Jamison through the dining room and out the kitchen door to the backyard.

"Hey, he used my story about us in shop class," Torp shouted, the delight obvious in his voice.

After they completed the inside of the house, they would build a smallish deck, because right now the homeowners only had a slab of concrete for a patio area at the foot of four old wooden steps. Jamison had their lunches unpacked and spread on the patio table before he noticed Torp frozen at the top of those steps. His friend wasn't smiling any longer.

In fact he was frowning. "I never said that." Torp looked up from the page to meet Jamison's gaze.

"What's wrong?"

LONNIE HADN'T been able to reach Jamison yet—*must be working hard to have his phone off*—but he was thrilled with the article so far. JP had done a good job, and Jamison looked so handsome. He had the paper spread out on the kitchen island, reading it out loud to Amber and his mother while Gran and Remmy took their naps.

He'd forgotten how well JP could write. The profile told Jamison's story beautifully. It captured the horror of the night Mr. Coburn had been killed, Jamison's heartbreak, but also his perseverance in the face of such pain and loss.

The story chronicled each step he'd taken to get where he was today, even including a funny story from Torp about Jamison's first shop class and how impressed his teacher had been with his novel approach to the standard birdhouse everyone in the class had to build.

"Hear, listen to this," Lonnie said eagerly. "Despite his early tragedy, Coburn has managed to build a good life for himself in

Overbrook, and this reporter credits Coburn's parents: the man who raised him until he was ten, a man who instilled in him the value of hard work, honesty, and being true to yourself, and the woman who has shaped him on her own for twenty years." Lonnie looked up at his family, and all three smiled broadly and nodded in unison, in complete agreement with the article. He went back to it. "Coburn has it all," he read, "good looks, a solid work ethic, and a staggering talent, which is why it's so surprising he has yet to find—"

Lonnie blinked, then read it again, this time to himself... and again.

"Lonnie?" Amber said.

"Dear?" Ginger asked. "Are you okay?"

Lonnie skipped ahead, but it didn't get any better.

"WHAT?" JAMISON asked.

"That's what it says, I swear," Torp said as he scuttled down the remaining steps and handed Jamison the paper so he could see for himself. "But I swear, Jam, I never said that. I wouldn't say that."

Jamison smoothed the paper out and read where Torp pointed.

COBURN HAS it all—*good looks, a solid work ethic, and a staggering talent, which is why it's so surprising he has yet to find that special someone to share his bright future with. According to his uncle, his boss, his best friend, and his mother, Coburn remains unattached. However, since young men have been known to keep secrets from those closest to them, I asked the man himself, and he confirmed it. There you have it, ladies. Jamison Coburn might just be Overbrook's most eligible bachelor. The queue begins to the left.*

NO NO no no. Jamison leaped to his feet and dug out his cell phone, his fingers shaking as he dialed, but Lonnie didn't pick up. Next he punched in the Palmers' number, but it went to voice mail too. He ran around to the front of the house, jumped in his truck, and peeled away as Lincoln watched in confusion. Jamison had to get to Lonnie before he read that. Lincoln would understand. It was his lunch hour. He could spend it any way he'd like, and if that meant tearing through the city streets to stop a misunderstanding with his boyfriend instead of eating… well, that's what needed to happen. This would hurt Lonnie, and that was the last thing he wanted.

As he drove, Jamison dug out his phone again, but the call went to voice mail… again. It was all wrong. *I told the guy I was in a relationship.* Maybe he hadn't said with whom, but he was clear, wasn't he? Jamison slammed on his brakes and took the intersection at Fallon Street a bit sharply. *Shit.* This was all Lonnie needed. He was already questioning everything. Add this to Delroy's little visit the other day, and….

Jamison heard the siren before he saw the flashing lights. He cursed at the top of his lungs but pulled the truck over. He dialed Lonnie again, and this time he left a message.

A CHILL crawled over Lonnie's skin as he felt the weight of Ginger and Amber watching him, reading his expression. He shook his head and shrugged, managing a weak grin.

"I'm sure it's some kind of mistake," he said. "Just a misunderstanding."

The two women glanced at each other. "What does it say, son?" He stared out the french doors at the backyard as he slid the paper to his mother. The two women quickly skimmed the article.

"Oh," Amber said. He could see from the corner of his eye she was looking at him. Her expression quickly shifted from concern to firm support. "You're right. It's a mistake," she said, shoving the paper back to him and tapping the page decisively. "Jamison will straighten it out."

The silence in the room shattered with another phone call. Instead of ignoring it this time, Amber jumped up to get it. Her gaze found Lonnie again, and she held out the receiver. "It's Bink."

"Of course it is. Honestly, you ladies," he said, taking the phone and chuckling. "Hello?"

"Have you seen—?"

"Yes, I saw. It's just some mistake. I don't—"

"And the author?"

Lonnie hesitated a moment. "Yep, that's him…. I was *going* to tell you, just hadn't had the chance." He turned to roll his eyes for the benefit of Amber and his mother but found they'd both vanished. "Huh?" he asked, Bink's voice drawing him back to the phone.

"You haven't seen him, have you?"

"Saw him the other day, but it was fine. He even apologized."

He heard a faint snort through the phone just as someone knocked on the front door, but Lonnie didn't see anyone heading to answer it. "Hang on, someone's at the—" Jamison entered the house, and their eyes met immediately. "Bink, Jamison's here. I'll talk to you later, okay?" Lonnie hung up without waiting for her answer. He stared at Jamison, who hadn't come any deeper into the house but stood frozen and fearful in the entry.

"Lon…."

He smiled and walked over to take Jamison's hands in his. "It's okay, babe."

Jamison swept him up in his arms and squeezed until it hurt a little. "No, it's not," he mumbled against Lonnie's neck. "I told him, Lon." He pulled back to stare into his eyes. "I told him I was in a relationship. And Torp swears he never said anything like that."

"I mean I'm okay." He reached up and kissed the tension out of Jamison, then said, "Trust me. It's all right."

Jamison stared at the floor and rubbed his hands up and down Lonnie's arms, an action clearly more a comfort to Jamison than to him. "I didn't want you to think I denied you." Their eyes met. "I'd never deny you."

"I know." He threw his arms around Jamison's neck, his legs around his waist, and Jamison laughed before they kissed again. Lonnie ground against him as Jamison's big hands gripped his butt, and Lonnie felt relief and delicious tension building at the same time.

"Ahem." They parted, and Lonnie smiled dreamily at Amber, who smirked back. "I take it all is well?"

The two of them nodded in unison, grinning like idiots at each other.

JP KNEW where Lonnie's sister lived. He'd dropped him off there several times when they were together. So when Lonnie wasn't at the university or his apartment or Coburn's place, he knew to try the Palmers'. He'd been tickled when Jamison raced up in his truck, but now he ground his teeth as he watched him and Lonnie exit the house hand in hand, practically hanging on each other, bright smiles on their faces.

It wasn't that he'd expected Lonnie to break it off with the guy over a sentence or two in an article, but it shouldn't have them so delighted with each other. There should at least be a fight to witness. But they hopped in the truck and drove off together. He waited a beat and followed, not too closely, because he had a fairly good idea where they were going.

Sure enough, less than ten minutes later, they pulled up to Lonnie's apartment building and parked. It was the same place Lonnie had lived when JP failed at rehab his first time out. He'd entered the program voluntarily after hurting Lonnie, but he'd also left when he tired of the "I'm powerless" bullshit. And no matter how much he'd apologized, Lonnie refused to move back in with him.

He gripped the steering wheel until his hands ached. That's why he'd relapsed. Lonnie's initial rejection. By the time he'd worn Lonnie down, getting him to agree to a dinner date, JP was already using again. And that night he'd needed just a little bump. Dinner had been a disaster, and a confrontation with restaurant staff—and the resulting property damage—had landed him in court-ordered rehab.

He'd lost everything, but now he was on his way back, back to where he'd been at his best, professionally and personally. Regaining Lonnie's love and trust were the first steps to making it all as if it had never happened. He waited until the two of them had disappeared inside, then drove away to profile the ex-con for the Community section. He needed to focus, not let himself get sidetracked by Coburn again, sidetracked by thoughts of him touching what was his.

"POOL!" STEWART shouted when he entered the newsroom later that day. He went directly to his editor's office instead of dropping his notes at his desk.

"Yeah?"

"Come in, close the door."

JP did and took a seat. "What is it?"

"Why were you late for your interview today?"

"I wasn't!"

"Yeah, you were. The guy's business is taking off. He has a full schedule, and you kept him waiting for nearly an hour."

"I don't know what to tell you, Stew. Maybe we got our times mixed up."

"Bullshit."

"Stew, listen—"

"No. First you fuck up the baking contest winners, have me promo a story you never produced on time—"

"I *told* you a computer glitch garbled it! Would have taken forever to get it cleaned up. We had to go with the Coburn piece instead. It was ready, and I apologized for that, man."

Stewart stopped talking and simply watched JP, who worked hard not to fidget beneath the scrutiny. He knew Stewart was looking for guilt or evidence he was high, so he met his gaze steadily. Finally Stewart sighed.

"You've done good work since you've been back. The Coburn piece was solid, as is the now-*ungarbled* version of the granny-and-grandson profile, and the story on the mom getting her degree actually made me smile, but—"

"I'll do just as well on the ex-con." JP smiled. "You know that, Stew."

"Don't fuck up, Pool."

Chapter 16

JAMISON SIGNED the note and silently carried it back into Lonnie's bedroom to leave on the pillow next to him. He paused in the doorway and watched him sleep for several moments. It was difficult to abandon such a beautiful sight—Lonnie warm and bare in bed—but he turned and left the apartment as quietly as he could. He had things to do, to take care of. He climbed in his truck and aimed it at his mother's house.

Rushing from the work site as he'd done, Jamison needed a shower, so earlier, when he and Lonnie arrived at the apartment, the two of them had shared a long, luxurious one, soaping, exploring, and enjoying each other. There wasn't much room to maneuver, but they'd pressed close, working slowly, reverently. But then he had noticed Lonnie wouldn't meet his eye.

"What is it, Lon?" He'd waited a moment. "I'm sorry about the confusion—"

"No, it's not that. There's something I need to tell you."

"Okay." But as Lonnie opened his mouth to speak, Jamison had crowded him suddenly, placing him beneath the spray and then laughed at his exasperated reaction.

"Hey!" Lonnie sputtered.

"Sorry, babe. Couldn't resist." They rinsed, stepped out together, and grabbed towels to dry off. "Okay, tell me."

He'd dried himself quickly and tied a towel around his waist, but Lonnie had stood there dripping and lost in thought. Jamison had taken another towel and began drying him, and Lonnie allowed it as if he were an inept six-year-old after his nightly bath. Jamison loved it, drawing the thirsty cloth over Lonnie's creamy, lean-muscled body. He'd grabbed a smaller towel and blotted his hair. *Ah, that hair.* He'd gotten hard again beneath his towel, but Lonnie hadn't seemed to notice.

"I went to see Jerry the other day."

Jamison had frowned. "Why?"

"I was...." Lonnie had shrugged. "I was angry, furious really, and wanted to tear into him."

"Uh...."

"I didn't want him talking to you, didn't want him in our lives." Lonnie turned and stomped into his bedroom, and Jamison chased after with the towel, eager to finish the job. "It feels wrong, the two of you even knowing each other." When he caught up to him and tried to wrap his arms around him, Lonnie wiggled free, saying, "No, I don't want to be cuddled right now." After jerking the towel out of his hand, Lonnie turned his back to him. "I just want...."

"Tell me what you want." Jamison had kept his distance, his hands held up in surrender. Lonnie's shoulders slumped, and he didn't seem to know where to look or how to settle himself. He finished drying himself as Jamison took a careful step closer. "You look like you want to punch something. I can understand feeling that way about the guy."

"No... I mean *yes*, I do want to punch something, but this other part of me is trying to be rational."

"Huh?"

Lonnie faced Jamison and glared. "Part of me doesn't think the mistake in the article *was* a mistake, but that would mean JP knew we were a couple and was just trying to start shit."

"How could he know?"

Lonnie shrugged. "I didn't even know he was back in town."

They stood in silence for several moments. Jamison didn't know what to do, so he said, "Can I cuddle you now?" Lonnie snorted, dropped onto the bed, and held his arms open to him. After Lonnie was securely embraced, Jamison asked, "Did you tell him about us?"

"No. Almost, but I stopped myself." Lonnie sighed. "I had just decided to go back and get the message I'd left for him, decided he was my past... when there he was. He seemed surprised to see me."

"What did he have to say for himself?" Jamison shivered happily as Lonnie gently drew his fingernails over his scalp.

"He apologized for the way things went down between us and wished me well." Lonnie was quiet for a few heartbeats. "How was he with you... during the interview?"

He thought about it, then said, "I was uncomfortable to begin with, but he put me at ease pretty quick."

Lonnie kissed the top of his head then. "The article was damn good... except for the bit at the end inviting all the single ladies in Overbrook to give you a call."

He laughed and rolled over onto Lonnie. "Yours is the only call I'll answer."

They had kissed then, long and slow, which led to other things, like making Lonnie call his name and moan like music. Only Jamison couldn't sleep afterward. His thoughts kept swirling, eventually touching on a comment JP had made about education and expanding your world beyond.... *What did he say?* College lets you see beyond your "ratty little neighborhood."

He had eventually unwrapped himself from Lonnie, crawled out of the bed, and called Torp to say he was sorry for bailing on him. Then he called Lincoln and begged forgiveness for rushing off the job like that. Lincoln had mostly wanted to know that Jamison was okay and said it wasn't a problem as long as the two of them put in the missed hours to meet the deadline next week. Jamison promised he'd make it happen.

There wouldn't have been any confusion, and Lonnie would never have been hurt, if he'd simply been honest from the start. Torp never said what the article claimed. JP had never been alone with him, so Jamison had heard every question he posed and the answers to them. But JP had been alone with Lincoln, his mother, and Uncle Ray. Maybe the guy wasn't that great a note taker. Maybe Jamison being an eligible bachelor made for a better story. Maybe Lonnie was right that the guy was trying to start trouble between them. Either way, there were a few people he needed to talk to. He couldn't blame his uncle or Lincoln. They didn't know how he felt about Lonnie, however....

As he pulled up to his mother's house, he noticed a bunch of people milling around the porch and side yard. The sun was setting, so he had trouble making out some of the faces. He could smell the grill working in the backyard. He parked and approached the house but froze when a smattering of applause greeted him.

"Jam Coburn! Son! Saw you in the paper today," Teensy Brooks shouted from the steps, where he was sitting. Jamison would know him anywhere. The older, and much rounder, man set his paper plate of barbecued chicken on the steps and struggled to his feet. He paused to tell one of the three children running by to keep the flies off his food and he'd give him a dollar. Then he waddled forward, a half-full beer bottle in one hand. Jamison braced himself before Teensy captured him in a bear hug that nearly squeezed the air from his lungs.

"Uh… yeah, that was me."

"Your mama is busting with pride, boy!"

"Yes, sir. Thank you, sir." Jamison looked around at the other faces on the porch. He spotted two neighborhood girls he'd grown up with, one or two older ladies from the block, and two or three guys he thought he recognized from his high school days.

"Come on in, boy. Let's find you a seat," Teensy said. "We're having this cookout to celebrate ya, after all."

"Uh…. Mr. Brooks, I'm just looking for Mama."

"I think she's round back with Frye."

Jamison pulled away. "Lincoln Frye?" he asked, noticing that the child tasked with keeping bugs from Teensy's food was now eating it with zeal. *That's one way to keep it safe, I guess.*

"Yeah, son. Your boss." He drained his bottle, and Jamison wondered how many he'd had. "Ya know," Teensy said, teetering forward, "I always thought Frye was a bit sweet on your mama." He laughed heartily, fogging Jamison's face with the stink of beer. Rushing up the front steps to escape, Jamison barely managed to slow enough to greet the two young women smiling sweetly at him.

Once inside the house, he found his Aunt Jo at the kitchen sink. Though she was a bit thinner and three years younger, he found her resemblance to his mother comforting. They had the same kind eyes, the same smile, the same laugh, and the same mannerisms. They were both Christian, but Aunt Jo believed love was love and didn't struggle with his relationship with Lonnie like his mother did.

"Jamison, I'm so glad you're here." Her expression was wary as she stared at him, wringing her hands as she apparently tried to gauge his mood.

He smiled weakly. "I'm okay, Aunt Jo."

She crossed the room and hugged him. "Oh, baby, the article was wonderful," she said, laying a hand to his cheek. "I'm so proud of you."

"Thank you." He kissed her cheek. "What is all this?"

"Everyone saw you in the paper, and this all sort of developed over the afternoon, until—" A burst of laughter sounded from the front porch.

"Is Jam here?"

God, no. Delroy entered the house from the front porch and made a beeline for the kitchen.

"Hey, Del," Jamison said, sighing. "Where's *your* Vinnia?"

"She's visitin' the in-laws in the next block. Good to see you, Jam."

"Thanks. I came by to talk to Mama."

"Did your friend give you my card? I was hopin' to talk to you before Sunday."

"Sunday? What about?"

Delroy gripped Jamison's arm and pulled him aside, away from Aunt Jo. "See, we're trying to get together a coalition of black churches to march on city hall."

"Why?"

Delroy lowered his voice. "I told you about the cupcakes and the lesbians, right?"

Jamison nodded.

"Well, last week a lady comes into my place and asks for a wedding cake for her son."

"So? You can do those with your eyes closed, can't ya?" He glanced back over his shoulder, eager to find his mother.

"Sure, but it's for a *gay* wedding."

Jamison waited, but Delroy didn't say anything more.

"What is it with you?" he snapped, causing Delroy to step back. "First it was the cupcakes and now this. We live in Maryland! We have marriage equality now."

Delroy stepped forward again. "Not in my shop, we don't. Hell no! My pastor said Christianity is under attack, and I have a right to stand up for my beliefs. Homos gettin' married just makes a mockery of the institution."

Jamison knew those weren't Delroy's words. He had never used the words *institution* and *mockery* in his life.

He pulled free of Delroy. "Who do you think you're talking to? Last year I saw your ad in the paper for a doggie wedding cake—two pugs in formal wear sitting next to a cake with a Milk-Bone on it! Count me out." He turned back to Aunt Jo. "Where is Mama?"

Her lips thinned in a grimace, and she nodded. "She's out back at the grill."

He turned to leave but stopped and told her, "I love you."

"Love you too, baby," she said, patting his back. "Now go give her what for." She turned and met Delroy's dumbfounded expression. "You! Back out on the porch." She made quick shooing motions and Delroy fled.

Jamison went out the back door and saw his mother standing by Lincoln at the grill. She held a plate at the ready as he filled it with grilled chicken and burgers. The smile on her face was one Jamison hadn't seen since he'd lost his father. She stared up into Lincoln's eyes as if he'd hung the stars.

Huh. Okay. He cleared his throat. "Mama?"

Her body jerked as though she'd been stuck with a cattle prod, and she nearly dropped the food. "Jamison? I… well," she said, glancing at Lincoln. "I wasn't sure I'd see you tonight, dear."

"I read the article, Mama. Torp and Lincoln—hello, sir—showed it to me."

Lincoln nodded at Jamison, uncertainty in his eyes. "I told her how you took off after that."

"Can I talk to you, Mama… alone for a minute?"

Lincoln turned back to the grill while she hesitantly handed Jamison the plate of food and entered the house. Aunt Jo had fled the kitchen, but he could hear her talking on the front porch. He set the food on the table, and they both took a seat at opposite ends.

"I thought the article was beautiful, baby," his mother said as she toyed with the fringe on a dish towel. "You looked so handsome, and your furni—"

"Mama? Did you tell the reporter I wasn't in a relationship?"

She didn't answer, didn't look at him, just folded and unfolded the towel. Then she got up and stood by the sink, watching her son. "Now, baby, I need you to keep your voice down. I don't want people to—"

"Is that what you said, Mama?"

She twisted her lips but finally said, "Yes! Yes, that's what I told him. What was I supposed to say?"

"The truth."

She scoffed, rolling her eyes. "You expected me to share your shame with that reporter?"

"Mama, I'm not ashamed. I love Lonnie, and he loves me."

"Then why didn't you tell that writer?" she demanded, narrowing her eyes. "If you're so all-fired proud of yourself, why didn't you tell him… everything?"

He stared down at his folded hands on the table. "You're right. I hurt Lonnie by not being honest, and I regret that." He sighed and rubbed his head roughly. "I guess I can't be upset with you if I didn't do any better." They stared at each other for several moments.

"What's going on in here?" Uncle Ray asked, coming through the back door with Lincoln close on his heels.

"Ray, glad you could make it," Alanna said, giving the man a hug.

He kissed her cheek but immediately turned back to Jamison. "Jam, why aren't you partying with everybody? That's why we're here, ain't it?"

Lincoln remained silent, apparently picking up on the tension in the room.

Ignoring Ray, Jamison stood, took a deep breath, and addressed his boss. "Sir, I get the feeling you're fond of my mother?"

Lincoln met his gaze steadily. "I am, Jamison. I am. Very fond."

He nodded. "You're a good man. I'm happy for you both." They shook hands.

Ray walked over to Jamison and put his arm around his shoulders. "Speaking of fond, I noticed several young ladies out front eager to make your acquaintance, Jam." He wiggled his graying eyebrows, and Jamison laughed. "That article really caught their attention, son." He and Lincoln laughed and nodded together in agreement.

"Thanks, Uncle Ray, but I'm already seeing someone." His mother gasped and shook her head in warning, her eyes wide. "His name is Lonnie Bellerose," Jamison said firmly and clearly.

The laughter died, the room falling silent save for Alanna's sob—until Delroy, who had reentered from the front of the house with his Vinnia now on his arm, asked, "Jam? You're a faggot?"

Chapter 17

LONNIE HAD woken to an empty bed, love bites on his chest, and a luscious ache in his backside. There was also a note from Jamison saying he'd be back for dinner and a movie. The note was signed with hugs and kisses, which delighted him so much he'd become inspired and sketched out his next two paintings while dinner cooked.

He strained the noodles and dumped them into the serving dish. Then he quickly chopped the grilled chicken and tossed it in along with the steamed broccoli before dousing the entire collection with a heart-healthier version of Alfredo sauce. It smelled heavenly.

Everything was ready. He just needed the man himself.

A knock at the door drew his attention, so he set the dish in the center of the kitchen table and went to answer it. The sight of Jamison leaning in the doorway, his left eye swollen shut, his lip busted, and his nose bleeding, hit Lonnie like a blow to the gut, locking the breath in his chest. He couldn't speak, but he pulled Jamison inside.

When Jamison tried to shuffle his way to the sofa, Lonnie kept him on his feet and said, "No. The light's better in the kitchen." After getting him seated, he ran to the bathroom to collect first aid items and came back with his arms full of alcohol, gauze, cotton balls, Band-Aids, and Advil. Upon his return he found Jamison holding a bag of frozen carrots to his face, and without a word, Lonnie dumped everything on the table and shoved aside the serving dish. Dinner could wait.

"Oh my God, that smells good," Jamison moaned.

Lonnie grabbed the bag of carrots and set it aside so he could work. "Later, babe." He focused on cleaning and disinfecting the cuts, wincing along with Jamison as he went. He didn't ask any questions, but he could feel Jamison's gaze on him, watching him as he cleaned away the dried blood. Lonnie swallowed past the lump of anger and fear in his throat, holding it in.

When Jamison was cleaned and bandaged, Lonnie silently collected and tossed out the scraps and refuse from his efforts. As he made another pass by the table, Jamison reached out, grabbed his wrist, and pulled him into his lap. Lonnie wouldn't look at him. He just stared at his fingernails.

"Dinner sure smells good." Jamison tilted Lonnie's face up he could look into his eyes. He stroked his thumb over Lonnie's bottom lip.

"So you said." He finally met Jamison's gaze. "What happened?" he whispered.

"I had a disagreement with Delroy—you met him in my driveway—and a couple of guys from the neighborhood."

Lonnie caressed Jamison's bruised face, his gaze clocking each mark. "A 'disagreement'?"

Jamison sighed. "I went over to Mama's to ask her what she'd said to Pool. There was a cookout going on, supposedly celebrating the article. My boss was there, and then my Uncle Ray showed up... so I took the opportunity to tell them about us."

Lonnie's heart quickened at the thought of Jamison outing himself to the rest of his family, to his boss. "Everybody?"

"No. Telling the whole neighborhood was an accident." Jamison smirked. "Delroy can be sneaky when he wants."

"How can you laugh about this?" Lonnie leaped to his feet.

"I'm not. Laughing hurts too much."

"Jamison!"

"Calm down, Lonnie."

"I will not! They beat you. They hurt you." He crossed his arms and glanced at the door. Maybe they should go to the hospital, get Jamison checked out. "You might have internal bleeding or a concussion." He went for the phone, his socked feet slipping on the hardwood floor in the entry, his arms and legs going chaotic for a second before he regained his balance. "I'm calling Torp, and we're going. Then we're calling the police and reporting this."

"Lon, I threw the first punch."

He stopped dialing and blinked. "What?" His gentle giant had punched someone?

Jamison got to his feet, walked over to him, and took the phone from him. "Delroy called me... a not nice word."

"And you hit him."

"Nope. Then he told me how ashamed my father would be of me."

"And you hit him."

Jamison shook his head. "I did take a step closer... but no. Then he said...."

He stared into Jamison's eyes for a moment before it sank in. "Something about me."

Jamison nodded slowly. "So I knocked him on his ass. Don't remember much after that, but I know everyone ended up in the backyard. Heard a lot of shouting, Mama screaming some words she'll never admit to. Ray and Lincoln jumped in too."

"Not hitting you?" Lonnie gasped.

"No...." Jamison frowned. "At least I don't think so. A couple of guys from the block—Teensy and two others—sided with Delroy when he told them about me. Teensy had hugged me earlier and felt... I don't know"—Jamison shrugged—"violated, I guess. I didn't stick around to sort everything out."

"You drove yourself here?"

"Yeah." Jamison sighed. "Mama was crying when I left, I know that much. Lincoln was taking care of her, though.... Oh yeah, Mama's dating my boss, just to get that out there."

Lonnie leaned in and carefully kissed Jamison's lips, wishing he could take his pain away. "We're going to the hospital."

Jamison groaned, but before Lonnie could get to the phone, Jamison's cell sounded. He peered at the screen. "It's Torp. Hello?"

Lonnie snatched the phone from him. "Torp, it's Lonnie," he said, rolling right over the frantic chatter coming from the phone. Apparently he'd heard what happened. "Please come by my place. I need help getting Jamison to the hospital." Lonnie gave him the address and apartment number, then hung up and stared into Jamison's working eye. "He's on his way."

"THEN LINCOLN told me he jumped in and tried to pull them apart, but he got shoved aside." Torp spoke at breakneck speed, filling Lonnie in on all he'd heard thirdhand about the incident, as they sat in the waiting area of Overbrook Medical's emergency room. "It's all over the neighborhood."

"What is?"

"All of it," Torp said, his eyes wide. "The fight at the Coburn cookout, the fact Jamison's gay, and that he's 'taking it up the ass from some university art dude.'" He winced. "Sorry about that." The look of shame on Torp's face brought a smirk to Lonnie's.

Not yet he's not. Lonnie massaged his temples and asked, "How's his mother?"

"She's upset but not for the reasons you might think. I mean...." Torp squinted. "She's not thrilled about everyone finding out about you two, but when those dudes jumped Jam, started calling him names? She whaled on them with a saucepan—one of her good ones too."

"She did?"

"Hell yeah, she did. She wasn't havin' that. Not at her house."

Lonnie nearly laughed at that image, not that he had any idea what Alanna Coburn looked like. As he thought it over, he realized his mother would do the same. She came off as educated, European, and refined, but Ginger Bellerose would cut a bitch. He chuckled softly to himself. That's what parents did. His father had defied his grandfather for Lonnie's sake.... *Because he loves me.* Lonnie sighed and vowed not to let anything overshadow that realization.

"Where's my boy?"

They looked up, and Lonnie saw two rather petite African American women headed their way—one a bit rounder than the other—followed by a tall, older black man.

Torp groaned. "Shit!"

"What?"

Torp leaned in and whispered, "That's Jam's mother, aunt, and our boss Lincoln."

The automatic doors hissed open again, this time ushering in Claude, wearing a BabyBjörn filled with Remmy. He moved at a more sedate pace as he approached. Lonnie had called the house once he'd reached the hospital, but Amber had taken his mother and grandmother to the airport to pick up his father. Lonnie and Torp stood to greet them all.

Stepping past Lonnie as if he weren't there, Mrs. Coburn asked Torp, "How is he?"

"Uh...," Torp began, glancing at Lonnie, then focusing back on Mrs. Coburn, "they're just checking him over right now, ma'am. Looking for a concussion or broken ribs."

"Oh Lordy!" she wailed, and Lincoln helped her to a chair when her knees seemed to give out. Jamison's aunt hung close, a hand on Mrs. Coburn's shoulder, but her gaze remained on Lonnie. She smiled at him and nodded.

Lonnie stepped away to greet Claude.

"You didn't have to come down here," he said.

"Everyone else is gone, and Amber would never forgive me if I weren't here for you, so I caught a taxi and... well, here we are." Claude blew a puff of air upward to get his blond bangs out of his eyes and swayed with Remmy.

"Thanks, but I think Amber's going to be pissed you came down here without a car seat."

Claude blanched and stopped swaying. "Damn, you're right. Oh shit," he whispered, staring at his baby boy.

Lonnie touched Remmy's fist, then stroked his soft curls. "Sleeping?"

"Yep. Nodded off in the car," Claude said. "How's Jamison?"

"Don't know yet. They're checking him out."

"I left a message letting Amber know where we are."

Lonnie widened his eyes. "You didn't."

Claude shrugged. "Sure. Why?"

"What did you say... exactly?"

Claude thought for a moment, still gently moving. "I just said we were at the hospital." His expression collapsed. "Oh."

"Yeah...."

Just then Amber and their parents rushed through the automatic doors. "Are you all right, dear?" Ginger asked, reaching them first.

"I'm fine, Mother. It's Jamison. He got into a bit of a.... Some guys jumped him."

"Oh dear!"

His father squeezed Lonnie's shoulder, then just pulled him forward and into a hug. Lonnie relaxed into the embrace and returned it, breathing him in. "Je suis certain qu'il ira bien, mon fils," Arthur murmured.

"Oui, Papa. He'll be fine." He smiled up at his father, but Arthur's gaze suddenly shifted beyond him, and Lonnie turned to find himself facing Lincoln Frye. Lincoln had a black eye and swollen lip, and despite what Torp had told him, he had to wonder, just for a second, if Jamison had given them to him. Torp stood at Lincoln's side, glancing between them.

"Boss, this is Lonnie Bellerose. Lonnie, Lincoln Frye."

They shook hands. "It's good to meet you, sir. These are my—this is my family," he said, gesturing to everyone standing by him.

Lincoln nodded to them and shook their hands, but then he focused on Lonnie again, making him squirm a bit. "Can we talk for a moment?"

"Uh… yes, give me a second." He turned to face his family. "Thank you… all of you, for coming down here. I appreciate it, but I'm fine. I should hear something about Jamison soon, and then I'll give you a call. Please, go home."

Ginger hugged her son and stroked his hair. "Call us as soon as you know something, dear."

He patted her hand. "Oui, Maman."

"I will stay with him," Arthur said. "I will take a taxi back if needs be."

"Give me the baby," Amber demanded, and Claude promptly unhooked the harness and handed Remmy to his mother.

I guess she made the car seat connection.

Amber and Ginger kissed Lonnie's cheek before they left, a mopey Claude following behind.

Lonnie joined Lincoln at the elevators.

"I suppose you heard what happened at the cookout," Lincoln said.

"I did."

Lincoln opened his mouth, then closed it and stared at Lonnie for a moment. He looked away. "I have to tell ya, I never would have guessed… about Jamison, that is."

Lonnie shoved his hands into his pockets. What was he supposed to say about that? He checked the time on the wall clock in the hall. How much longer before he could see Jamison?

Lincoln continued. "He was always such a good man."

Oh, he knew what to say to that. "He's still a good man, a damn good one!" He was a bit taken aback by the fire in his own voice, but he didn't back down or school his features. Lonnie kept the stink eye going strong.

"Yes, yes, but…." Lincoln glanced down the hall at Mrs. Coburn, who sat in a chair, her back ramrod straight, staring at the wall in front of her. Torp and her sister were on either side of her, and they watched Lonnie and Lincoln like fretful hawks. Leaning against the wall by a water fountain, Arthur also watched the exchange.

"Maybe it would be a good idea for you to…." Lincoln glanced twice at the automatic doors.

Lonnie raised an eyebrow and waited.

"Oh goodness." Lincoln rubbed his hands on his jeans and stared at the ceiling. "Are you going to make me say it?"

"Absolutely. I know you're important to Jamison. I know you've known him all his life, and he thinks of you as a father of sorts. But I believe I'm important to him too, and I'm the one who insisted he come here to get checked out."

"He took off before we could—"

"So if you're suggesting I leave this hospital because I make his mother uncomfortable…? Yep." Lonnie nodded. "You're gonna have to say *that*."

"Son?" Mrs. Coburn said, getting to her feet as Jamison exited a room down the hall and approached them.

"Mama," Jamison said, his gaze moving from her to pass over the faces around him in search of…. "Hey, Lon." He smiled and opened his arms, and Lonnie went to him.

"Are you okay?"

"Doc says I have a mild concussion and two bruised ribs."

"Which will be very painful for a while," a doctor said as she joined them. "I'm Dr. Rossini." She extended her hand. "You must be Lonnie?"

He nodded, then turned to introduce everyone else. "This is Jamison's mother, Mrs. Coburn, his aunt, his boss, and his best friend. And this is my—"

"Okay…." Dr. Rossini chuckled, and Lonnie tried to calm his racing thoughts. Was Jamison okay? He had to be or they wouldn't be releasing him. *Wait. Are they releasing him?* "Well, it's good to meet you all." She looked up at Jamison. "You have quite the entourage, Mr. Coburn."

"Yes, ma'am. I'd certainly like to leave with them."

"Let me get your discharge papers started. Be right back."

Lonnie relaxed a bit.

"You'll come home with me," Mrs. Coburn said, nodding firmly.

"No, Mama. I'm going with Lonnie."

"Jamison!" She looked as if her heart were breaking, and Lincoln frowned.

"I'll see you tomorrow after work," he said, then leaned over and kissed her cheek. "I promise." Then he fixed his gaze on Lincoln. "That is if I still have a job."

"Of course you do," Lincoln said quickly. "You're a good worker. Who you… uh, who you're…." He waved his hand in Lonnie's general direction but couldn't seem to finish his thought.

Jamison and Lonnie smiled, then Jamison said, "Thank you, sir."

"I can't believe you'd choose him over your own mother."

"I love you, Mama, but I love Lonnie too. The sooner you accept that, the better."

"I'll get my truck," Torp said, heading for the doors.

Arthur looked concerned. "I hope there is room for one more. My days of riding in truck beds, they are over."

Lonnie shared a smile with him, but it fell from his lips when two uniformed officers entered just as Torp exited.

"Jamison Coburn?" one asked at the intake window, his voice rivaling Jamison's in its depth. He was older, tall, muscular, with short sandy-brown hair sprinkled with gray.

"That's me," Jamison said.

Both officers joined their group. The second was a black cop, cute with light brown skin and hazel eyes. Obviously a junior officer, he glanced at each of them, tension building in his shoulders as his gaze settled on Jamison. He looked as though he was working hard not to touch his gun. Lonnie reflexively tightened his grip on Jamison's arm, as if he could hold him in place, prevent them from taking him away. Mrs. Coburn took hold of his other arm.

"I'm Officer Nathan Gagnon. This is Officer Robert Cosgrove. We have a warrant for your arrest."

"For what?" Lonnie, Mrs. Coburn, Lincoln, Torp, and Aunt Jo demanded in unison.

The officers blinked at them for a moment. Then Gagnon said, "Assault of a—" He glanced at the warrant. "—a Mr. D. Pritchard."

Everyone rolled their eyes and moaned, "Delroy."

Chapter 18

"POOL! FLINT! Get in here!"

JP jumped to his feet immediately, startled out of a deep sleep, while Rodney Flint just sat at his desk and blinked in confusion. *What a fucking loser*, JP thought as he headed for Stewart's office.

"Yeah, boss?" JP dropped into one of the chairs provided.

"Where's Flint?"

JP shrugged. "Sitting at his desk, trying to decide if he wants to come in here." He waggled his eyebrows. "Is he in trouble?" he asked with a smile.

God, he hoped so. Flint currently covered the police beat, and JP wanted to take that over in the worst way. Stewart held up a finger, rounded his desk, and stopped when his bulk filled the doorway. "Flint! Get your ass in here. Now!"

Once Flint joined them, he took a seat beside JP, and they both waited for whatever news Stewart had for them.

"Just got a tip from downtown. Pool, that profile you did on the furniture guy… what was his name?"

"Coburn. Jamison Coburn."

"My source at the courthouse says a warrant was issued for his arrest."

"What?" This was even better than he'd hoped. "What's the charge?"

"Assault."

JP's stomach twisted. *Not Lonnie.* "Who… uh, whom did he…?"

"Some guy named Pritchard filed the complaint."

Relief flooded him from head to toe.

"Why am I here?" Flint asked.

"I've often wondered the same thing," JP said.

"Fuck you, Pool!"

JP laughed. "Not even if you could suck peanut butter through a garden hose."

Flint sputtered for two seconds before Stewart, failing to hide a smirk, said, "Guys, please." He sighed. "Pool will cover the story, and you're here, Flint, for a courtesy heads-up. He's gonna be on your turf."

"Luckily I know that turf well."

"This isn't Baltimore." Stewart jabbed a fat finger at JP. "Try not to piss anyone off."

"Oh, that ship has sailed," JP said, rising and leaving the room.

"THIS IS your fault!" Jamison's mother shouted, wagging her finger at Lonnie, who felt as though he'd been slapped. Their entire group had followed the officers and Jamison outside. Torp immediately stood between them.

"Ma'am, this isn't Lonnie's fault."

"How do you know? You weren't even there."

"Neither was he."

She huffed and stepped away to continue her pacing as she watched Jamison being handcuffed and read his rights. "He's never been in trouble before, and after knowing you for a few weeks… look! Just look at this!"

Was she right? Lonnie wanted to pull his hair out; in fact, he was tugging on it something fierce while he paced as well, only in a different direction than Mrs. Coburn. Arthur talked rapidly on his cell to a colleague. Arthur's specialty was international corporate law, and they needed a criminal attorney.

"I have to call Ray," Mrs. Coburn said, digging into her purse. "Maybe he knows a lawyer. I can't have my baby spending the night in jail."

"Alanna," Lincoln said, trying to calm her as she dialed, "I doubt Jamison will be arraigned to—"

"Ray? Can you hear me?" She held the phone away from her ear for a second, then went back to talking. "No! Listen. Jamison needs a lawyer… yes, a lawyer…. Who do you think after what happened at the house…? Ray? Are you still drinking, Ray?"

"Lonnie?" Arthur said, drawing his attention. "Find out what… erm… where…." He frantically waved his hand up and down in the direction of the police officers.

"Oh. Yes!" Lonnie said, springing into action.

"No!" Torp hissed, missing a grab for Lonnie's arm.

Lonnie ran toward the cruiser as Cosgrove squeezed Jamison into the backseat.

"Excuse me—"

Gagnon whirled on him. "Step back, son," he ordered, one hand on the butt of the gun at his belt, the other raised in Lonnie's face.

Lonnie froze and turned back to his father, who looked as if he'd stopped breathing, his eyes wide with horror, what little color he possessed gone from his face. In fact, everyone in their group looked like a photograph of shocked rubberneckers, all of them immobilized as they stood, lined up outside the emergency room, waiting to see if Lonnie would be shot. He slowly turned back to Gagnon and spoke very calmly and clearly. "I just need to know where you're taking him… please, sir."

The man relaxed. "Main station house, on Bola Avenue."

"Thank you," Lonnie said as he backed up, his heart stuttering out the words *fuck me* before regaining its normal rhythm. When he rejoined Arthur, his father wrapped him up in his arms and spoke quickly into his cell phone. When he ended the call he said, "Tomas Redking représentera Jamison, fils. Il le retrouvera au commisariat."

"Merci, Papa."

"What did he say?" Jamison's mother demanded as she rushed over to them, her eyes red and puffy from crying. "Talking this gibberish, how's a body to unders—?"

"Alanna!" Jo said, stepping in front of her sister. "I swear if you don't shut your mouth right now, I'm gonna slap you!" Alanna bit her bottom lip and dissolved into tears. Jo hugged her and said softly, "I know you're scared, but we'll get this straightened out. I promise."

"He's been…," Alanna muttered. "He's been a good boy all his life. Never in any trouble. Never raised a hand to anyone in anger."

"I know, dear, I know." Jo hugged her tighter and rubbed her back.

Lonnie approached the women carefully and said, "A friend of my father has agreed to represent Jamison. That's who was on the phone." Aunt Jo smiled gratefully at him and nodded at Arthur as she continued to comfort her sister.

Lonnie joined Lincoln and Torp, who spoke quietly together away from everyone else.

"Can we go now?" he asked, tugging on Torp's sleeve. He was exhausted and starving, and he began to choke up. *Dinner. Our dinner….* He closed his eyes, feeling as if his thoughts and fear were drowning him.

Torp squeezed Lonnie's shoulder. "I'll drive you."

"No, just take me to my car, please. I'll drive myself, but can you drop my father off at my sister's place? He just flew back into town. He must be worn out." Lonnie met Arthur's eyes beyond Torp. He did look tired.

"Sure thing, Lonnie."

JAMISON TURNED in the seat to watch out the back window of the cruiser as they drove away. He saw only chaos among the people he cared most about, and his heart ached. He wouldn't be holding Lonnie tonight. He faced forward again, a bit unsettled. What happened next? He'd never been arrested before. He knew guys who had been, of course, but it wasn't as though he sat down with them after and quizzed them on the procedures. He was entering a black hole of uncertainty, and it terrified him. Hopefully that didn't show in his eyes.

All his life he'd tried not to frighten people, to not play into the initial image most had of him: big, black, and scary. Yes, he'd used it to keep the thugs at bay, but he'd never raised more than his voice, and that was only to cheer on his favorite teams.

Gagnon glanced back at him in the rearview mirror several times before saying, "Hey, aren't you the guy from today's paper?"

"Yeah, that's me."

His partner snorted. "We have a celebrity in the car, Gag. What do you think about that?" Cosgrove turned a bit in his seat to look at Jamison and asked, "Bit of an inauspicious end to your day, huh?"

He didn't know what that meant, so he shrugged and gazed out the window instead of talking. *I'll finally see the inside of a jail cell. Yippee!* Jamison had been interviewed at the police station after his father's murder years ago, and his stomach knotted as he recalled the smell and bustle of the place. A lady cop had brought him chocolate milk and asked him endless questions in a soft, patient voice. He didn't think that was going to be the case tonight. He sighed.

"Aw, it ain't that bad, buddy," Gagnon said. "Is this your first offense?"

"Yes, sir."

"What are you? Twenty-five? Twenty-six?"

"I'll be thirty in a few weeks."

"So you've had a solid run of good citizenship. What happened?"

"A long-time loudmouth said something about me, then my late father, then…."

"Yeah?" Gagnon glanced in the rearview again, waiting.

Jamison sighed. "Then he said something hateful about my boyfriend."

The officers mulled that over in silence, then Cosgrove said, "So you punched him."

Jamison nodded.

"Did he go down?"

"Yes, but not out. I was angry, but I didn't want to hurt him too bad. He's smaller than me, so I pulled the punch at the last second. Then I walked away."

Cosgrove smirked. "I'd say everyone is smaller than you, buddy."

"He can't have been too smart to rile up a guy your size," Gagnon suggested.

"He was surprised about the gay thing, sort of walked in as I told my family." Jamison leaned back in the seat and stared at the roof of the car. "I guess he had trouble wrapping his head around it."

Cosgrove asked, "If you walked away, why were you at the hospital?"

"The loudmouth and some other guys from my old neighborhood jumped me behind my mama's house. I'm big, but three to one is still three to one."

Both officers nodded.

"When I got back to Lonnie's apar—"

"Lonnie?" Cosgrove said.

"My boyfriend. Been together a month or so. When I got back there, he made me go to the hospital."

"Smart man," Cosgrove said. "You don't want to fuck around with head injuries."

"Language," Gagnon admonished as they pulled into the station house parking lot.

"I didn't see nothing about your boyfriend in the article," Gagnon said as he helped Jamison out of the cruiser.

"Yeah, that was my fault. I wasn't exactly ready to come out to the whole town, so I wasn't as clear as I shoulda been." He shrugged. "Guess the writer got it wrong." His eyes widened as they neared the entrance. "What happens now?"

Gagnon stared at him for a moment, probably reading his expression and seeing deeper than Jamison wanted. *Cops can do that, right?* "We're going to book you, which means we'll take your picture, fingerprint you, remove any personal items—keys, watch, belt, and the like—then put you in a holding cell until you can be arraigned, which probably won't be until tomorrow. But you'll be able to talk with your lawyer tonight."

Jamison nodded, took a deep breath, and they entered the building, a police officer on either side of him.

THEY CONVERGED on the station practically at the same time. Lincoln drove Jamison's mother and aunt; Lonnie pulled up in his Beetle; and JP was leaning on the intake desk when they entered.

"Lonnie?" JP said, sounding surprised. "What are you doing here?"

"I… uh, I came to see—"

"You're Lonnie?" the officer from the hospital said. *What was his name again?* "Sorry about earlier, kid, but you don't run up on an officer making an arrest."

Lonnie nodded and gulped. He would remember that lesson for the rest of his life. He glanced at the man's uniform. *Gagnon. Okay, got it.*

Gagnon looked around the room as though he was making certain everyone else was too wrapped up in their own worries to listen in. "Your man is in with his lawyer right now," he said softly, "but I'll take you back to say good night once they're done."

"Thank you." Tired and so hungry…. Lonnie sighed, nodded, and stopped himself from tugging on his hair just in time. *Wait.* Had he heard right? "Good night?"

"He won't be arraigned until morning, I'm afraid."

Lonnie worried his bottom lip as he looked around at all the sad and angry faces in the main lobby. Jamison's mother glared at him while Lincoln hovered at her elbow. *My fault.* "But… but he hasn't eaten." He began to wring his hands. "Will he get something to… to…?" Lonnie teetered on his feet as the floor tilted beneath him.

"Whoa there, little fella."

"Lonnie? I got ya." Strong arms held him upright, and someone guided him to a seat. He looked up, focused on JP's handsome face, and recoiled.

"Jerry." He held his hands up to ward off JP. "Please, step back. Thank you…. I just need to clear my head for a moment."

"You two know each other?" Gagnon frowned down at them.

"JP's my ex."

Lonnie caught JP tossing a smirk Gagnon's way.

"Is that right?" the cop asked. He turned to face JP dead on, and JP backed up. "Is there something I can help you with, Pool?"

"I'm just getting the details on Coburn's arrest. My editor gave me the story because of the profile I did on the guy. Any chance I could see him?"

"Not tonight. Sorry."

"I doubt you're sorry, Gag."

"You'd be right. Get what you can from the desk and scat."

JP saluted Gagnon and headed back to the front desk, smirking. Lonnie watched the exchange curiously. Of course, odds were the cop would know JP from his drug-using days. He appeared to not like him very much. *No surprise there.*

"Be right back, kid." Gagnon patted Lonnie on the shoulder and went to speak with Mrs. Coburn's group. He heard a shrill "What!" from her before the room quieted and heads turned her way.

The place wasn't bustling like he'd seen on TV shows. It was Overbrook, after all. There were a total of two people handcuffed to chairs in the room. A scantily clad woman, who winked at Lonnie when she caught him looking at her. He snorted and looked away. The other was a man who kept nodding off as a detective asked him questions. He had to weigh at least five hundred pounds and was sporting a black eye.

Lonnie slumped in his seat and stared at his shoes. The floor was dirty, scuffed linoleum—*Is that blood?*—with a large white-and-brown-checkered pattern. As he stared, losing himself in the lines, he soon noticed a pair of expensive Italian shoes pointing at his ratty sneakers.

"Are you Alonzo Bellerose?" the man asked.

Lonnie stood as though he'd been stuck with a needle. "Yes."

"I'm Tomas Redking." The man was tall—tall, slender, blond… and terribly handsome. He could pose for a Nazi poster except, instead of gazing off at some horizon he wanted to conquer, he smiled warmly down at Lonnie, his soft blue eyes twinkling. "Your father asked me to represent Mr. Coburn."

"How is he?"

"Please. Sit." Tomas sat next to Lonnie on the bench and crossed his legs elegantly. "He's fine, but we won't be able to get him in front of a judge until tomorrow at 8:00 a.m."

"What will happen to him?"

"Well, that really depends on Mr. Coburn. He plans to plead guilty."

"What!" Mrs. Coburn stormed over to them. Lonnie fervently wished she'd stop screaming like that. "I'm his mother. You should be telling me all this."

Tomas stood and spoke politely. "Yes, ma'am, however I'm representing your son as a favor to the Belleroses, and Jamison has made it clear to me that this young man"—he gestured to Lonnie—"is the party I should be speaking with. If you'd like to have a seat, I'm sure we'd be happy to have your input."

"*Input?*" She drew herself up, preparing to let loose with another tirade, but Jo headed her off.

"Sit down, Alanna. Sit down and listen."

Mrs. Coburn sat and folded her hands in her lap on top of her purse. Lincoln and Jo hovered, creating a tiny huddle, and Lonnie thought he saw Gagnon and JP milling about close by.

Tomas sat back down. "As I said, Jamison plans to plead guilty. He says he threw the first punch, therefore...."

Mrs. Coburn began to cry softly.

"What will that mean?" Lonnie asked, unconsciously patting Mrs. Coburn's hand, then giving it a gentle squeeze.

"It's his first offense. He assaulted the gentleman and walked away, but as I understand it, he was subsequently set upon by three men, and Mr. Coburn is the one who went to the hospital. He would most likely get probation." They all nodded. "However, another avenue we might consider is filing hate crime charges against Mr. Pritchard and his cohorts."

"How so?" Lincoln asked.

"As I understand it, there were some antigay slurs used prior to the fight and during."

They all nodded, except Lonnie, since he hadn't been there. "Would that prompt Delroy to drop his complaint?" he asked.

"I think so, yes," Tomas said. "It carries a heftier penalty than second-degree assault."

Lonnie turned to everyone and managed a hopeful grin before looking back at Tomas. "Can we see him before he's… uh…?"

"Sent to holding?"

"Yes, can we?" Mrs. Coburn asked in a much softer voice. She had clearly run out of steam.

Tomas nodded, and Lonnie told Mrs. Coburn to go first.

Chapter 19

JAMISON FOLDED his arms on the cold metal table he was cuffed to and used them as a pillow. He had to rest. Talking to his mother had drained him. Nothing he said would calm her, and he needed some calming of his own. His lawyer seemed to think everything would turn out just fine, but… hell, he didn't know. Second-degree assault? He knew he was wrong to hit Delroy—he smiled to himself—but he was *right* not to kill him. It had definitely run through his mind. Maybe they'd take that into account…. *But I probably shouldn't mention considering it.*

"What's so funny?"

He looked up to find Lonnie holding a big greasy takeout bag and two large sodas.

"Lonnie," Jamison moaned.

"Hang on, Coburn," Gagnon said as he squeezed past Lonnie and around the table. He produced some keys. "Let me free you up a bit here." He unlocked one of Jamison's hands and left the room with a grin on his face and a whispered thank-you from Lonnie. They stared at each other for a moment, and then Lonnie set down the food and walked around the table to kiss him, to stroke his face and stare into his eyes.

"Everything will be okay, you know that, right?"

The desperation to believe it was thick in Lonnie's voice, so Jamison nodded and ran his fingers through Lonnie's hair. "I know it, babe."

They kissed again, then embraced—or the best Jamison could manage with only one arm free. His grip tightened as he remembered how terrified he'd been when Lonnie startled Gagnon outside the hospital. But as they held on to each other, Lonnie's hair tickled Jamison's cheek, and he laughed, relieving some of their distress. Then Lonnie's stomach growled ferociously, and they laughed and snorted together.

Lonnie disentangled himself, took his seat again on the other side of the table, and began unwrapping the food. "I know you're starving because I am, and you're a lot bigger than me." Jamison bit his big burger in half, and Lonnie laughed. "Chew your food, babe."

"Thanks for this," he said around his mouthful.

"Wasn't me. Officer Cosgrove ran out for it." Lonnie leaned across the table and whispered, "I think Officer Gagnon might be *family*." Then he took a big bite himself.

Really? Jamison hadn't thought about it. "I expected to be in holding by now," he said as his wiped his mouth.

"Nathan thought it would be better for me to visit you in here."

"Nathan?" Jamison said, lifting an eyebrow.

"Officer Gagnon." Lonnie rolled his eyes. "You know what I mean."

"I'm not complaining, but why?"

Lonnie paused, then wiped his mouth with a napkin. "He seemed to think my coming back to holding to see you might… cause a ruckus, make things harder on you?"

Jamison got it. "Well, you *are* awful pretty," he said, smiling, "but there's probably nothing more than a few drunks back there, Lon. No hardened criminals."

They sobered and went back to eating silently for a few minutes. Then Lonnie said, "Your mother seemed quieter when she came out."

"She wasn't when she was in here. Just kept crying and looking at me like I was dying."

"Jamison—"

"But I don't know if it's because I'm in jail or gay."

"Probably a little bit of both."

They laughed together again. Lonnie reached out and took his hand. "I wish I could sleep in your arms tonight, more than anything."

"We've slept apart plenty of times."

Lonnie took his hand back. "Yeah, but I always knew you were tucked safe in bed." He glanced at the walls as if they were diseased. "Not surrounded by strangers and… criminals."

He nodded. "Speaking of strange, I saw Pool when they brought me in." The face Lonnie made nearly caused Jamison to choke on his soda.

"I saw him too. I didn't say who I was here to see, but he has ears like a cat, so he probably overheard me and Redking."

Jamison thought for a moment, then changed the subject, saying, "I like Redking. We talked a lot. He's in Maryland to finalize his divorce from his 'harpy of a wife.'"

"Yikes."

"Uh-huh. He moved here with her to be near her family about seven years ago. He'd just felt settled in the States when he found her in bed with some old high school boyfriend."

"Okay...."

Jamison blinked. "What?"

"Did the two of you talk any more about your case?"

"Sure." But Jamison didn't want to talk about that. "He's originally from France, a place called Province—"

Lonnie sighed. "Provence?"

"Yeah. That's it."

"It's in the southern part of the country. It's beautiful there but pricey. You've heard of the French Riviera, right?"

"Seen it in movies."

Lonnie nodded quickly but slowly reached for Jamison's hand again. He must have sensed time ticking away for them tonight, just as Jamison did. "That James Bond movie *GoldenEye* was filmed there, *Ocean's Twelve*, ooh, *Dirty Rotten Scoundrels*, hilarious! *The Transporter*.... Lots of films," Lonnie said.

"Get over here."

Lonnie was up and sitting on the table in front of Jamison in two seconds, cupping Jamison's face in his hands. Jamison held him as best he could, stroking his thumbs along the outside of Lonnie's thighs and smiling weakly.

"We'll watch those when I get out of here. It's just a few more hours, Lon."

Lonnie nodded and kissed the top of his head. When the key turned in the door, Lonnie gripped him tighter and laid a deep kiss on his mouth, and Jamison's dick filled. He groaned at the prospect of going into the holding cell waving that flag. The kiss grew deeper, and Lonnie raked his nails over Jamison's skull.

The door swung open.

"*Ahem*."

They parted and found Gagnon smirking at them. "I told you no touching, Mr. Bellerose."

Lonnie got up and gathered the trash from their meal. "Did you? I must have missed that."

Gagnon met Jamison's gaze. "Time to take you back." He seemed almost apologetic as he freed Jamison completely from the table and cuffed his hands behind his back again. Lonnie choked off a sob, but when they looked at each other, he winked and smiled bravely. Jamison decided to ignore the sparkle of tears in his eyes.

JUST A few hours, Lonnie repeated to himself as he walked out to his Beetle. *He'll be out and home safe in just a few more hours.* He unlocked the door and climbed in. He faced the station house, staring at the brick structure as if it were a castle he needed to storm. He dug out his cell and called his sister.

"Tell me," Amber said.

"He'll be arraigned tomorrow morning. Mr. Redking seems solid. Thank Dad for me. Jamison's settling in for the night, and I think I'll stay here too."

"Lonnie, it's not a hospital. There's no waiting room, and I don't think the officers will appreciate you being underfoot."

"I'm not underfoot. I'm sleeping in my car." He turned in his seat and felt blindly along the backseat. "I have a sweater and everything." He pulled the old sweater into his lap.

"What's 'everything'?"

"Uh… a sweater."

"That's what I thought. I can bring you some coffee, donuts?"

"Maybe in the morning. Oh, get this. JP was there when I arrived."

"What? Why?"

"I'm guessing since he did the profile, he's been assigned Jamison's fall from grace."

"Anyone else I can call for you?"

"Nah. Jamison's boss took Mrs. Coburn home to rest, though I expect her to get about as much as me tonight—" He frowned. "Wait, that didn't come out right."

The two of them dissolved into laughter. When they sobered, Lonnie said, "He's going to plead guilty because he threw the first punch, but Redking might seek hate crime charges against Delroy and the others for jumping Jamison after he walked away."

"Good!"

After smiling at his sister's support, Lonnie yawned. "Now, if you'll excuse me," he said, snuggling beneath the sweater, "I need some sleep. Talk to you tomorrow after court."

"Lonnie, are you sure you don't want to just come over here and crash?"

"I'm parked in front of the police station. What could happen?"

JAMISON WAS happy to see his two cellmates cringe when he entered their space. He glowered at them, making sure they stayed in their corner. They were both a pretty good size, and he didn't want any trouble... well, any *more* trouble. He took a seat on one of the benches along the wall of the cell and had just begun to nod off when he heard a door open, footsteps, and hushed words.

He peeked out one eye and saw Jerry Pool standing outside the holding cell chatting with a policeman. He saw a flash of green as money changed hands. The cop turned and looked right at him. "Coburn!"

Jamison rose and went to the bars. "Yeah?"

"This guy has some questions for ya." The cop nodded to Pool. "Make it quick." Then he left them alone.

"I've got nothin' to say to you," Jamison said.

"I thought my profile was a hit."

"It was great until the end. I told you I was in a relationship."

"Did you?" Pool appeared stunned. "I'm sorry, Jamison—"

"Mr. Coburn."

"—Mr. Coburn. My mistake. I guess when I was going over my notes and writing it up, I went with what everyone else told me. I figured as close as they were to you, they'd know the truth, so I erred on their side. I apologize, truly."

"I was there when you talked to Torp. He never said—"

JP pulled out his notepad and a pen. "Just give me the lady's name, and I can include a correction in the story I'm writing about your arrest. About that, care to tell me what happened?"

Jamison regarded him for several moments. Searching his pretty eyes, he saw no sign of a trick, just bright blue sincerity. But instead of looking away, he held Pool's gaze for several more seconds and saw the façade crack. He made his decision.

"You knew about me and Lonnie."

Pool dropped the act and smiled, his eyes narrowing and no longer so pretty. "I did. Saw you out at a club together."

"You've hurt him." Jamison's voice grew more threatening, and Pool took a step back from the bars.

"I regret that, and I'll treat him better next time."

Jamison snorted. "He'll never come back to you." *At least I hope not.*

Pool stared at him for a moment, then said, "Listen, Coburn, you seem like a nice guy. In fact, according to everything I've learned about you, that's exactly what you are. But nice isn't enough." He lifted his hand and began counting off on his fingers. "Lonnie is talented. He's traveled the world. He's educated." He looked Jamison up and down. "And you've made it only as far as the other end of town from your neighborhood, which happily sucked you back down into the muck this afternoon." Jamison hadn't realized he'd gripped the bars until his hands began to ache. "I can see your appeal, certainly, but is it all fucking? What do you two even talk about?"

"We talk about how I'm not an addict, how I've never raised my voice to him, belittled him. Can you say the same?"

"You've been with him for how long? A few weeks, right? Wait until it's been a year or two, then tell me how much fun he is."

"Doesn't sound like he means much to you."

"I'm working on getting my life back, and Lonnie's part of that life."

"He's not the man he was. He won't put up with your bullshit again."

"We'll see. Right now he's sitting in his little fucked-up car in the parking lot, waiting for your hearing tomorrow." Jamison glanced at the window at the top of the wall outside the cell. He could see a sliver of the night sky and the glow of the lot lights through it, and he hated the thought of Lonnie out there alone. But the last thing he wanted was this guy keeping him company. "You know his doubting nature, how insecure he is," Pool continued. "And just look at what he's done to your life in the short time you've known him."

"This isn't his fault!" Jamison rumbled.

"You're not good enough for him, and he's a wrecking ball to your existence. It's a match made in hell, and I'm gonna show him that."

"Pool! What the fuck are you doing back here?" Gagnon said, suddenly filling the doorway at the end of the hall.

The reporter looked unperturbed, though Jamison did see him tense slightly. "I needed to get a quote for my story."

"Come on, get the fuck away from him."

Tapping a front tooth with his pen, Pool taunted, "Such language, Gag." He strolled away from the cell and toward the officer.

"I'm not going to be in here forever," Jamison said.

Pool paused in the doorway and looked over his shoulder. "If I've learned anything in my research, it's that you're not a violent man, Mr. Coburn."

Gagnon leaned into Pool, causing him to flatten his back against the doorjamb and stare at him, startled. "Until someone talked shit about his man," the cop rumbled. "Imagine if someone were to hurt him."

Pool quickly scooted past Gagnon, and Jamison nodded his thanks to the officer.

Chapter 20

LONNIE TURNED again. His legs were too long to lie down in the backseat, so he made do in the front, eyes closed, listening to the muffled night sounds around him, the occasional car, and constant cricket song. Maybe it was time to get a new car. After it slipped down yet again, he pulled the sweater back up over his shoulders like the inadequate blanket it was. What was Jamison doing right now? He probably couldn't sleep, either.

Their day had gone to shit so fast. The article was glowing, and seeing Jamison's smiling face in the paper and his beautiful furniture showcased had filled Lonnie with joy... until the last paragraph. That had been disheartening to say the least, but then they'd made love, followed by the cookout and confessions and confrontations.

More like a roller coaster, I guess. Shit! Focus on the making-love part, he told himself. *Sweet dreams.*

A tap on the passenger window startled him, and he sat up. Frowning, he reached over and cranked down the window. "What do you want, JP?"

"Why are you loitering in the Overbrook Police Station parking lot?" The smirk on his face was familiar. He'd often found Lonnie amusing or exasperating.

"None of your business."

"Come on, Lonnie, open up. Tell me what's going on."

Lonnie looked away from him, back at the station house. "Why are you still here?"

"I'm covering Coburn's arrest. That's the guy I profiled in today's—"

"I know who he is."

JP reached through the window and unlocked the door. "You read it?" he asked as he slid inside. Lonnie nodded curtly, and JP grinned. "Fuck, I didn't think you would still read my stuff."

"It was a nice piece," he said through clenched teeth. "He came off well."

JP shrugged. "He's a good guy. After all he's been through in his life, he's finally on the road to somewhere. Well… until today, that is." He sighed heavily.

That stung. "What are you talking about?" Lonnie said, looking at him sharply.

"Just that Coburn's luck has taken a turn for the worse recently. A criminal record is never something you want to have. Trust me, I know."

"Yeah, you would." He glared at JP, who sighed.

"Lonnie, I've apologized. I don't know what else I can do."

"I accept your apology," he said, rolling his eyes, "but that doesn't mean we're gonna be buddies."

"I understand, and thank you."

They sat in silence for several moments, Lonnie working the question through in his head and finding no way around it. "Did you see him, speak to him?"

"Who?"

"Jamis—Coburn?"

"Just for a couple minutes. He seemed fine. Tired, but fine. He'll be glad to get out tomorrow."

"You think he will?"

JP frowned. "Be happy to get—?"

"No… be released."

"Oh. Sure. Remember, this used to be my beat in Baltimore. It's his first offense, and he caught the worst of it." Lonnie grinned gratefully, but then JP continued. "Then again, it sort of depends, as everything does, on how hard the plaintiff wants to push it and who he has in his corner."

Lonnie blinked at him. One moment awash in relief, the next finding it difficult to breathe. Who did Delroy have in his corner?

"I did a little background check on this Pritchard guy," JP explained.

"He owns a bakery," Lonnie offered, biting his tongue too late. JP narrowed his eyes and smiled at him. *Damn, that smile.*

"Two actually," JP said. "Just opened a second location, but he's also toying with the idea of trying to sue his way around the city's nondiscrimination ordinance. Doesn't want to bake a gay wedding cake or something."

"So he's an all-around homophobe."

JP shrugged. "Says he's exercising his religious freedom, and his church is behind him on it."

"Bullshit."

JP blinked. "Lonnie! I'm not sure I've ever heard you swear like that before."

He gave JP a reluctant grin. "A lot's changed since the last time you saw me."

"It's sorta sexy."

He snorted, then stopped smiling. JP had always hated it when he laughed like that. "I told you—"

"Yeah, yeah, you're seeing someone. Let me guess. Professor?"

"Nope." He looked at JP, trying to read him like he used to. He'd been at the front desk of the station when they arrived. Like everything else in Overbrook, the police station was a small one, and the longer he stared at JP, the more certain he became that he knew everything.

"Doctor… surgeon maybe?"

Lonnie shook his head, trying not to be amused by or curious about his guesses. He looked at the station house, concern about Jamison thrumming through him.

"Not another artist." JP frowned.

"Of sorts. Why?"

"That would just be too weird."

"He doesn't do what I do, but his work is elegant and created with a load of skill and love."

JP was silent for several moments. "You sound smitten."

He ignored the odd note in JP's voice. "I am." He could feel his ex watching him and realized too late how he must appear gazing at the station house with such longing.

"Jesus Christ! It's Coburn, isn't it?"

"Jerry—"

"Really, Lonnie?" JP shook his head, as if to clear it. "Wow."

"Wow what?"

"Well… um," JP said, appearing to tamp down his surprise, "you're just so different, I guess. Two different worlds and all that."

"Listen—"

"I mean, he's a gorgeous piece of ass, but—"

"Stop." He couldn't have him talking about Jamison like that. "I'm fairly certain you figured out who I'm here for, so why don't you give up this charade?"

"Sorry," JP said, grinning.

Anger had heated his skin, and he turned to face his ex. Crossing his arms over his chest, he said, "Jamison and I work just fine, thank you. Better than you and I ever did." JP made a face that said he didn't believe him, and Lonnie shot him a death glare. "Jamison thinks I'm miraculous, and all you ever did was pick me apart."

JP remained silent for several moments, then said, "True. I was struggling with my own shit at the time, but you didn't deserve the way I treated you. I'm learning not to hate myself, and hopefully, the next time I find someone who's willing to give me a shot, I'll be the man he deserves."

Lonnie blinked, letting JP's words sink in. "I can't tell whether that's your usual line of bullshit or not."

"You could always just give me the benefit of the doubt." JP wiggled his eyebrows.

"Not likely."

"Lonnie, you have to know I wish the best for you…. Which is why—"

"No!" He'd had enough.

"Lon"—Lonnie cringed at JP using the nickname Jamison had for him, but it was better than his old, overused Loonie—"you've been out since you were, what? Three?" JP snorted. "Coburn's just not there yet. If he were, he would have told me he had a boyfriend instead of that lame pronoun-less 'I'm in a relationship' crap he tried to pull. No one else important to him knew about you."

Lonnie gripped the steering wheel. "Get out of the car."

"Yeah, yeah. I'm going." JP opened the door and slid out but paused to lean back in the window after he shut the door. Lonnie refused to look at him. "Sorry, Lonnie. I'm sure it'll all go well. See you in court." And JP was gone, walking across the lot to his late-model SUV and leaving Lonnie with only his thoughts and doubts to keep him company.

LONNIE'S SLEEPLESS night was written in his tired, puffy eyes the next day as he stared into the mirror above the sink in a city hall men's room. Freshening up there wasn't perfect, but it got the job done. Lonnie splashed cold water on his face and patted it dry with a rough brown paper towel. He'd been shocked awake by his cell phone around 7:30 a.m., when Redking had called to tell him which of the two courtrooms Jamison would be arraigned in.

He'd gotten there just as the building was unlocked and gone straight to the bathroom. He wanted to see Jamison before the proceeding, but he'd been told by a courthouse clerk that Jamison would be brought directly from holding to the courtroom.

Upon leaving the men's room, he spotted Redking in the hall. He and Mrs. Coburn stood chatting. *Oh goody.* Lonnie approached carefully, not wanting to startle them. When Redking saw him over Mrs. Coburn's shoulder, he smiled, encouraging Lonnie forward.

"Mrs. Coburn. Mr. Redking," he said, managing a weak smile. "What's the word?"

Jamison's mother regarded him with thinly veiled hostility. *I see this is still all my fault. I seduced your son, led him astray and into a life of sin.*

"I was just telling Mrs. Coburn we're waiting for Mr. Pritchard to arrive."

"Don't you need to speak with the prosecutor?" Lonnie asked.

Redking ran his fingers through his blond hair, which fell right back into place, briefly reminding Lonnie of JP. "The prosecutor is already inside," Redking said. "It's Pritchard we need to discourage. Without him, there's no case."

Lonnie began wringing his hands but stopped the moment he noticed Mrs. Coburn watching him worriedly. "What will you say to him? I mean, isn't blackmail or threatening someone illegal?"

"Yes, but I'm not doing that."

"You're not?"

"Of course not, Mr. Bellerose. Bringing hate crime charges against Mr. Pritchard is as legitimate as charging Mr. Coburn with second-degree assault."

Lonnie smiled, but at that moment the elevator doors opened and discharged three African Americans—two men in expensive suits and a beautiful woman, equally stylish. They looked as though they were on their way to church. Hell, maybe they were going after court.

"Oh Lordy, that's Pastor Jackson!" Mrs. Coburn said, and Lonnie grimaced when she gripped his hand to steady herself, but he held on, supporting her. He wanted to ask who Pastor Jackson was, but he could tell by how shaken Mrs. Coburn was that the guy was some bigwig—at least to her.

"Please excuse me," Redking said with a short bow. He walked quickly over to the trio and shook everyone's hands.

"Is he your pastor?" Lonnie asked Jamison's mother as he watched the conversation Redking was having with the trio.

"No. Pastor Jackson heads the biggest Baptist church in town and has his own Sunday telecast. I watch it sometimes. He's colorful."

Lonnie nodded as Redking maintained his pleasant expression while the others began to frown, growing angrier, eyes darting about. Then the pastor spoke, and Lonnie wished he could hear what was being said, because the body language was a bit blustery. When the pastor quieted, he held his mouth in a tight-lipped grimace as he looked from Redking to Delroy and back again, and then he pulled Delroy aside.

Lonnie and Mrs. Coburn glanced at each other, then back to the group. Redking waited patiently, standing next to the very confused-looking woman. Delroy's conversation with Jackson ended with the pastor giving him a curt nod. Delroy turned and wordlessly held out his hand to the woman, who came directly to his side. The two of them and the pastor walked into the courtroom, not sparing one glance at Lonnie or Mrs. Coburn.

"That went so-so," Redking said, rejoining them.

"What just happened?" Mrs. Coburn demanded, gripping Redking's wrist.

"Pastor Jackson nearly withdrew his support. It seems his church is raising funds to campaign for a 'religious freedom' ordinance, and they're willing to support the complaint against Jamison, but the pastor isn't happy about the possible hate crime charges Delroy could face." Redking smiled. "Seems he doesn't want Trinity Baptist tarnished with the bigot brush. But he's willing to see what the judge will do."

"What now?" Lonnie asked.

"Now we go to court and see just how determined Mr. Pritchard is." The elevator opened again, producing Torp and Lincoln. Lonnie smiled. Jamison would have a lot of good people in his corner today. Lonnie's family had offered to appear as well, but he'd promised them a phone call when everything was settled. He didn't want them crowding the courtroom as they'd crowded the hospital the night before. He loved them, but his family could be overwhelming at times—especially when they got worked up.

As a unit, his group pushed open the courtroom doors.

SITTING BEHIND his desk in chambers, Judge Dennis Gino popped two aspirin and stretched his back until he heard and felt a pop. *Another day, another collection of degenerates.* The party his wife had thrown last night was a doozy, and he wasn't looking forward to the day ahead. Saturdays were short days, everyone out by noon, but somehow they didn't feel all that short lately. He scrubbed his hands through his short gray hair and thought fondly of the nap he'd be taking in a few hours.

After donning his robe, he checked himself in the mirror, first facing, then profile, smoothing his hand down over his belly to see how much farther it stuck out today. *Oh well.* He allowed the robe to billow loosely again. *No one will see.* He went to the door, took a deep breath, and stepped into the courtroom.

"All rise! The Honorable...." *Blah, blah, blah....*

He didn't meet anyone's eyes as he climbed to his seat on the bench. He slowly filled a glass with ice water from a pitcher waiting for him at his left hand. Then he whacked his gavel. "We're in session," he said. "Thank you, Billy. Everyone sit down." *Now....* he gazed out at the occupants of his courtroom.

Mr. Mault, a city attorney, sat in his usual spot, waiting, appearing tired. He looked miserable, and he probably was because he'd been at the party last night too, though how he'd wrangled an invite, Gino didn't know. A young African American couple sat in the gallery behind Mault, and an older, large barrel-chested man sat next to them. He looked as though he belonged in a pulpit with his swept-back hair and brightly colored suit. Dressed to the nines, the trio appeared determined, even smug. *Plaintiff. Check.*

Then he took note of the young man who looked like a linebacker sitting at the defendant's table, but he didn't look angry or threatening. He just looked nervous and... *and beaten to a pulp.* Directly behind him sat what looked like a nice mix of spectators: a mother and father, a younger brother with rather exciting hair—all African American—a Hispanic man, and a Caucasian police officer. They all looked on, concerned.

Next to the defendant stood... *well, well.*

Aside from those folks, a motley collection of others was sprinkled throughout the gallery, waiting their turns before him. One man sat in the very back of the room in the corner. He was blond and stank of reporter.

"What do we have to start, Billy?"

"Delroy Pritchard versus Jamison Coburn," the bailiff said.

"Ah yes." Gino donned his reading glasses, and after skimming the file, he peered at the defendant over his frames. "Mr. Coburn, you are charged with second-degree assault. How do you plead?"

"Guilty, your honor."

He'd seen a lot over the years, and it was difficult to surprise him, so that plea caused him a ripple of confusion. He wasn't sure he'd heard right, so he paused for a sip of water. To cover, he decided to chat and allowed his gaze to slide over to Redking. "Hello, Tomas."

"Your Honor."

"How are you?"

"Very good, sir. You?"

"Eh… left knee is acting up."

"Sorry to hear that, Your Honor."

He focused on Coburn again. "Guilty, huh?" There was something familiar about him, but Gino couldn't quite put his finger on it.

"Yes, Your Honor."

The judge silently read the file again, then looked to the prosecutor. "Hello, Mr. Mault."

"Your Honor. It's good to see—"

"Says here, Mr. Coburn attacked Mr. Pritchard?"

"Uh…." Mault glanced at the defendant's side of the room. "Yes, Your Honor. That's correct. Mr. Coburn assaulted Mr. Pritchard."

"And where is Mr. Pritchard?"

The smaller of the impeccably dressed men he'd noticed earlier sprang to his feet and rushed forward to stand next to Mault. "Here, Your Honor. Here I am."

Gino motioned for Pritchard to approach the bench, and he came forward, glancing over his shoulder at Mault, who was on his heels. Gino peered at Pritchard's face. There was swelling and a fat lip. "Show me your hands, son." After making his examination, he looked up at Coburn and told him to approach as well. Coburn rose and moved stiffly toward him, holding his arm tight to his ribs.

Once he and his lawyer stood before the bench, Gino said, "Tell me what happened, Mr. Co—"

"Uh, Your Honor, I don't think—"

"No, Mr. Mault, you don't. Otherwise you wouldn't be telling me what I can and can't do in *my* court." Mault fell silent, and they all looked to the defendant.

Coburn cleared his throat and said, "Your Honor, I punched him… Delroy… uh, Mr. Pritchard." Coburn glanced quickly and apologetically at the court reporter.

"Then what?"

Mault tried again. "I have to object—"

"Noted. Please continue, Mr. Coburn."

"That's all, sir. I punched him and walked away." The big man looked down sheepishly. "He was saying... some things."

"He disrespected you?"

"Uh... yes, sir, but when he *disrespected* someone I... care about...."

Gino pointed, indicating Coburn's puffy face and stiff posture. "You look in worse shape than the plaintiff, with your breathing, the way you move, and the shape your face is in. Also his knuckles are a mess, while yours—" He gestured, and Coburn raised his basically unmarked hands so Gino could get a better look at them. "Why is that, if you walked away?"

Coburn glanced at his lawyer, who simply nodded. "Delroy and two other guys jumped me in my mother's backyard."

Gino tsked and turned to the plaintiff. "Why'd you do that, Mr. Pritchard?"

"Your Honor, he punched me."

"Yes, we've established that."

"Well, I couldn't let some fag—" Mault grabbed Pritchard's arm hard to shut him up.

"Excuse me?" Gino raised an eyebrow.

"Nothing, sir," Pritchard mumbled, staring at the floor.

"Okay," Gino said with a deep sigh. "Plaintiff, defendant, back to your seats. Counsel, stay where—wait." Everyone froze. "You, Coburn, why do you look so familiar to me? Have you been in my courtroom before?"

"No, Your Honor."

Redking smiled. "You might have seen him in the newspaper, Your Honor."

Gino stared at Coburn for a moment, then said, "Ah, yes. Now I remember." He shooed Coburn and Pritchard away, then looked deeply into Redking's eyes. "Are you bringing hate crime charges against the plaintiff?"

Mault began to sputter. "Your Honor!"

"Save it, Mault."

"It's possible, Your Honor." Redking glanced sideways at his colleague. "I'd have to confer with my client, of course, see what he'd like to do."

"Do so."

The two men walked back to their separate camps for a huddle. The preacher joined the plaintiff's huddle, and after some discussion, straightened and walked out of the courtroom, shaking his perfectly coiffed head. Gino smirked at Billy, who stood at his post, also grinning. The judge waited as the two groups conferred for several more minutes. Then he spoke up.

"Let's go, gentlemen."

Mault smoothed his suit and faced him. "Your Honor, at this time… we won't be pursuing any charges against Mr. Coburn."

"Excellent. And Mr. Coburn?"

"That's great, sir."

"No, son," Gino said, chuckling. "Will you be bringing charges against Mr. Pritchard?" The plaintiff's table watched and waited as Coburn made up his mind.

"No, Your Honor. I just want to go home, please."

Gino banged his gavel. "Case dismissed. Next!"

Coburn smiled and, once he got the okay from his lawyer, rushed toward the young man waiting for him, who squealed in delight, embraced, and kissed Coburn.

Okay, not *his little brother.*

He couldn't be sure, but the lady he took to be Coburn's mother might have smiled, ever so slightly. Redking nodded to Gino and followed the family out the door.

Chapter 21

JAMISON HELD tight to Lonnie, burying his face in his hair and oblivious to all others around them, as he walked out of the courtroom with his arm around his man. His relief made him as light-headed as Lonnie's scent. Once they were in the hallway, he pressed Lonnie against the wall just outside the doors and kissed him deeply. Alanna grimaced. Lincoln looked everywhere but at them, while Redking, Torp, and Gagnon smirked, and JP scowled. Lost in Lonnie, Jamison didn't want to be found.

The doors swung out, and Delroy exited with Vinnia on his arm, looking as though he still had plenty of venom to spit, but he kept his mouth shut as they waited for the elevator, their backs to the group.

Pool slowly made his way to the stairwell door, then paused, looking at them. "You've been apart less than twenty-four hours," he said. "You'd think he'd just come home from war." Jamison stopped kissing Lonnie and took a menacing step toward Pool. "Now, Coburn, you don't want to end up behind bars again."

"You stay the hell away from us."

"If that's what Lonnie wants…."

They all turned to Lonnie—who stood against the wall, a finger on his lips and his eyes glazed—for his answer. "Huh? Y-yes, it's what I w-want."

"Didn't seem that way in your car last night," Pool said before vanishing through the door.

Jamison ignored that shot across his bow and opened his arms so his mother could fill them. Next he shook his lawyer's hand rather briskly. "Thank you, sir."

"You're m-most wel-welcome, Jamison. I'm g-glad to help." Once Jamison released him, Redking shook out his hand and flexed his shoulder in relief.

Torp, Lincoln, and Gagnon came forward to slap Jamison on his back, and he thanked them for their support, but he was eager to get Lonnie back home, and they all seemed to understand that. Well, not all.

His mother wanted to take him back to her house and feed him, baby him, but Jamison firmly and lovingly declined.

"Mama, the next time we have dinner together, it'll be with Lonnie there next to me. Do you understand?" At first she bristled, glancing Lonnie's way, but then her shoulders slumped. She nodded, and Jamison kissed her cheek. "You'll like him, Mama," he said gently. "He's miraculous."

They ended up at Jamison's apartment, which looked so forlorn from the street without his truck filling the driveway. He'd have to retrieve it from Lonnie's place, but for now, he unfolded himself out of Lonnie's Beetle, and the two of them, bone-tired but thrilled to be able to touch each other, made their way to Jamison's bed, where they stripped to their shorts and collapsed with equally deep sighs.

"Tired?" Jamison mumbled.

"Yeah, didn't sleep much."

"Me either."

"Should call… m'family."

"Later, babe." Jamison pulled Lonnie against him and fell asleep to the steady rhythm of his heart.

WHEN JP got back to his desk, kicking over his chair probably wasn't the best thing to do. It brought Stewart out of his office and frightened the intern handling the phones.

"Pool, in my office!"

JP righted his chair and dropped into the one in his boss's office seconds later.

"Are you using again?"

"Of course not." *Absolutely.* "Don't be ridiculous."

Stewart gestured to the door, indicating the outer office. "So what was that all about?"

"Lousy day in court."

"For you?"

"No, that…." He sat forward in his seat. "You know I went down there to cover the Coburn arrest." Stewart nodded. "He got off." He huffed and pounded the arm of the chair.

Stewart frowned. "I thought he was a nice guy. That's good news, right?"

"Good news doesn't sell, Stew." JP ground his teeth but relented. "Yes, yes, it's great for him, it's just... I was hoping for something a bit more exciting than 'case dismissed.'"

"Look, JP, I know you're eager to be back on the meatier stories, but honestly, this was a one-shot deal. Until you've completed probation, you won't be covering the police beat. And definitely not city hall. They're the biggest bunch of cokeheads in town."

"What?"

Stewart shook his head. "Sorry. It's for your own good, and you know it." He wrote something on a notepad and passed the sheet to JP. "This is your next assignment. New director of the gallery on campus. Give me the basic profile and what she hopes to accomplish in her first year. Shit like that."

JP stared at the contact information. "You. Are. Killing. Me." He tugged on his hair, and Stewart laughed.

"Go on." Stewart waved to the door, dismissing him. "Get it done."

He hauled himself out of the chair, moving as if he'd been beaten.

"Oh, and JP," Stewart said.

"Yeah?" he asked, pausing.

"Give me your best, and we'll revisit the police beat in a year or so. Nice job on the ex-con mechanic, by the way."

"Thanks," he mumbled as he walked out. Once back at his desk, JP opened a new file for the paragraph of information on Coburn's arrest and release. *Riveting.* He hadn't lied—about the drug use, yes, but not about being pissed... just the reason for his anger. The display Coburn and Lonnie had put on outside the courtroom was ridiculous. But he had another angle in the works, an angle that should be nearing fruition soon. *Time for a little bump,* he thought, fingering the tiny vial in his pocket. He had an inside man in the lab that handled his drug testing, and as long as JP kept him in cash, he would always test negative.

Now what to do about Lonnie. Had Coburn's manhandling wiped away all the doubts he'd planted the night before? *Knowing Loonie, probably not.* So he just needed to keep up the pressure, show them how bad they were for each other, and stay out of Coburn's reach.

He read the contact information for the new director of the gallery again. Why did her name sound familiar?

WAKING HOURS later, Jamison was hungry, but Lonnie had wrapped around him so tightly, he couldn't move without waking him. So he lay there, stroking Lonnie's hair and staring at the ceiling. Despite the warm man lying against him, Jamison's thoughts quickly filled with Jerry Pool. The man had known they were a couple and written the article's ending just to drive them apart, to make Lonnie doubt Jamison and his feelings.

Then there was that crack about "in your car last night." What had that been about? He didn't believe Lonnie would cheat…. But would it be cheating at this stage, so early in their relationship?

His stomach growled, and Lonnie jerked awake, looking around. "Wha…?"

Jamison couldn't help but laugh. "It's okay, just my empty belly making itself known." Lonnie stretched long and slow, and Jamison watched, smiling, dick stirring.

"Gosh, what time is it?"

He glanced at the clock. "It's thirteen after five."

"Shit! I never called Amber." Lonnie leaned over the side of the bed, his pert ass pointing at Jamison, much to his delight, and rummaged through his jeans pockets. He reappeared clutching his phone, brushed his hair out of his face, and called Amber. After a few moments, Lonnie said, "Sis? Yeah. Sorry."

Jamison rolled out of bed and headed for the shower. He made the water as hot as he could bear and soaped and rinsed repeatedly, trying to get the feel of the jail off his skin. He'd only been in there for a few hours, but when he imagined how long he could have stayed…. Just the idea of being locked away, another faceless black man in the system, seemed to have settled under his skin.

Pool would probably love that. Me locked up. Lonnie on his own. But Lonnie wouldn't be on his own. He never was. He had his parents, sister, grandmother, and even Claude's parents. They wouldn't let him sink back into something with Pool, not from Amber's reaction when Lonnie had explained the old relationship to him. The reporter liked his mind games, made clear by their conversation in holding. He wondered what Pool had said to L—

Bacon. I smell bacon… and coffee. Every other thought fled his mind. He rinsed for the last time, exited the shower, dried off (for the most part) and stumbled into his bedroom to get dressed. Less than a minute later, he was standing in the kitchen watching Lonnie place a pancake on an already healthy stack of them. The bacon was nearly done and the juice was poured.

"How long was I in the shower?" he asked.

"Not very. I cooked while I filled Amber in, and you had a carton of readymade batter in the fridge. We're having breakfast for an early dinner. Sit. Eat."

Jamison did. "This is amazing." He ate and had to make a conscious effort to slow himself down, to chew, to enjoy the meal. "God, I was so hungry." Lonnie watched him, smiling. "Aren't you going to eat?"

"Sure." Lonnie grabbed a fork and aimed it at Jamison's plate, then laughed at Jamison's warning growl. "Fine. I'll make my own." He worked quickly, Jamison grinning at his back as Lonnie moved about the tiny kitchen. It felt good having him in the space, felt right, and he didn't want to let thoughts of Pool disturb it, but….

"Lonnie, Pool knew about us before he wrote the article. He ended the article the way he did—"

"To start some shit, make me doubt you and us." Lonnie flipped his flapjack. "I suspected as much, but I couldn't figure out how he'd know. Last I heard he was living the high life—pun absolutely intended—in Baltimore before ending up in rehab again. I certainly didn't expect him to land in Overbrook."

"He saw us out at Skulduggery."

Lonnie nodded, then suddenly turned to face him, dripping a bit of raw batter on the floor. "And that thing he said about us in the car last night…."

"He told me you were waiting in the lot, so I figured he'd come out there to whisper Pool shit in your ear, just like he did to me when I couldn't get to him."

Lonnie snorted and turned back to his breakfast. "That man's a pill." Jamison didn't like Lonnie laughing the guy off, but instead of saying so, he decided to take care of something that had been bothering him all night.

"Hey, Lon?"

"Yep."

"Do you know what *inauspicious* means?"

Lonnie turned and slid four pancakes on a plate. "Yeah." He frowned and took his seat. "Why?"

Jamison shrugged and passed him the syrup. "I heard it the other day and…." His face heated.

Lonnie seemed to think about it for a moment before slicing a hunk out of his short stack and spearing it with his fork. "It has to do with success. It basically means something doesn't bode well."

"Huh?"

Lonnie blinked. "Oh… well, just because I know what it means doesn't mean I can explain it. Give me a second." Jamison watched him mull it over further. "If, for instance, your morning has an inauspicious beginning, then odds are your day is gonna suck." He filled his mouth with pancake and syrup, looking satisfied on several levels.

"Got it." Jamison nodded. "Thank you, babe."

"Now for the auspicious." Lonnie poured himself some orange juice. "I'm calling Bink today and accepting the job."

"You'll be great."

They clinked juice glasses and sipped, but it wasn't enough goodness, so Jamison stood and leaned over the table to plant a tangy-sweet kiss on Lonnie's lips.

HE WATCHED him work for a while. Lonnie—his hair bound up in a red scarf—bending and stretching as he measured the gallery space, was a sight to behold. JP hung back, smiling at the way the denim hugged Lonnie's ass. He remembered that ass, remembered it well. When he caught a glimpse of Lonnie's abdomen as he spread the tape up a wall, his cock began to fill while his thoughts filled with memories of touching and kissing Lonnie there, on his way south. JP got lost recalling how vocal and expressive Lonnie could be when touched the right way, so he had a smirk on his face when the man himself finally caught sight of him.

"What are *you* doing here?" Lonnie demanded as their gazes met, the measuring tape in his hand snapping back across the room like a whip.

"I'm interviewing the new gallery director." He smiled. "What are *you* doing here?"

Lonnie turned away from him and knelt by his pencil and pad to put in the last dimensions he'd collected. "I'm the assistant director."

"Now I know why her name sounded so familiar. Bink was your professor." Unseen, JP moved closer. "And here you are, still her flying monkey."

Lonnie straightened and glared at him, and it turned JP on just as it always had. "What did you say?"

"You're still her flunky." He smirked.

"Mr. Bellerose is the assistant director of this gallery, Mr. Pool," Bink said, striding into the room, "and you will treat him with the respect he deserves."

"Yes, ma'am. I apologize." She glanced at Lonnie, and JP got the hint. "I'm sorry, Lonnie. Forgive me?" Lonnie said nothing, just went back to his measuring. "Where would you like to talk?" JP fingered the camera around his neck.

"My office will do."

With Lonnie at his back and Bink leading from the front, JP pressed a hand against his crotch, trying to calm his cock. Glancing back over his shoulder at Lonnie didn't help.

Chapter 22

JAMISON TUGGED on the glass door of Lincoln Frye Home Improvement. As he walked into the much cooler showroom, he noticed more customers seemed to be milling about than usual. Business was good for so late on a Saturday.

"Hey you!" Cartha, Lincoln's pregnant office manager, waddled up to him and hugged him tight, long enough for him to feel the baby kick. Then she pulled him down to her level and planted a sloppy kiss on his cheek. She'd never done that before. "I think all your pieces are gone!"

"What?"

"That article in the paper brought folks in to see your work, and most of them walked out with something. Isn't that great?"

"Uh… yeah." Jamison looked around the room, seeking a glimpse of something he'd built. His heart beat faster when he realized he couldn't find a single item. "Damn," he whispered.

She continued to smile up at him, clearly thrilled for him, her ginger hair shining from the overhead lights. "You looking for Lincoln?"

He nodded, still glancing around. *How could it all be gone?* He felt strangely sad. "I wanted to see where he needed me Monday." He looked down at her. "We haven't finished the Waldor place."

She pooh-poohed that. "He has Torp, Rodney, and Carter finishing that up, but I'll call him for ya." She waddled away and took her seat behind the reception desk with a relieved sigh.

He came over. "Almost time, huh?"

"Yep, and boy am I ready." She laughed and then sobered when Lincoln answered. "Where you want Jamison on Monday, boss?" She winked at him. "Yes, I told him. He's tickled!"

Jamison still couldn't believe it. Selling so many pieces at the same time meant thousands of dollars. His mind felt ready to explode.

"You're the guy from the paper, aren't you?" Jamison looked down to see a beautiful young man, no older than twenty, gazing up at him. He was slender, with big brown eyes and a pretty face framed with shoulder-length, straight brown hair, which he quickly tucked behind ears that stuck out considerably.

Jamison cleared his throat. "Uh… yeah, that's me." He held out his hand. "Jamison Coburn."

"Temple Schrodinger." The man smiled when he said his name, as if anticipating the same from Jamison at the sound of it. They shook hands, and then another man walked up and placed a muscular arm around Schrodinger's shoulder. This man had buzzed jet-black hair and a similar build to Jamison's, his biceps testing the sleeves of his red T-shirt. He looked Jamison directly in the eye with his piercing blue ones.

"This is Staz… just Staz," Schrodinger said.

Jamison shook his hand as well. "Nice work," Staz said.

"Thank you. I appreciate that."

Schrodinger stepped free of Staz's arm, took Jamison's instead, and steered him away from the reception desk. "We came to this little town of yours to get a piece for my loft in Baltimore, but alas"—he pouted—"the pieces I saw in the paper are gone, spirited away by opportunistic heathens."

"You're just pissed they beat you to them," Staz offered as he leaned on the reception desk.

Without turning around, his gaze going hard, Schrodinger froze and said, "And whose mani-pedi made us late getting here?"

Jamison glanced at Cartha, seeking help, but she only smiled and stepped away to file something.

"What can I do for you, Mr. Schrodinger?"

"Call me Temple, please." Temple had a deeply Southern twang, so he definitely wasn't from Maryland. The sound of it reminded Jamison of distant relatives on his mother's side, ones he'd spoken to on the phone when he was a child at Christmas or on his birthday, ones who'd traveled north for his father's funeral so long ago. "I'd like to commission a piece. A dining table. You do that, right?" He snapped his fingers, and Staz appeared at his side, producing a business card. Temple gave it to Jamison, then pulled out his smartphone. "What's your number?" Jamison recited it for him. Temple hit a few buttons, and Jamison's phone buzzed in his back pocket.

"Now… I'm right at your fingertips." Temple gave his bicep a squeeze. "I'll just need you to stop by my place in Baltimore to get a feel for the space, to check the dimensions and whatnot."

He stared down into Temple's big brown eyes, then back up at Staz, who was glaring now. "I've... I've never made something specifically for someone before." He tried to hand back the business card. "I wouldn't know the first thing about how to price something like that."

"Jamison—may I call you Jamison? *You* are an artist. I trust your judgment. I could e-mail you photos of my loft, show you where I'd like the table to go, but I think you'd get a better feel for everything if you were to visit my place. It's on the Inner Harbor. You'd love it." Temple smiled up at him, and he was momentarily mesmerized.

Momentarily.

"Temple, I don't think I—"

"Listen, we'll talk, we'll discuss, we'll make plans, but if it doesn't work out, no hard feelings, okay?" Temple released Jamison and followed Staz to the door. As Staz held it open for him, he turned and graced Jamison with another smile, a knowing smile. "Hope to hear from you soon." Then they were gone.

Jamison read the business card. It seemed Mr. Schrodinger was a computer programmer and gamer.

"Jam. Earth to Jam," Cartha called, waving to get his attention. He pocketed the card and joined her at the desk. "Lincoln says to show up bright and early for demolition Monday at the Pendock Avenue site, okay?"

"I'll be there. Thank you, Cartha."

"You're welcome, hon, and congratulations on the sales."

"Thanks."

"Whatcha gonna do with the rest of your weekend?" she asked. He thought about it for a moment, thought about how nice the weather was this late in September, remembered the picture he'd seen in Lonnie's book about rural France. They should do something outside. Then he grinned softly.

"Uh-oh, looks like trouble," Cartha mused.

He wondered briefly if he should go into detail. Had Lincoln told her about Lonnie? *Well, so what if he hasn't?*

"I'm thinking of taking my boyfriend on a picnic."

"Ooh, he'll love that," she gushed. Then she narrowed her eyes. "Now, that's Amber Palmer's little brother, right?"

"They're twins."

"Yeah, but he's ten minutes younger, and believe me, Amber counts. We were all in school together on and off. They traveled a lot between here and France. She was always a nice girl... a bit rowdy, but nice."

He left Cartha with a pleasant smile on her face, lost in memories of her youth, and headed straight for his aunt's house.

"WILL THIS do, dear?" Aunt Jo asked.

"That's perfect," Jamison said, taking the picnic basket from her. He examined it. There were nooks and crannies, specific spots to hold everything, just like a toolbox. "Hey," he said, looking at her, "this is fancy."

"It was your grandmother's. She used to take your mother and I on Sunday picnics after church in the summer. We were all dressed up, and we sat on a blanket and had tea and tiny sandwiches while wearing these little white gloves." She held her hands up and wiggled her fingers. "Quite proper." She smiled at him and mimicked sipping tea with a pinkie extended. "I think Mama had seen it in a movie once somewhere… the tea-and-tiny-sandwiches part, I mean." Aunt Jo laughed softly, covering her mouth.

Jamison tried to imagine his mother as a little girl, sitting in the sun in her Sunday dress and sipping tea with her sister. He frowned. "Where was Grandpa in all this?"

"In his shirtsleeves, tossing a football around with the neighborhood boys." He liked that image, a big family out in the park together on a Sunday. Though his original idea leaned more toward romance than family time, it began to expand. He decided to run his new plan past Lonnie and see if he could help get everyone else on board.

In bed that night, side by side on their stomachs and playfully knocking their bare feet together, the two of them got on their phones and called everyone they cared about, asking them to bring something to a picnic in Overbrook Park after church.

Torp and Kimmy were bringing macaroni salad, a football, and Frisbee. Amber and Claude were bringing Remmy and a cooler of drinks. Ginger, Arthur, and Grandma Bellerose would bring a big bowl of fresh fruit. And Jamison was delighted to discover his mother was willing to bring a bunch of her deviled eggs. He could hardly wait for those. It had been quite a while since he'd tasted them. Lincoln planned to grill up hamburgers and hot dogs—provided by Ray—and run them over to the park. Lonnie and Jamison would be providing all the condiments.

Lonnie hung up the phone, sighed, and flipped onto his back. "What do you think?"

"I think it'll be a perfect day," Jamison said, nuzzling at Lonnie's neck.

Lonnie stared at the ceiling. "You hope. It'll also be the first time everyone is together sharing a meal."

"Uh-huh. Listen, I have more good news."

Lonnie turned on his side to face Jamison, pressing playfully against his front while idly tracing the tattooed sleeve on his shoulder and upper arm. "And what would that be, my dear?"

"Met a guy today," he explained as he dug into his back pocket to retrieve Temple's business card, "who wants me to design and build him a dining table for his apartment. At least I think it's an apartment." He passed Lonnie the card. "He wants me to drive into Baltimore and look at the space."

"Jamison! That's—"

"And I sold all my pieces on Lincoln's floor!"

Lonnie's beautiful green eyes went wide and round, and he suddenly smashed their lips together. Jamison chuckled right through it. "That is amazing!" Lonnie shouted. "You're a star, you are." They spent the rest of the night celebrating, never leaving the bed.

"WHAT DID you think?" JP asked into his phone, feet propped on his desk and smiling up at the cheap drop ceiling.

"You were right, JP. The furniture is beautiful and well crafted, though none of the remaining pieces interested me."

JP grinned to himself. "Sold out, did he?"

"No doubt because of your article. He a friend of yours?"

"So what did you decide?"

"Left him my card. We'll e-mail, and he'll visit the loft to get an idea of the space and my needs."

JP chuckled.

"What?"

"Your *needs*."

"Oh please. You're such a scoundrel."

JP didn't fill the silence that followed, letting his old acquaintance's wheels turn unimpeded.

"He's straight, right?"

"Nope. Bye!"

"Don't you dare hang up on me, Jerald!"

JP laughed again.

"Now, if he's family, why didn't you—?"

"Not my type. *You* should know that better than anyone."

"Mmm, I think he's just right—big and strong and handsome and quiet. Yum. You always talked too much, that is, until you hooked up with that art student. Lewis? Larry?"

"Lonnie."

"Whatever happened to that guy?"

"Oh, he's still around. On another subject, what would Staz have to say about you setting your sights on Coburn?"

"I don't belong to anyone."

"Good luck with the table."

"Thanks for sending me the article. I appreciate it."

"No problem," JP said. "Looked like something you'd be into."

"The furniture or Mr. Coburn?"

JP chuckled and hung up. Things were nicely in motion now. Lonnie wouldn't stand for someone cheating. He was too insecure for that, so putting someone as tasty as Temple in front of Coburn—a healthy all-American boy—might accomplish what his earlier efforts had not. And he'd be there to pick up the pieces... familiar, handsome JP. Jamison and Lonnie had only known each other a short while. No way were they truly in love, not that JP would necessarily recognize it if they were. He was careful to keep any salient details from Temple, like the fact that Jamison was dating someone. Temple was the honorable type and wouldn't knowingly interfere with a relationship.

He went back to writing up his interview with Bink. *That bitch.* Her contempt for him was evident during the entire hour, peering at him over her glasses as though she was some old, pissed-off librarian and he was a noisy, disrespectful, book-destroying child. Apparently Lonnie had told her everything about their relationship, so he didn't exactly come off as a knight in shining armor. But things would be different the second—no, the third—time around. Jerry Pool could be shiny, goddammit.

Chapter 23

LONNIE PAUSED in his sketching to shield his eyes from the sun as he looked over his glasses and watched Jamison leap into the air and catch the pass Torp threw him. Jamison landed hard, crumpled to the ground, and rolled several feet before coming to a stop, the ball sitting on his heaving chest. Lonnie grimaced, thinking about Jamison's ribs, but he could see the smile gracing his face. Hooting and laughing, Torp ran to Jamison's side and helped him up.

Lonnie looked around at his family and friends. Ray chatted—about what, he had no idea—and sipped coffee with Arthur on a park bench. Aunt Jo spoke to his grandmother about her haircut, with Ginger translating. And Mrs. Coburn goo-gooed at Remmy as Amber held him. For his part, Lonnie had almost completed a sketch of Amber and Remmy sitting on the blanket near him. He heard a car door slam and looked up to see Lincoln walking their way with trays of grilled burgers and hot dogs. Thank God. He was starving.

The clouds were few and far between, but the sun wasn't uncomfortable. It was the best day he'd had in a long time, especially coming after Jamison's arrest.

"It's hard to believe my boy was ever this tiny," Mrs. Coburn said, drawing Lonnie's attention back to her. She now held Remmy in her arms, and Amber had fled to the picnic table for some goodies. Now alone except for Remmy, who could hardly participate in a conversation, Mrs. Coburn glanced up at him. "You and your sister are close?"

He shrugged. "Twins. We couldn't help it."

She tickled Remmy's pudgy chin. "I can't imagine if Jamison had been twins," she said, gazing at the baby. Lonnie sucked in a deep breath as his mind reeled at the idea. Mrs. Coburn apparently caught the smile on his lips and the dazed look in his eyes. "You cut that out, you," she commanded, smirking. Lonnie's face heated, and he leaned over his sketch to focus and finish it.

"What's happening over here?" Jamison crashed down next to Lonnie, startling him.

"We were just wondering what our lives would be like if you'd been twins," Mrs. Coburn said.

"Uh… no, not me." Lonnie affected his most innocent expression, but Jamison just snorted, rolled over, and stared at his mother holding and smiling at Remmy.

"Is he smelly yet?" he asked.

Mrs. Coburn smirked. "Babies are sometimes smelly."

"Not me." Jamison winked at Lonnie. "My sh—poop smelled like roses. Isn't that right, Mama?"

Lonnie burst into laughter, and joining him, Mrs. Coburn said, "In your dreams, baby. In your dreams."

Jamison gave him a peck on the lips. "You wanna toss a few?"

"What am I tossing?"

"The ball." Jamison held up the football and spun it on his finger.

"My hand-eye coordination can be… destructive to those around me."

Jamison got to his feet. "Come on, babe. Give it a go." Lonnie set his pad and pencil down and let Jamison help him to his feet.

"Good luck," Mrs. Coburn called after them before going back to baby-talking Remmy.

They ran into an open area of lush grass, where Jamison showed Lonnie how to hold the ball for passing.

He looked over his shoulder at Jamison. "You know, if you want to tackle me, this football is completely unnecessary."

Jamison laughed and placed Lonnie's fingers on the laces of the ball. "Torp, go long!"

"Long?" Torp shouted, appearing dubious. "Are you sure?"

"Hey?" Lonnie whined. Torp took off running, then cut right. Lonnie drew back and drilled the ball to the center of his chest.

"What the…?"

Lonnie glanced at his mother, who gave him a thumbs-up. He turned back to a dumbfounded Jamison. "Mother's a football fan, always has been. Maybe I can't dribble a basketball or run without tripping, but that? I can throw *that* fucker." He winked and went back to the blanket, feeling Jamison's appreciative gaze on his backside. Kimmy had arrived after finishing up some Sunday school business, and it was her turn to cuddle

Remmy while Amber and Mrs. Coburn sat close by eating their burgers, picking at a plate of fruit, and flipping through…. *My sketches!*

"These are beautiful," Mrs. Coburn said. "Looks just like my b— Oh my!"

Lonnie rushed over and liberated his sketchpad and the nude drawings contained within of Alanna Coburn's baby boy. "Sorry about that. I forgot those were in there." She didn't look him in the eye as she popped a grape in her mouth.

"I loved the one you did of me and Remmy," Amber said quickly. "Will you paint it?"

He nodded without a word. He could feel Mrs. Coburn peering at him from the corner of her eye. It's one thing to learn your son is gay, but it's another to *know* he's actively fucking another man. Lonnie grimaced. The only thing worse would have been her walking in on the two of them. They were almost getting along, but the chill coming off her now would take time to thaw. There was only so much cute magic Remmy could wield.

"How you doin', baby?" Torp asked Kimmy as he ran over.

She gazed up into his eyes and, after a quick kiss, said, "I want one."

"One wh—?" Remmy cooed and kicked, and Torp's eyes grew wider. "Oh… uh, okay?"

Jamison appeared at Lonnie's elbow with a plate of burgers and hot dogs to share. At least Lonnie *thought* he intended to share. "I dressed up a couple the way you like."

"Thank you." Lonnie grabbed a burger and took a big bite. He was famished, and it was cooked to perfection. Feeling Mrs. Coburn watching, Lonnie said, around a mouth of burger, "Have you told everyone else your news?"

Jamison looked startled, then glanced at the people sitting nearby.

"What news?" Mrs. Coburn asked.

Jamison gobbled down his last bit of hot dog and said, "I sold most of my furniture at Lincoln's."

"Oh, baby, that's wonderful!"

"And he might be doing a commissioned piece for some guy in Baltimore," Lonnie piped up.

Jamison nodded in the face of his mother's glowing pride, and Lonnie gave him a congratulatory kiss, which soon lingered and softened and hardened and softened again as their tongues played against each other. Their surroundings faded to nothing as they lost themselves in each other.

"Fucking faggots!"

They jerked apart as a familiar twist hit Lonnie's stomach and ice ran through his veins. He wondered if Jamison felt the same as they joined their friends and family in glaring at the interlopers. Three college-age boys jogged by—one white, two black—obviously part of some sports team from the university and working out together. They weren't bulky enough for football or tall enough for basketball, so Lonnie guessed baseball.

No one said anything. What did one say when faced with such ignorant bullshit? Hurling back one of the insults whirling through his head would only escalate the situation. Jamison's fingers came up and caressed his cheek, gently guiding him back until their eyes met. The angry noise in Lonnie's head faded. They kissed again, lost themselves to it, shutting out the world.

But then the cursing began, and their attention was drawn toward Torp as he ran forward to retrieve his football, which he had apparently bounced off the head of one of the college kids. Lonnie jumped to his feet just as Jamison did, and they found themselves facing off with the athletes.

"What the fuck, man?" one of them said to Torp, crowding up in his face. "You gonna tell me your hand slipped?"

"No, dumbass," Torp said, smiling. "I meant to hit you 'cause you called my friends names. Next time, maybe you'll check yourself before you spout off."

The athletes moved forward as one, but Jamison stepped between them and Torp. "Back off, boys." Lonnie smiled at the pleasant depth and rumble of Jamison's voice. "You were out of line, and my buddy reacted."

"It's a free country! I can say what I want," the taller of the two black guys declared.

"Yes," Lonnie said, stepping forward, "and we can react to what you say."

Jamison smiled. "You know what consequences are, right?" Lonnie couldn't be sure, but he thought Jamison punctuated that statement with a minute flex, his T-shirt growing tighter across the chest.

Arthur, Lincoln, and Ray joined them. "Is there a problem?" Lincoln asked.

"Nah, man. No problem," the smallest of the athletes said after tearing his gaze away from Jamison. The three of them ran off to continue their jog, glancing over their shoulders repeatedly.

The men at the picnic watched them go, and then Lonnie said to Jamison, "I don't think you looked quite as big lying on the ground."

Torp chuckled when Jamison snatched the ball from him and told him to go long. Arthur put his arm over Lonnie's shoulder as they watched the ball climb into the sky, seeking its target.

"TEMPLE SCHRODINGER," Lonnie said from his perch at the kitchen island.

"Never heard of him," Amber said as she stirred her pasta sauce. She scooped some into a wooden spoon and blew on it before carefully taking a taste. Through the french doors, Lonnie could see his grandmother and Ginger hovering over Remmy in his bouncy chair on the deck. Lonnie tapped a few more keys on the laptop, bringing up several entries about the mysterious Mr. Schrodinger. "What does he do?"

"According to this he's a programmer or something…. He's worth— holy shit!"

"He's worth holy shit? What does that mean?"

"He's worth millions." Lonnie found several photos. "And he's… adorable, gorgeous even. Says here he's in his early thirties, but…. Jesus! He looks like he's twenty or twenty-one, tops."

Amber fumbled a tiny jar free of the spice rack. "So he's rich and gorgeous, huh?" She sprinkled a dash of something Lonnie couldn't identify into the pot. "At least you know he'll be able to pay Jamison for the dining table. When's he due back?"

"I'll see him tomorrow," he answered absently, turning back to the screen. "He drove into Baltimore after work, and he's driving back tonight, so he'll be wiped." He continued reading, trying to absorb as much as possible. He was fairly certain he already hated Temple Schrodinger. The man had accomplished a lot at a young age, developing and selling a security software program to a banking giant. There wasn't much available online about his childhood or his origins, but Lonnie kept looking.

What he found most disturbing were the accounts of Temple's playboy ways, that he cut through clubs and bars and men like some sort of hurricane. The photos he found usually showed Temple surrounded by a collection of burly gym bunnies, all around Jamison's size and appeal.

"Stop it," Amber whispered in his ear, startling him.

"Huh? Stop what?" He turned to her.

She placidly dried her hands with a dish towel. "Stop comparing yourself to this Temple person, seeing how you measure up."

"I'm not—"

"Jamison loves you."

"I know that."

"Really? Because you've been doubting it for weeks now, questioning why he would want you over every other soul out there."

"Amber—"

"Save it, Lon. I know you better than anyone. What is it that makes you doubt his feelings for you? How often does he have to tell you how special you are before you believe it?"

He couldn't deny it, so he shrugged.

"Is it because of how that asshole treated you, making you question every step you took?"

"I… I think that might be part of it, but…." He sighed and lied. "I don't know." He could trace it all back to his grandfather and his rejection and ridicule, Lonnie's willingness to be JP's doormat, afraid he'd never find anyone else who might want him. But he wasn't that Lonnie anymore. He deserved to be loved. *I'm miraculous.*

Amber reached out and closed the laptop. "It doesn't matter how rich or pretty this Schrodinger is. He's not *you*. Got it?"

"I get it." Lonnie smiled and stood to join the other women in his life out on the deck. Remmy, that little bundle of love, could brighten any mood.

Chapter 24

JAMISON HOPPED out of his truck, armed with his iPad and tape measure. He paused to take in the impressive harbor view as several boats drifted by, some heading out to sea and others heading home to dock. He took a deep breath and sighed at the beauty of it, the sun playing off the water, the city rising up, shiny and bright around him. He turned to face the moderately sized brick structure that housed Temple's loft. It had the look of a former factory, but the windows facing the street were huge and probably let in a lot of natural light.

After looking both ways, he jogged across the street and hit the buzzer on the big red barn door. The street noise kept him from hearing clearly, but he was fairly sure someone shouted and was moving around inside. The door swung open to reveal Temple standing there barefoot, in sleep pants and a baggy T-shirt. His hair was a mess, as if he'd just woken up.

"Jamison! Glad you could make it." Temple stepped back, allowing him entry. After closing the door behind them, he said, "This way. I was just making dinner. I hope you're hungry." Temple led the way up a black metal flight of stairs.

"I hadn't planned on staying for dinner, Mr. Schrodinger," Jamison said, trying to avoid watching Temple's pert ass as they climbed. Temple gathered his hair into a high ponytail as he went, securing it with a blue scrunchie.

"Puhlease! What's this 'mister' bullshit? We're just about the same age, aren't we?"

Yes, Jamison had been surprised during his Google searching to learn that Temple was much older than he appeared. "Sorry, but as the client, it's gonna have to be 'mister' and 'sir' all the way." Lincoln had taught him that.

They emerged into a main living area, which smelled fantastic. Whatever Temple was cooking had Jamison rethinking his refusal of dinner.

"That's a shame," Temple said. "So impersonal."

The place was open concept and covered from end to end with blond hardwood floors, awash in the natural light Jamison had expected. A dining table sat to his right upon entering. It was a good size, but the space could accommodate a much bigger piece.

"Is this the space you want to fill?" he asked, approaching it.

Temple glanced up from his kitchen island. "That's it." He turned the heat down beneath a sauce pan and joined Jamison. "I like to host the odd party now and then, so I need a table that will seat eight to twelve people comfortably but also complement the space. This one was just a placeholder, and it's too small."

Jamison whipped out his tape and began taking measurements. He could feel Temple's gaze on him as he took the dimensions and made his notations. "How long have you lived here?"

"I've lived all over Baltimore for several years, but I bought this place just last year."

Jamison nodded and recorded another measurement. "You know, I've never made a piece on request before, so I'm gonna need as much information as you can give me." He looked up from his iPad. "Have you thought about what material you'd like to use?"

Temple thought for a moment. "Uh… wood?"

Jamison chuckled. "Yeah, but what kind of wood? Black ash is inexpensive and—"

"Cost isn't an iss—" Jamison grinned as Temple bit his lip and color rose to his face. "I probably shouldn't have said that, huh?"

Distracted by a familiar sensation in his crotch, Jamison didn't answer. Instead, he focused on Temple's abused lip, his tongue darting out to lick it, trying to soothe it, his slender, fit build. *Like Lonnie, only smaller.* He sighed. *Lonnie.* His gaze drifted to the outline of Temple's cock within the cotton sleep pants. "Is your sauce burning?" he asked.

Temple started and dashed back into the kitchen to remove the pan from the heat. He stirred whatever was in it, then blew on a spoonful and took a tentative taste. "It's fine. No harm done. But I should"—he grabbed a bright orange oven mitt and removed a tray of chicken breasts from the oven—"grab these before they dry out." He set the tray on the island, then reached in a drawer for a sauce brush to baste the breasts with.

As Temple worked, Jamison explained, "Reclaimed wood would give the table a rustic look and more character… a little bit of history." He looked around the large, open room, taking in the feel and atmosphere of the space. The surrounding walls were brick. The kitchen area was all deep blue tile, gray-blue granite, white cabinets, and stainless steel. The black matte ceiling had an industrial look. "You have a sleek kitchen, rough brick walls, and exposed ducts on the ceiling, while your floors are pretty light hardwood, so I think…." He began typing on his iPad.

"Yes?" Temple continued his food prep. "You stopped talking… what do you think?"

Jamison glanced at Temple. "Sorry. My mind runs faster than my mouth when I get an idea." It was true. His thoughts raced ahead, outpacing any doubts or concerns he had about taking on the job.

"You're the artist here. Do share."

"I was thinking I would use reclaimed wood but build the table in a modern style."

"Combining the character with the sleek?"

Jamison beamed. "Exactly!" His enthusiasm dimmed when he caught sight of Temple's appraising expression.

"Let's eat," Temple purred.

"WHAT DO you want?" Lonnie asked, frowning at the sight of his ex standing in his doorway. "You have some nerve showing up after what you pulled."

"I took a chance," JP said, holding up a giant pizza box and six-pack. "Just got off work. Didn't want to eat alone. Thought the three of us might share this pie and make up. Whadya say?"

Lonnie shook his head. "Not gonna happen."

JP smiled at him. "Shouldn't you ask your man first?" He smiled and wiggled the box in Lonnie's face. "He might be hungry. He's a big guy. I bet he's hungry a lot."

"You can't appease Jamison with that. Not after what you did."

"Not even"—he opened the box to reveal a pizza loaded with meat—"for a meat supreme pie?"

"Not even. Good-bye, JP." Lonnie tried to close the door in his face.

JP stuck his foot out, blocking it. "Now, Lon, I—"

"Don't call me that!"

"I'm just trying to apologize for the mistake in the article."

"It wasn't a mistake. You did it on purpose to fuck with us."

"Can't I be sorry?"

Lonnie snorted. "Nope."

"Coburn!" JP shouted suddenly. "It's Pool. I've come to apologize, but your boyfriend won't let me in." His outburst was met with silence, and he turned a perplexed glance Lonnie's way.

"He's not here. Good-bye, and take your pizza with you."

JP shoved the door open and walked in. "Awful late for him to be working, isn't it?"

"Actually, he's doing a commissioned piece in Baltimore," Lonnie bragged. He was proud of Jamison. No harm in letting JP know that.

JP spun to face him. "Ohh, look at *him*… getting work because of *my* article." He dropped the pizza box on the kitchen table and set the beer down next to it. He glanced at Lonnie, then looked around the kitchen. "I've only been here a couple times. You still keep the glasses…. Ah! Here they are." After removing two from a cabinet, JP grabbed a bottle opener and took a seat at the table. Lonnie couldn't help smirking as he watched JP open the pizza box and take a long, deep appreciative sniff of the pie.

"You need to—"

JP looked up at him and popped the cap off a bottle of beer, then filled one of the glasses. "Come on, Lonnie. Let's bury the hatchet."

"You're lucky I don't have one handy." He entered the kitchen but didn't sit down, gripping the back of the chair instead. "If Jamison finds you here—"

"What?" JP took a big bite of pizza and chewed slowly, grinning, his blue gaze capturing Lonnie's green.

"There's no telling—"

"Bullshit," JP said so quickly he nearly choked on the food in his mouth. He swallowed. "Your man's not a fighter, remember?"

"What I remember is the last guy who pissed him off got punched." Lonnie folded his arms across his chest. "That guy was built like a fire plug." He looked JP up and down. "You're not."

"I'm not exactly a twig," JP said, flexing an impressive bicep. "Remember?"

Lonnie sighed and took a seat. "Do you really believe being charming—?"

"You think I'm charming?" JP beamed.

"—and flexing is going to win me over? Come on. Have you forgotten everything that happened between us? You don't want me. I was never good enough. Everything I did was wrong."

JP's playful expression sobered. "I'm sorry, Lonnie. I wasn't myself then."

Lonnie shook his head. "You can't blame it all on the drugs, JP."

"I know that, baby." JP reached across the table, opening his hand for Lonnie to grasp. He didn't. "I blame it all on me, my insecurities."

Lonnie narrowed his eyes. "Insecurities? You?"

JP shrugged. "We all have them. I just wish I'd handled it all better." He met and held Lonnie's gaze. "I wish I hadn't hurt you."

"Yeah, me too." Lonnie grabbed a slice of pizza and the glass of beer. He leaned back in the chair, and they ate in silence for a while, occasionally grinning at each other as old, more pleasant memories skipped through their thoughts.

"So," JP said, waving a half-eaten slice in Lonnie's direction, "you really into this Coburn?"

Lonnie nodded and gulped half his beer, then belched loud and long. He was tickled to see a grimace play across JP's features. "I'd say the two of us made it crystal clear how we feel about each other outside the courtroom on Saturday. It seemed to catch your attention."

JP smirked. "But you and I, Lonnie. We're… on the same level."

"What the fuck is that supposed to mean?"

"Did Coburn even graduate high school?"

"Oh please." Lonnie jumped to his feet. "Are you serious? That! That right there. The coke didn't make you a snob, JP. That's all you."

"Bullshit! I grew up in the same situation Coburn did, but I made something of myself. I saw the world. He seems content right where he is, and you're going places, Lon. You'll leave him behind, baby. He can't keep up."

Lonnie rolled his eyes. "I'm not your baby."

"Not to mention, he's newly out."

"You just mentioned it." Lonnie fought hard not to let the doubts bubbling inside him show. It was important that JP never know he'd given voice to most of Lonnie's primary fears.

"He doesn't know what it is to live out and proud, has no idea of the men who would line up for him. Awfully tempting."

And there was his secondary fear. *Shit!* "JP—"

"But you and me? We've navigated those waters already. We know who we are. We fit."

"I want you to leave. Now."

JP stood and walked toward him. "Yeah… because you know I'm right."

As JP hovered ever closer, Lonnie slowly backed into the kitchen doorway. "What I know is you sound desperate," he said, trying to keep the quiver out of his voice.

They stood face-to-face now, JP close enough for Lonnie to catch the scent off his heated skin. They stared into each other's eyes for several seconds, and Lonnie managed not to flinch when JP reached up to brush a lock of hair out of Lonnie's face.

"I lost so much, Lon," JP said softly. "Not the least of which was you, but I'm working on getting my life back… *all* of it." He wrapped an arm around Lonnie's waist, pulled him tight against his front, and kissed him. For just a second Lonnie relaxed into the pleasure, the familiarity of it, but then he noticed how different it was from Jamison's taste and touch, and he shoved JP away.

"Get out!" he growled.

JP gazed into his eyes for a moment longer before turning abruptly and heading for the door. "See ya, Lonnie."

He heard the self-satisfaction in JP's voice. He knew it well. Lonnie slammed the door after him and locked it, then fell back against the door, closed his eyes, and pressed his hand to his excited crotch. *Fuck!* His thoughts swam, and more than anything he wanted to talk to Jamison, see him, touch him. He felt disgusted by his apparent attraction to someone who'd hurt him. Jamison's words echoed in his mind: *They go back.*

Because I don't deserve better?

He grabbed his car keys and fled the apartment. No Jamison at hand. He didn't want to bother Amber. Definitely not his parents. Lonnie drove to the campus gallery and let himself in. No Bink. A few lights along the base of the walls helped relieve some of the darkness in the room, but the bare partitions standing sentinel throughout the space threw sharp shadows. The air-conditioning unit kicked on, cutting the silence but drowning out his breathing and the pounding of his heart.

Lonnie sat on the floor against the back wall and stared out through the windows at the front of the gallery. As he unconsciously tugged at his hair, he imagined seeing Jamison rushing to join him as he had on the night of his thesis show. He felt so tiny in the big room, tiny and alone. Unwanted. Lonnie took a quick, deep breath. *No. That's not true. Hang on. I'm not alone. Not unwanted.*

He dug out his cell phone and called Jamison, but he didn't pick up. *He's probably driving*, he told himself. *On his way back home.* The call went to voice mail, and Lonnie said, "Hey, babe. Hope the job went well. I miss you. See you tomorrow. Love you." He closed his eyes and shoved the phone back into his pocket, disappointed, maybe even a little angry. If he could have just heard Jamison's voice, something. He hated feeling so… panicked, so needy.

He opened his eyes and gazed out at the dark campus beyond the windows. It made him feel as if not another soul existed in the world. He knew what he needed and where to go.

Chapter 25

"THAT WAS delicious." Jamison sighed and relaxed back in his seat as Temple smiled and licked sauce from his finger.

"Thank you," Temple said, rising to clear the table.

"Let me help with—"

"I got it." With his hands full of dishes, Temple gestured toward the living room. "Why don't you pour us some more wine, and I'll meet you on the sofa." Jamison hesitated, and Temple noticed. "Come on, you let me blabber on about myself during dinner. You have to give me a chance to learn about you."

Jamison relented, saying, "Just one more glass wouldn't hurt, I guess." He felt good. His belly was full, and the wine gave him a pleasant warmth. He felt more relaxed than he had in a while—without Lonnie at hand, that is.

Temple loaded the dishwasher while Jamison refilled their glasses and carried them into the living room. He sat on the sofa and tried to ignore the uneasy tickle at the back of his thoughts, tried to settle it with a sip of wine. *Damn that's good*, he thought, staring at the glass, impressed. More of a beer man, he didn't know anything about vintage or types of grapes, and during dinner he'd been more focused on the food and Temple's life story.

Temple Schrodinger's early years were oddly vague. Jamison only got a sense of poverty with a general undercurrent of homophobia. But as Temple described his success with game development and programming, explained how being the smartest person in an ignorant Southern town wasn't always painless, Jamison became captivated. The stories and Temple's quick wit had them laughing 'til it hurt. Temple Schrodinger was good company, lovely company.

"So," Temple said, startling Jamison as he set the wine bottle on the coffee table, grabbed his glass, and curled up next to him on the sofa, "tell me everything about you that wasn't in the article I read." Temple sipped his wine, watching Jamison over the rim of the glass, his brown eyes warm and... inviting.

It was a big sofa, L-shaped, but Jamison noted how awfully close to him Temple sat, so he turned to face him and brought his knee up between them, hoping that would create some distance from any bad decisions he might make.

"I'm afraid there's not much more to tell." As he looked Temple over, tension replaced his all-is-well fog, and the clarity of impending disaster slammed into him. He stretched his arm along the back of the sofa, feigning an ease he no longer felt.

Temple immediately danced his fingers along Jamison's hand and slowly up his arm. "I find that hard to believe."

He withdrew his hand and gulped the rest of his wine. "I should probably get back."

Ignoring Jamison's protective knee, Temple was suddenly straddling his lap, wineglass in one hand, the other caressing his face as he kissed him. Jamison froze, melted for several moments, then froze again.

Temple drew back, his puzzled gaze searching Jamison's stunned one. "Have I read you wrong? Not interested?"

It took a moment for Jamison to find his tongue. "No!" Temple frowned. "Wait... I mean, yes... I find you... *amazing*, but I'm... I'm with someone." He tried to force his swelling cock to behave. *Think of Lonnie. Think of Lonnie.*

"Oh...." Temple slid away from him and sat much farther away than before. "I wasn't even sure you were gay, but I got the feeling, the way you looked at me—"

"No. I'm gay... just attached."

"Huh." Temple sighed and gulped the rest of his drink. "Well damn!"

"Disappointed?"

Temple's eyes widened, and he smiled. "You have to ask?"

"I'm flattered, but... well, honestly, he's it for me."

Running his hand back through his long brown hair, Temple said, "Sorry for the confusion. I had the impression you were single...."

"And *possibly* gay?" Jamison chuckled.

Temple laughed. "Hey. A guy's gotta take chances, right?"

"What about Staz?"

Temple waved that question aside. "We're not a couple. Just fuck buddies."

He wasn't sure what to say to that, so Jamison said, "Uh... *okay*," and set his glass on the coffee table. "I've had a good bit to drink. I don't suppose I could—"

"Of course you can stay over."

"—get some coffee?" Jamison laughed, and Temple blushed. It didn't look like something he did often.

"Sorry. Yes! Just a moment." Temple dashed into the kitchen to brew a pot, then returned and curled on the sofa again. "It'll be a few minutes. Now... tell me about him?" Those brown eyes had taken on a bit of sadness, and Jamison again relented. "Please?"

Smiling, Jamison said, "His name's Lonnie, Lonnie Bellerose, and he's a fantastic artist."

Temple frowned, holding up his hand. "Stop. His name is... *Lonnie?*" Jamison nodded, confused, and Temple's expression slowly twisted into anger. "Well fuck me."

Nearly an hour later, after Temple had stopped ranting about "being used," "being manipulated," and some "rancid son of a bitch," Jamison was able to piece it together.

Jerry Pool.

He sipped his second cup of coffee, watching Temple pace in front of him. Temple stopped and glared. "Why aren't you angry about this?"

"I am."

Temple snorted, much like Lonnie did, and that made Jamison smile. "You don't seem angry."

"This is me angry."

Temple plopped back down onto the sofa. "Well, your way's no fun." He folded his arms across his chest and pouted.

"I don't like to lose control."

"Oh, I love it. Letting off steam is cathartic." Temple tapped his chin in thought as he looked around the room. "That reminds me, I need to buy some more breakies."

"Huh?"

"You know," he said, smiling into Jamison's eyes, "cheap dishes, vases, stuff I can shatter without regret."

"I'd suggest a punching bag."

"Oh no. That's what Pool is for."

Jamison laughed. "I'm sorry, but I don't think you'd do much damage."

"No, silly. Staz would do the punching. My job is to indicate which kidney."

Jamison's laughter filled the space, and Temple soon joined in.

"You're a dangerous man, Mr. Schrodinger."

Temple sobered and met Jamison's eyes. "I can be. I don't take shit from anyone. Learned that lesson early. And… I don't come between lovers. JP knows that, which is probably why he didn't mention you were involved." He glanced away. "You have to believe… I never would have—"

"It's okay, Temple."

"Hey, what happened to 'the client is always mister'?"

Jamison grinned and finished his coffee. "Well, I don't normally kiss my clients, so I think we've moved beyond that." Color rose to Temple's cheeks. "You can call me Jam. My friends do."

LONNIE PINCHED the webbing between his thumb and index finger, massaging away the ache as he stared at the image before him, the image he'd created during the night. He rubbed his eyes and glanced across the studio to the windows flooding the room with sunlight. Blinking in the glare, he turned back and smiled at the way his canvas seemed to glow. A couple embraced behind a foggy shower door, just the suggestion of their forms as they caressed each other. He could practically feel Jamison's arms around him, the hot water and soap making their skin slippery beneath their fingers.

Despite his lack of sleep, Lonnie felt 100 percent better than he had last night. Then he was alone, uncertain, unnerved by his physical reaction to JP. But after capturing a favorite moment he and Jamison had shared, his head was clear of the doubts crowding it the night before. As he painted, as he remembered all the times and ways Jamison had touched him, shown him how he felt, Lonnie repeatedly reminded himself that he did deserve better than JP. Jamison was infinitely better, and he deserved that man's love.

In fact…. He glanced at his watch. Just now 7:10 in the morning. *That's enough sleep, right? I could go over there, give him an extra-special wake-up call.* He'd stop and get some pastries and Jamison's new favorite coffee. Jamison had grown curious—or possibly bored with his standard cup o' joe—one day at Knotty's Coffeehouse, and Lonnie had shared a cup with him. Ever since then, Jamison was hoping for a cup all of his own. Life and work (and court) had been such that they hadn't returned, but this morning, Lonnie decided he'd make the effort.

He scratched his signature on the painting and set to work cleaning his brushes, giddy with the prospect of a satisfying tumble in the sheets with his man.

JAMISON YAWNED and rubbed his eyes, trying to keep the road from blurring in front of him. He and Temple had stayed up for hours talking about Pool and his antics, about Lonnie, about their first times and when they *knew*. They'd discussed what it meant and felt like to be open and honest about who they were in the world, about who they loved. Temple had hinted that being out hadn't always been rainbows and butterflies, but it was worth it to be able to look himself in the mirror each morning. Though Temple gave no real specifics, Jamison got the impression the rest of the Schrodinger family was no longer in his life, his siblings and his parents all lost to him.

For his part Jamison was able to ask all the questions and express all his doubts to Temple. They'd talked through everything he didn't feel he could say to Lonnie without sparking any broken hearts, and that talk led him to a decision.

Still too drunk and tired to drive home safely, Jamison slept on Temple's big sofa. He didn't bother pulling out the hide-a-bed, but Temple covered the couch cushions with pricey sheets and provided blankets and pillows. Jamison had fallen asleep in mere moments, forgetting to let Lonnie know he wouldn't be home as expected.

Now nearly home, he was looking forward to losing himself in Lonnie. He didn't like sleeping away from him and saw no reason for that to continue. He dug his phone out of the glove box and saw he'd missed a call. He listened to the message and smiled. *Aww, I miss you too, babe.* He saved it and immediately punched in Lonnie's number. It rang twice, then went to voice mail.

Trying to decide if he should head straight for Lonnie's or stop at his place, he put his phone away and concentrated on the last ten miles before Overbrook. Asking someone to move in with you should probably be done face-to-face. Ten minutes later he hit Overbrook, and five minutes after that he was delighted to see Lonnie's Beetle parked on his street. He pulled into the driveway and right up to his garage apartment.

The place they rented would have to be a lot bigger than his little hole-in-the-wall. Lonnie would need studio space because it would take a while to save enough money for a down payment on a house. He cut the engine, laughing at how quickly he had planned out their future.

"Lonnie!" he shouted, jogging around the truck and heading for his stairs. Jamison was halfway up before he spotted Lonnie sitting at the top. He held two cups of coffee, and he was not smiling. Jamison paused, and Lonnie got to his feet as if he were eighty years old. "Lon?" Jamison asked. "Are you okay? You look—"

"What? I look what?"

Jamison took a hesitant step forward. "Upset?"

"You're goddamned right I'm upset! You're just getting home? You were with Schrodinger all night, and you're surprised I'm upset?"

"Now, hang on—"

"No! *You* hang on." Lonnie stomped down the stairs. "You're going to tell me nothing happened, right? Bullshit! I've seen him, read about him."

"Lonnie, I swear—"

Lonnie held up a hand. "Save it. Here!" He shoved the cup of coffee into Jamison's hand. "It's probably cold by now, but what the fuck ever!" Jamison followed him, trailed after him all the way to his Beetle.

"Lon!" he bellowed, regretting it instantly when Lonnie jerked and froze. He wouldn't meet Jamison's eyes, however. Lonnie just braced his hands against the roof of the car and stared at the ground, as though he was about to get frisked. "I did not sleep with Temple."

"Then what *did* you do?"

Their eyes met, and the hurt in Lonnie's gaze nearly did him in, but he said, "I measured for the table, asked his preference in materials. We had dinner, and—"

"Dinner?"

"He was cooking when I got there. We talked. That's it."

"All night? Really. What did you talk about all night, Jamison?"

He shrugged. "We talked about… everything, life, relationships, being gay, you and me."

"Why the fuck would you talk about us?"

"He was curious. I… I don't think he has anyone in his life like we do. He's cut off from his family, he's—"

Lonnie snorted. "I'm not about to feel sorry for him." He swung open the car door, but Jamison was there in seconds, wrestling him back out of it. "Get off me!" Not thinking clearly, panicked by what Lonnie believed, Jamison pulled him out of the car and threw him over his shoulder. "I swear to God! Put me down!"

Wincing at the volume, Jamison glanced at the Standleas' kitchen window and thought he caught movement there. Lonnie struggled fiercely, nearly throwing them both to the ground, but Jamison maintained his grip. "I'm sorry you're hurt, but what you've got in that head of yours is wrong, and dammit, you're gonna listen to me." He marched toward his apartment.

"I deserve better than this!"

"So do I!"

Lonnie stilled and went limp. "What?" he asked softly.

Jamison continued walking. "I deserve better than you thinking I fucked Temple, Lon, and you know it. You *know* me."

"Put me down."

"No." He started back up his stairs.

"I kissed JP."

Chapter 26

WHEN THE light hit his eyes, JP groaned and rolled over. He reached out for the other pillow, but instead of cool Egyptian cotton, his hand slapped skin—warm skin, warm stubbled skin. "Holy—!"

The stranger in his bed mumbled something in his sleep as JP scooted quickly backward and off the edge of the mattress, then hit the floor with a *thud* that rattled the window. He lay, staring up at the ceiling, trying to recall the previous night.

He had kissed Lonnie, had felt Lonnie's interest hard against his thigh. To celebrate that spark of success—and completely ignoring being tossed out of the apartment right after—JP went drinking, dancing, snorting, and fucking until the wee hours of the morning. Ah, the fucking. As he'd had his way with the latest trick whose name he currently couldn't remember, his thoughts, as always, were filled with Lonnie, with Lonnie and that kiss.

They'd be together again soon, especially if Temple had managed to take Jamison to bed as JP had planned. He wondered if Jamison would answer the phone if he checked in with Temple right now. He chuckled quietly to himself, then his mattress moved under the weight of the nameless occupant crawling over to JP's side of the bed. A handsome young face topped by a mop of brown hair and dusted with dark scruff came into view and smiled down at him.

"Hey, last night was tasty."

JP detected a slight accent. *British? Australian?* "You're welcome."

The man eyed him for a few seconds, then said, "You've got a lot of stamina for an old fella." The trick winked.

JP frowned. "You can go now."

"Ah, come on, pops, don't be like that," he groaned. "I thought we could share a soap, rinse, and repeat in the shower—"

JP considered it, then looked more closely at the guy. "How old *are* you, kid?"

"Isn't that something you should've asked me last night?" The guy sighed and disappeared as he rolled off the other side of the bed and headed for the bathroom. "The stubble burn on your upper thighs should tell you I'm old enough."

JP growled when he heard the bathroom door slam and the shower start. He slowly rolled onto his stomach and got to his knees. He heard and felt them pop. When he finally stood up, he went through his nightstand drawer, searching for one of several tiny brown vials he had around the apartment. The fog in his head was clearing too slowly for his tastes, and he had a couple of articles he needed to write, or Stew would have his head and his ass would be behind bars again. Aside from work he had places to be, men to do, and Lonnie to woo. JP's fingers closed around a vial, which he held up to the light and shook. The thin layer of white powder at the bottom would do the job for now. He could get more later.

"WHY THE fuck would you do that?" Torp asked.

"What? Kiss Temple?"

"No. Tell Lonnie you did? Are you outta your fuckin' mind?"

The two men sat side by side on the steps of Jamison's apartment, plowing through a six-pack. The shade cast by the garage left Jamison chilled, that and missing Lonnie. None of his calls had been returned, and he was losing patience. How much time did Lonnie need on his own since admitting kissing JP and enjoying it?

"He told me he kissed Pool!"

Torp shook his head. "That's just because he felt guilty, ya jackass."

"And I didn't?"

"People don't break up over a kiss."

Jamison frowned and looked away. "It's so much more than that."

"How?"

He shrugged, then spread his arms wide. "All I know is right here in Overbrook. Lonnie has traveled, he's got degrees. Pool is like him, familiar, educated." Jamison sighed deeply. "He's done things, been places."

"Yep, one thing he did was treat Lonnie like shit."

He couldn't deny that. They sat quietly for several more moments, but eventually Torp broke the silence.

"Why *did* you kiss Temple?"

"I don't know."

"Bullshit. You did it because you thought he was hot." Torp drained his bottle and belched. "No matter how we feel about someone, a pretty piece of ass is the reason we do stupid shit like that."

"I *love* Lon."

"Of course you do. And he loves you. You two just happened to get stupid at the same time." Torp shook his head. "What a pair—sorry, trio you make. Two idiots who think they're not good enough for the other and one jackass who thinks he's God's gift…."

"Lonnie's avoiding me." He yanked another beer from the six-pack, popped the top, and took a few gulps. "Hell, it's not like I'd know what to say to him if he *did* answer."

"SO?" AMBER asked Lonnie between mouthing Remmy's tiny toes and watching the baby squirm.

"He *kissed* him." Lonnie passed her the baby powder.

"Again, so? You kissed Jerry. I'd say you're even."

He grimaced. "JP said—"

"Stop." Amber fastened the diaper, wrestled Remmy's legs back into his outfit, and snapped the onesie closed. It was one Lonnie had bought, and it read: *Poop! There it is!* He planned to go back and get the *I'm proof my mommy puts out* one later. "Just listen to how that sentence began and then start over."

Lonnie grimaced. "Maybe Jamison should date for a while, see what's out there. Why should he get tied down to the first guy he feels something beyond scratching an itch with?"

"Has he called you?"

"He called a couple times. Left messages, but I didn't return them."

"Why not, Lonnie?" Amber gathered Remmy in her arms and swayed with him while giving her brother a solid, sisterly scowl.

"I needed time to think, and I suppose Jamison does too. Plus he has a lot of work with Lincoln and that table to finish for… *Schrodinger*."

"Did you mean that to sound like a curse word?" Lonnie smiled through his lashes at her. "Men!" Amber looked down at her baby boy. "Oh, not you, sweetness. You're Mama's perfect little man, yes you are." She cast a disapproving glare Lonnie's way and huffed. "It was only a kiss." Lonnie bit his lip and felt his face heat. Amber didn't miss it. "Wasn't it?" He remained silent. "Alonzo Bellerose."

"When JP and I kissed... I felt...."

"No. Uh-uh. No way in hell are you still into him!" she growled softly, angry but trying not to startle Remmy. "If he comes near you, I'll... I'll...." She glanced down at Remmy. "Je vais éviscérer de fils de pute!"

"The baby is learning French, ya know. Do you really want Remmy knowing that kind of language? And calm down, sis. I'm not going near JP again, no need to slice him open." He turned away from her and stared at the mural of the family farm he'd painted on the nursery wall. He sighed, drawing peace from the image. It didn't used to have that effect, not while memories of his grandfather lingered. He turned back to Amber. "However hot and sexy JP might be, he treated me like shit, and I deserve better."

Amber beamed at her brother but spoke to Remmy. "You hear that, sweetness? Uncle Lonnie took his smart pills this morning."

They left the nursery and headed downstairs where their parents were cooking dinner. Lonnie could hear their laughter and muffled conversation. He had no doubt they were flirting with each other, giving each other a taste of whatever they were whipping up.

"Are you certain you want to do this?" Amber asked as they reached the foyer.

Lonnie nodded. "Gotta clear my head."

"Cognac the only place you can do that? What about your fancy new job?" He shrugged. "I'm surprised Bink okayed it so soon after hiring you."

"She's all for me working this out. Besides, we'll keep in touch on Skype. I'll get Gran settled, maybe paint a bit—"

"Lie in the grass, wander around the vineyard... missing *him*...."

"Probably." Lonnie sighed.

"You're gonna tell him good-bye, right?"

"I'll call him tomorrow once we're in the air."

"And you'll be back when?"

"Not sure. Jamison needs—"

"You!"

Lonnie huffed, ignoring his sister. "He should hit a couple of clubs, flirt, something... without me tagging along."

"I'd hardly describe you as tag—"

"You have a better idea?"

"Yes. You need to go to him and ride him until he can't move."

"Sis!" Lonnie burst into laughter. "I can't talk to you about this."

"Yeah, maybe Mom and Dad would listen. Let's ask." Chuckling, she walked quickly into the kitchen, Lonnie on her heels. But a knock at the door drew his attention, so he went to answer it instead of pursuing her.

"Jesus Christ! JP, what do you—what happened to your eye?" Lonnie asked, gaping at the shiner.

JP strolled in. "Must you always frown so when you see me?"

"Yes. Go away!"

The man was a mess. Aside from the black eye, JP's hair was tangled and sweaty, his clothes rumpled, but he was smiling as though it was Christmas. "Thought maybe we could pick up where we left off the other night." JP grabbed Lonnie by the forearms and tried to pull him in for a kiss, his lips grotesquely puckered and insistent.

Lonnie pulled free and shoved him, hard. "We left off with me kicking you out of my apartment. Seems you've conveniently forgotten that." Lonnie peered into JP's eyes. The pupils were blown, and… and he smelled. "You're high!" *Jesus! How long was this bender?*

"Aw, Lon." JP tried to grab him again, tried to slither his hand up Lonnie's arm. "Don't be like that. I was out late again but thinking only of you."

"Bullshit!" Lonnie peeled free… again. "How long? Have you been partying since I kicked you out, JP?" Concern twisted Lonnie's gut as he took in the wreck that had been Jerry Pool. "You can't… you can't do that," he warned.

"Oh hell no!" Amber said, rushing toward them. With no Remmy in her arms to be cautious for any longer, she was battle ready. Eyes wide, JP stumbled backward to the open doorway. "This is my house! You have some nerve."

"Relax, Amber," JP said, lifting a placating hand he was likely to lose. "Don't start cursing me in French or nothin'. I just stopped by to ask Loonie out to dinner."

"You did?" Amber and Lonnie asked, then looked at each other in shock.

"Yeah. Thought we might talk." He glanced around the foyer. "Or is your big bad boyfriend lurking nearby?" Lonnie avoided JP's gaze. "He can come along if he wants. Did you tell him about our kiss?" JP smirked and puckered up again, closing in. Lonnie punched him in the nose, and JP staggered back into the doorframe, where he clutched his face and slid down to settle on his ass. "Hey!"

Lonnie shook out his hand and massaged the pain from it. Then he squatted next to JP and looked him in the eyes, waiting until JP focused on him. Lonnie reached out and brushed a tangle of blond hair out of JP's blue, bloodshot eyes.

"Jerry," he said softly, "I'm calling a cab, and you're going back to rehab… now."

"The hell I am!"

"It's that or you explain your condition to the cops."

"You wouldn't dare…," JP said, checking the structural integrity of his nose.

"You're fucked if you don't get clean," Lonnie said while Amber stood back, watching in silence. He could feel his parents' eyes on him too.

JP grasped at Lonnie's sleeve feebly a couple of times. "I just need you, babe. Take me home and I'll sober up. I promise." He blinked up at Lonnie with his best pouty face. "Things can go back to the way they were."

Lonnie shook his head slowly, keeping eye contact with JP. "I don't want that. I've moved on."

"With Coburn? With that—"

"Watch it!" Lonnie barked, and JP froze. "Jamison and I are taking some time apart."

JP grinned and said, wiggling his eyebrows, "'Cause you liked that kiss I laid on ya, right?"

"Yeah, I liked the kiss, JP," Lonnie said, speaking clearly and slowly, "but I never liked you yelling at me, belittling me, and shoving me around. I never liked you hitting—"

"That was just the once!"

"Once was enough." He continued looking JP over, taking in the wreck he had become. "Jamison needs time to figure out exactly what he wants.

JP smirked. "That what he said?"

"That's what *I* decided. I want him to be happy. That's what you want for the man you love."

JP grimaced and looked away. "I'm not going back to rehab," he mumbled, trying to get to his feet. Lonnie shoved him back down.

"I remember the day we met. Do you?" JP tangled his fingers in his hair and shook his head, trying not to hear what Lonnie had to say. "Sure you do," Lonnie whispered as he took a seat next to him. "You'd come into the Coffee Coop to interview some detective, and you flirted with me as I took your orders." JP grinned weakly but still didn't look Lonnie's way. "I thought you were so handsome and commanding talking to that tough old cop the way you did. You had him laughing his ass off within minutes." JP looked down at himself, plucking absently at his stained shirt. "Look at you now, Jerry. You're nowhere near the man I fell so hard for, the man I was so charmed by."

Through the still-open door, Lonnie saw a taxi pull up. Amber must have called it. It honked, and he helped JP get to his feet.

"I didn't tell Temple…," JP said almost too softly to hear.

"What?"

"I didn't tell Temple you and Coburn were together."

"Ah…," Lonnie said, nodding, "That was your doing, was it?" JP had the decency to look ashamed. "You're a real prick, Jerry."

"I know." He looked into Lonnie's eyes. "I'll be better, Lon, I promise."

"Be better for you and you alone because we're done." Before leading JP out of the house, Lonnie paused and addressed his family. "I'll be back for dinner."

Chapter 27

THE SANDER drowned out every other sound around Jamison, but his thoughts were loud and clear, bouncing around inside his skull. He'd hoped focusing on Temple's table would keep his mind off Lonnie, but it hadn't worked. Even exhausting himself on assignments for Lincoln failed to bring him a good night's sleep. He desperately missed having Lonnie next to him in bed, and the man refused to return his calls, but Jamison was tiring of giving Lonnie his space. He thought he heard something and shut off the sander. Turning, he spotted his mother leaning out the back door.

"I'm sorry, Mama. What did you say?"

"Jamison? There's someone on the porch to see you."

Lonnie!

He was a bit miffed his mother hadn't just shown Lonnie through the house to the backyard, but he was too excited to dwell on that for long.

"Some skinny white boy," his mother added.

Oh. He dusted himself off as best he could and, wiping his hands on his jeans, rushed around the side of the house. The first thing he spotted was a shiny black BMW. The next thing he saw was the owner.

"Heya, Jam." Temple rose from the porch swing and removed his sunglasses. "Ooh, look how sweaty you are," he quipped. "Personally, I think the days are getting chilly." Temple clutched his fitted gray-tweed blazer shut.

Jamison couldn't help but grin, even at Staz, who sat on the front steps, glowering like a massive guard dog. "What are you doing here? How did you find—?"

"Stopped by Lincoln's place. He gave us the address. How's the table coming?"

"Uh, come on back, I'll show you." They followed him to the garage.

"You mother's a delight."

Jamison glanced over his shoulder. "What did she do?"

"She looked at us like we were from Mars."

"Well, in this neighborhood, you might as well be." They surrounded the tabletop. "As we discussed, the wood is from that hundred-year-old church on Cowrie Road taken down last year."

Temple ran his fingers over it. "This is gorgeous, Jamison," he said as he caressed it. "It'll contrast with the light floors perfectly."

"That's the biggest piece of wood I've ever seen," Staz said. He looked at Temple. "How the hell is a table that size supposed to get into your place?" He glanced at Jamison. "I mean, can we even get it up the stairs?"

"We'll take the top up first," Jamison explained. "The stairs don't turn, so it's a straight shot to the top. Then we'll attach the feet in the loft."

"You can do that?" Temple asked.

"Sure, just need my tools. You still okay with the stain we decided on?"

"Oh yes," Temple said, nodding quickly. "Lighter than the ceiling but darker than the hardwood."

All three stopped talking at the same time, and then Temple said, "Lonnie not around?"

Jamison felt a stab to his gut. "We… had a… a…."

"Fight?" Staz ventured.

Jamison shook his head. "Not really that," he said, squinting in thought.

"Spat?"

"That's closer." He nodded and grinned sadly.

Temple stared at him long enough for Jamison to think he was reading his mind, and then he said, "He thought we slept together, didn't he?"

"How—?"

"Please," Temple said, waving his hand. "That's what I would have thought if I had a man that looked like you and he stayed out all night." He didn't appear to notice Staz's scowl. "You need me to talk to him?"

"No." Jamison covered the wood and then shut off the lights. They exited the garage, and he locked everything down. "I appreciate the offer, though. We have other… things to work out, I guess."

"Well, thank you, Jam, for showing me my beautiful table. I can't wait until it's installed." Temple hugged himself and twirled as Jamison and Staz looked on. "I'm going to have a dinner party, which you and Lonnie will be invited to, of course."

"What about chairs?" Staz asked. "You're gonna need more chairs, Temp."

"We'll shop for them once the table's set up. I'm thinking we'll mix and match."

Jamison nodded. "I like that idea, but I'd suggest having them all stained or painted the same shade."

"Guess I should Google thrones for sale, huh?" Staz quipped. Temple feinted a jab to his midsection, and Staz flinched. Jamison smiled at the two of them, how easy they were with each other. *Fuck buddies, my ass.*

"Keep it up and your seat will be a beanbag," Temple warned.

Staz laughed loudly and turned, smiling at Jamison. He stuck out his hand. "Thanks again." They shook. "Time to go, Temp, if you want to take care of that business."

"Oh yeah. Gotta see a man about trying to play me." He winked.

As they headed back around the house, Jamison said, "I didn't think you made the drive just to visit me."

"Oh, I—sorry—we have something to take care of at the *Overbrook Times.* I've been trying to pin down JP for several days now, but no luck."

"So," Staz said, "we thought we'd corner him at work." Staz rolled his shoulders, cracked his neck, and then his knuckles.

"Uh...."

"Don't worry, Jam," Temple purred as he took Jamison's arm, "we won't cause any permanent damage. Pinky swear." Temple fluttered his long eyelashes.

"Good, because if you mark him up, Lonnie will think it was me, though I didn't tell him about Pool setting us up."

"No worries. Jerry has loads of people who like the color bruise on him, trust me. Lonnie knows that."

They reached the car and said their good-byes. Once they were out of sight, Jamison caught glimpses of several neighbors peering through curtains or standing at their screen doors, probably wondering who the hell he knew who owned a car like that.

"Baby, come inside," his mother said from the front porch. He did as he was told, following her through the door. "Have a seat, and tell me what's the matter."

"Mama—"

"Tell me, boy!"

He froze. In all their years together his mother had only raised her voice to him once, and that was when he'd come out to her. He sat. She served him a slice of peach pie. Everything was easier with peach pie. He cut a bite with his fork.

"I think I screwed things up with—are you sure you want to hear this?" She nodded and patted his hand. "The guy I'm making the table for?"

"That was him and his… *friend* at the door?"

He grimaced at the inflection in her voice. "They're not a couple… well, he says they're not, but… yeah, friends. Anyway, when I went to take measurements at his place, we got sort of close."

"Oh…." Alanna pressed a hand against her chest and watched her son warily, waiting for him to continue.

"Nothing happened beyond a kiss, Mama."

"And Lonnie found out about it."

"I told him but only after he told me he had kissed his ex."

His mother remained silent in the face of that information. She leaned back and yanked open a drawer to grab a fork. After scooping up a bite of Jamison's pie, she looked him in the eye and asked, "Why Lonnie?"

"Huh?"

She chewed slowly, thinking, swallowed, then said, "Baby, you'll be thirty soon. That's a lot of years, and I have to wonder…."

He sighed deeply. "If Lonnie's the reason I'm gay or the reason I came out?

She shrugged. "You *say* you love him."

He thought about it for several bites. "First, Mama," he said, taking her hand, "I'm not gay because of anyone else. I was born gay—" She started to speak, but he cut her off. "—whether you believe that or not, it's the truth. I've never felt for women the way I'm attracted to men, and," he continued, holding up a hand to forestall her again, "there is not a *right* girl out there for me."

He set his fork down. He'd lost his appetite for the pie. "Now, as for coming out?" Jamison closed his eyes and thought of the moment he'd seen Lonnie, stunned by his beauty, amused by his clumsiness, curious about his talent. He opened his eyes and looked into hers. "Lonnie is beautiful and funny and talented and smart and kind and strong and fierce, though he doesn't seem to know those things about himself. I look at him, Mama, and I see magic. When he smiles at me…."

"Yeah, baby?" Her eyes had gone wide.

Jamison placed a hand on his chest. "I feel like my heart's gonna burst it's so full. With Lonnie I'm not alone anymore." She opened her mouth, but he cut her off again. "I know, I know…. I have friends and family who love me, have always loved me, but at the time, none of you knew the real me. I've been lying to you for years. And when I met Lonnie? I felt like I could breathe."

She nodded. "I'm sorry you felt you couldn't be honest with us."

"I struggled for so long. Didn't know how to be a man like my father and be myself. Didn't think it was possible."

They sat together, silently finishing off the pie, their forks occasionally tapping each other. When they were done, Alanna softly said, "A couple of kisses couldn't have torn me and your daddy apart."

"It's not that simp—wait. Are you comparing you and Daddy to me and Lonnie?"

She shrugged and rose from the table to pour herself a mug of coffee. "All that you just told me…," she said, leaning against the kitchen counter and staring at him over the rim of her cup, "have you ever told him?"

"Not in those words." She frowned. "Well, no. Why?"

"You said he doesn't believe it about himself."

"He knows how I feel, but all that other stuff…?" He shrugged. "I'm not much of a talker, you know that."

His mother returned to her seat but kept her gaze fixed out the window. "Jamison, you know how I feel about this, but… that boy held my hand at the police station *and* in court. He…." She sighed. "He seems like a good man, and he for sure cares about you." She gripped his hand and locked eyes with him. "Sometimes people need to hear the why of things, baby."

SCREECHING TO a halt in his truck, Jamison jumped out and ran up the front steps of the Palmer home. He pounded on the door until Claude answered it. Then he strode right past him into the foyer and held his phone in front of the man's face. "Please tell me this is a joke!"

Claude blinked, staring at the screen. "It's a… it's a phone?"

"Lonnie's in France? France!"

"Come outside," Claude insisted, ushering him back out the door. "Amber and Remmy are taking a nap." They sat side by side in silence on the steps for several moments as the light afternoon traffic passed. Finally, Claude said, "I'm sorry, Jamison, but he flew out this morning around three."

"But… but…." He held his hands out, pleading. "Why would he do this?" he asked, staring at the ground. "We should talk, work things out, get past this."

"What did he tell you?"

He shook his head. "Missed the call. His message said something about settling his gran back in at the farm and maybe getting some painting done. He said we should 'take some time to figure out what we want.'"

"Is that such a bad idea?"

He stared at Claude, stunned by the question. "I *know* what I want!" Jamison quickly sobered, shaking off the anger and taking control of himself. "But," he said with a deep sigh, massaging his temples, "I guess Lonnie doesn't. He kissed Pool, ya know." He lifted his gaze to stare off across the street at the neat homes, much like the one he sat in front of. "Probably still has feelings for him."

Claude laughed suddenly and loudly. "Yeah, I'd say he has feelings, all right. Jamison, Lonnie punched JP in the nose when he showed up here yesterday, then hauled the idiot off to rehab."

"What?"

"The guy had the nerve to show up high, and he got a bit… uh, *grabby*. If he doesn't stay in treatment, he'll never get his life back."

Jamison sighed. "I wish I'd seen that."

"You and me both. Amber told me."

They didn't say anything for a few moments. Then Jamison asked, "What do I do?"

Claude thought for a few seconds. "Well, if it were Amber… I know what *I'd* do." They looked at each other, and a smile slowly spread across Jamison's face.

Chapter 28

LONNIE RETIED the yellow scarf containing his hair and watched the workings of the farm play out in front of him as he sat at the base of the big oak near the main house. It was the same tree he'd painted on Remmy's nursery wall, the same tree Amber had climbed as a child. The farmhands were returning after a long day of tending the vineyard. Normally his Uncle Benoit would be directing them, but he was away for the day, though Lonnie had no idea where.

His father's brother lived at the farm and managed everything for Gran, who was too old to handle the operation now. Unfortunately Benoit resembled Lonnie's late grandfather, Hubert, and seeing him again after so many years, Lonnie found that slightly unnerving at first, considering Hubert's treatment of him as a child. But within moments, Benoit had put Lonnie at ease with his warmth and honest joy at seeing him again. He was a big man and embraced Lonnie, swinging him around off his feet as he cheered his arrival.

Lonnie had never received such a reaction from Hubert. From the old man, he'd only gotten revulsion and rejection: his hair too long, too much like a girl, his skin too dark. It didn't matter that Amber had the same coloring, and much the same hair. For her, Hubert could muster some warmth. There was just too much wrong with Lonnie. He shivered at the memories, but then his thoughts went elsewhere.

He'd been back at the family farm for three days, but not an hour had gone by that he didn't miss Jamison. *It'll get easier*, he thought. *The longer I'm here, the better it will be. It's another world here.* He tugged a long blade of grass free of the ground and rubbed it between his thumb and finger. The color was rich, saturated. He thought he could almost smell the hue. The grass surrounding him and waving in the breeze as far as his eyes could see looked like a green ocean spread out before him, the whisper of its movement reaching his ears.

Surprisingly, he didn't feel much like drawing the beautiful scenery at the moment, so he gave up. He took a deep breath and gathered his sketchpad and pencils, tucking them away in his art box and then heading for the main house. When he entered, there was no one about, but Lonnie thought he heard his gran mucking around in the kitchen. Dinner would be ready soon.

He headed straight for the guestroom at the far end of the structure, not wanting his mood to darken her day. Once inside the simple but lovely room, he dumped his supplies, kicked off his sandals, and fell facedown on the handmade quilt covering the bed. The lace curtains on the window stirred in the unusually warm breeze that flooded the space with the smells of earth and plants, and the sound of birds.

It was so different from Overbrook, Maryland, not that the birds didn't sing there. They were just quickly drowned out by traffic noise. Not so on the Bellerose farm. Lonely thoughts filled his head again, and he wished Jamison could be beside him, listening to the sounds of the farm, breathing fresh air, holding him, touching him, kissing….

Lonnie woke with a start, momentarily perplexed by the wild shadows dancing across the walls of the room. The sun had gone down, and he sat up, remembering reading somewhere that sleeping too much was a sign of depression. The scarf he'd worn earlier had fallen off during sleep, and he retrieved it from the floor to secure his hair once again. More sharp shadows flared across the walls, and he realized a car was approaching, because there could be no shadows without light.

He got up and padded barefoot into the main entry hall to see who their visitor might be. He found his gran perched in front of the TV, knitting. The sound on the set was low, probably so as not to disturb him during his impromptu nap.

"Ah, c'est une vraie marmotte," Diane said with a warm smile.

"Oui, Grand-mère." He went to the front door and peered through the curtains, asking if she was expecting anyone. She didn't answer, so he turned back and found her focused on her craft but grinning slyly. Perplexed by the sound of tires on the rough-paved courtyard, Lonnie opened the front door.

The courtyard was dark except for the headlights of his uncle's old pickup. *Ah. Okay. He's back. I wonder if he needs help carrying anything.* He turned back to his gran to tell her it was just Uncle Benoit, but she had disappeared.

Huh? "Grand-mère, où es-tu?" He laughed in confusion as she reappeared, carrying her bag and wearing a light jacket.

"Benoît m'emmène dîner en ville." She patted his cheek and walked right past him into the courtyard. "Passe une bonne nuit, mon cheri."

He stared after her as she slowly made her way to the truck. Benoit jumped out and ran around to help her in. Then he waved good-bye, smiling the entire time, and got back behind the wheel. *That's odd. Maybe I'm dreaming.* As Lonnie watched the truck back out of the courtyard, his gran and uncle deserting him, Jamison stepped from beside the door and blocked his view. Lonnie stared up at him. *Yes. I'm still asleep. I'm dreaming—*

"*Bonsoir*, Lonnie," Jamison said, smiling.

Or not.

JAMISON HADN'T flown before and soon learned that sitting scrunched in coach on a flight to France was the antithesis of comfort, but he'd managed somehow. Lonnie would be at the end of the road, and wrapping him in his arms was all that mattered. He'd made arrangements, via Claude and Amber, for Lonnie's Uncle Benoit to pick him up at the train station. He'd used some of his windfall from furniture sales to pay for his first trip outside the US, but he had Temple's payment for the dining table to take some of the sting away.

From the jet to the train to the old pickup, and then, thankfully, to standing in front of the man he loved, the man with his beautiful mouth hanging open and his big green eyes wide with shock.

"Wha—?"

"Can I come in?" Jamison asked, brushing past Lonnie.

"What are you doing here?" Lonnie asked as he moved decisively toward Jamison, placed his hands on his broad chest, and pressed him back against a doorway leading to some other part of the farmhouse. As Lonnie kissed him, he unbuttoned Jamison's shirt and tugged it free of his pants. "God, I'm so happy to see you," Lonnie said, panting, shucking the cotton off Jamison's shoulders.

"L-Lon, hey. Wait!" Jamison laughed as he tried to fend him off.

"Why? You're here. Why would we wait?" Lonnie kissed him again, playing his eager tongue against Jamison's.

"D-don't… don't we need to talk?" Jamison asked after freeing his mouth from Lonnie's.

Lonnie froze and met his eye. "Oh." He stepped back and hugged himself, kept his gaze focused on the floor.

"Babe, why did you leave?"

Lonnie shrugged but didn't meet Jamison's eye. "Seemed logical at the time."

"Lon—"

"I wasn't trying to be dramatic or anything—"

"Which means you were."

"—I honestly thought you should probably meet some other men. Might be good for you." Lonnie finally looked up. "I mean, you settled for me pretty quickly."

He grinned and closed in on Lonnie, reaching out to caress his arms. "Nothing about you is 'settling,' babe. Tu es le seul homme que je veuille."

Lonnie stared openmouthed at him, tears welling in his eyes.

"Amber helped me," Jamison said. "Made me a recording, and I practiced all the way here." He freed Lonnie's hair from the scarf and ran his fingers through it. "I needed you to hear me when I said you're all I want or need."

Lonnie stepped close again and pressed his body against Jamison, running his palms over his now-bare chest. "I bet you got some strange looks on the plane, huh?"

"A couple, but I wanted to get the words just right." Jamison leaned down and took Lonnie's lips gently. "Where's your bedroom?"

Lonnie beamed and gripped his hand to drag him down the hall. Once inside, Lonnie flicked on the bedside light and began quickly undressing Jamison, who simply stood there and let it happen. Inch by inch, Jamison's dark, smooth skin was revealed until he was butt naked and standing there with his cock at attention.

"Uh… your gran isn't coming back any time soon, is she?" he asked.

"She went to dinner with Uncle Benoit," Lonnie said, taking hold of Jamison and stroking him. "Aw, you're so happy to see me."

"You have no idea, but I was upset with your little message."

Lonnie's hand stilled, and he had the presence of mind to look ashamed. "I took the coward's way out, I know, but—"

"But you thought it was best for me." Lonnie nodded, and Jamison reached out and touched his face. "How could us being apart ever be best, babe?"

"You kissed Temple."

"Sorry about that."

"And he's gorgeous and talented and rich and sexy."

"He's got a sexy Southern twang, that's true."

"Hey!"

Jamison chuckled and pulled Lonnie against him. "It was one kiss. It didn't go any further."

Lonnie rubbed against Jamison's swollen cock. "Why not?"

He groaned and then put a finger under Lonnie's chin to gently lift his gaze so their eyes met. "He's not you, Alonzo Bellerose."

Lonnie sighed and shoved Jamison so the two of them fell on the bed. Then he began to strip in earnest as Jamison watched appreciatively.

"However…," he continued, and Lonnie stopped, his shirt halfway off.

"What?"

"About Pool."

Lonnie snorted. "That idiot kissed me—"

"But you *liked* it."

"*Maybe*… for a moment." Lonnie bit his lip, grinning. Then he tossed his shirt on the floor and slid his hands over the expanse of Jamison's body. "But then I remembered everything he put me through, and standing next to you, he falls way short"—Lonnie straddled Jamison's lap and gently rocked his ass against him—"in more ways than one, Jamison Coburn." He nibbled a nipple, drawing a gasp and full-body quiver from Jamison.

"Dammit, Lon, you need to get these pants off."

"That's all you have to say?"

"Huh?"

"Make me feel good."

"I can do that," he said, beaming.

"Tell me a failing of… Schrodinger."

Oh. Jamison thought about it, which was the wrong thing to do. When he saw Lonnie's expression growing stormy, he quickly said, "His hair's too straight, boring."

Lonnie raised an eyebrow. "Really?" he asked in apparent disbelief.

"And he's not interested in a one and only."

"Ooh," Lonnie said, nodding, "I can see that being a problem."

"It's awful," Jamison added before capturing Lonnie's mouth again and working him out of his pants. Next he rolled them over, pinning Lonnie beneath him. "Heard you punched Pool." He nibbled at Lonnie's neck, breathed him in. He'd been without Lonnie for too many unpleasant days.

"JP? Hell yeah! He wouldn't let go of me, literally and figuratively speaking. He kept saying he wanted his life back, and somehow he got it into his head I needed to be part of that life to make it work."

"We need to make sure he backs the fuck off."

"He has... I took him to rehab." Lonnie's face clouded for a moment. "You should have seen him. He wasn't going to come back from this last bender if he didn't take action right away."

"He's lucky you were there... and still cared."

Lonnie focused on Jamison's gaze again and kissed him deeply.

When they parted, Jamison said, "Move in with me."

"Say what?"

"You heard me. That's what I was rushing home to ask you that day we... we walked away from each other. I'd spent the night at Temple's—"

Lonnie blew a raspberry, and Jamison smiled.

"—and I didn't want to spend any more nights away from you."

Lonnie stared at him, apparently seeking the truth of the statement. "Roll over," he whispered, and once Jamison had, Lonnie slid down his body and took Jamison in his mouth.

"I... I, uh... g-guess that's a y-yes?"

BENOIT TIED the vine, and Jamison copied him on the next one, then looked into his eyes, as if he understood what the man was saying.

Lonnie explained, "He says you're a quick learner."

This was how they'd spent portions of the past two days: Lonnie translating every conversation Jamison had with Diane and Benoit and any other farmhand they happen to meet as they explored the property. The rolling hills and boundless blue sky made him fill his lungs deeply and smile as he gazed around him. It seemed to go on forever, and he just wanted to roll in the grass with Lonnie in his arms. In fact, they'd done just that a couple times when no one else was about.

They were flying home tomorrow morning, back to their lives together. He was eager to find a place they could rent as a couple, a place they could call their home... at least until they were ready to buy a house.

"I forgot to ask. Did you finish Schrodinger's table before you left?" Lonnie stopped and suddenly cackled. "That sounds like some kind of formula, doesn't it? But... did you? Finish, I mean?" His chuckles died off.

"Nearly," Jamison said as he tugged on a branch from the big oak on the property. A leisurely evening stroll was on their agenda. As they made their way to the single-lane road, the sunset blazing on the horizon almost brought a tear to Jamison's eye. "Temple gave me an extension. Said love was more important than furniture."

Lonnie frowned. "That was nice of him, I guess."

"I could see you and Temple becoming friends someday— *someday*."

Lonnie snorted. "Sure," he said, twirling in the road, arms thrown wide, "we'll be the best of buddies. I can see it all now."

Jamison took Lonnie's hand, and they made their way to the wide dirt road. A breeze stirred the trees that lined the road, and Jamison gazed up, enjoying the wind and the pleasant rustle it created. The lights of the farmhouse didn't reach very far, so they lingered, alone among the shadows. Tonight there was a decided chill in the air, but Lonnie told him it had been unseasonably warm up until Jamison had arrived. The family expected the vineyard yield to be fine despite the shifts in temperature.

"Okay, okay. Message received." Jamison laughed softly and peered through the trees at the stars beginning to appear. He sighed. "It's so beautiful here." He looked at Lonnie. "How do I say that in French?"

"C'est tellement beau ici," Lonnie said, and Jamison repeated it, or tried to. "We'll... have to work on the pronunciation." Lonnie stepped into Jamison's arms and backed him against a tree. "Here, let me show you how to use your tongue."

Epilogue

"STOP COMPLAINING!" Lonnie commanded, gently slapping Jamison's smooth head.

"I'm not," Jamison insisted. "I just think it's silly for a grown man to make a wish and blow out candles on a cake."

"Well, something needs to happen," Torp said, standing to the side with his arm around Kimmy and a drink in his other hand. "There's thirty candles on that thing. You don't want to burn the place down!"

Everyone who had squeezed around Alanna's kitchen table—Lincoln, Amber with Remmy, Ginger, Temple, Staz, Aunt Jo, and Uncle Ray—laughed, then fell silent as Jamison silently made his wish. He blew out the candles, and his gaze immediately found Lonnie's as they all applauded. Alanna and Ginger went to work cutting and passing out the cake to the guests, while Lincoln and Ray hustled back out to man the grill.

"I told him it's too cold to be grilling out," Alanna admonished, shaking her head at Lincoln's retreating form. But he caught the smile gracing her lips as well.

When she passed Lonnie a slice, she leaned in and whispered, "I cut you a corner piece. They have the most frosting."

Lonnie blushed and accepted the cake. "Thank you, ma'am."

Jamison wrapped his mother up in his arms, lifted her off her feet, and kissed her cheek, then said, "Thank you, Mama."

She squealed and slapped at his shoulders. "You're welcome, baby. Now put me down!" She was still chuckling softly when she asked, "So now you're a thirty-year-old man. How do you feel?"

Jamison looked around the room, noting the animated faces, laughter, conversations—even Lonnie was speaking to Temple—and suddenly foremost in his mind was his father. "I miss Daddy. I wish he could be part of this, see where I am, see who loves me." His gaze drank in Lonnie, and he smiled to see Temple making him laugh.

Alanna squeezed his hand. "He sees it, baby. Believe that. Your Daddy sees it all."

HAIR HANGING heavy with sweat, hands slipping on sweaty skin, Lonnie clawed at Jamison's shoulders, locking eyes with him as he lifted and lowered himself, as he rode him, filled by Jamison. Angling himself just right to strike his sweet spot, Lonnie gasped and grinned, his head swimming.

"*Uh...* so good, Lon," Jamison panted.

"Yes... *yes* it is," Lonnie whispered. Jamison squeezed his eyes shut, bit his lip, tightened his grip on Lonnie's waist. "That's it, baby. Come! I'm ready. Come for me!"

They came together shouting, grunting, panting, then laughing softly as Lonnie collapsed on top. The chuckling continued, and Lonnie asked, "What's so funny?"

"Nothing." Jamison shook his head. "Just thinking of something my mother said the other day."

Lonnie sighed. "That was a great party, but all I heard from Temple is 'Why couldn't we have this at my place? I've got this kickass new table and loads of room.'"

"We'll christen the table at some point, but it was nice to have everyone I care about there."

Lonnie snuggled closer. "Worlds collide."

"Uh-huh." Jamison yawned and stretched.

"Mmm, you sound content," Lonnie mused.

"You have no idea."

"I know exactly what it feels like, thank you very much." Lonnie stroked Jamison's chest and pressed his crotch against his thigh.

"Hey, I'm thirty now. I'm gonna need a bit more recovery time, babe."

Lonnie laughed. "I just like being close to you. No expectations, no pressure."

"While I catch my breath, why don't you tell me which apartment you liked best out of the ones we've seen so far?"

"That's easy. First floor of the duplex on Doulton." It was a great old white-and-dusty-blue house split into two apartments, first floor and second. Jamison laughed softly, which perplexed Lonnie. "Something else amusing?"

Jamison rolled over to face him, or at least that's what Lonnie thought he was doing. "That's my favorite too. It's in a nice neighborhood between the university and Lincoln's, lots of natural light, especially in that back room." Jamison stretched over Lonnie to reach the nightstand. "I'll make the call."

"What?" Lonnie exclaimed as Jamison dug through the drawer for the number. "Now? Really?"

Jamison looked into Lonnie's eyes. "Yes, Lon. I don't want to wait any longer, not for anything. We've been together two months, and we've filled most of that time with questions and doubt. But you and me... trusting in us? That's the answer, babe... puts it all to rest." After dialing, he smiled at Lonnie, then kissed him, and Lonnie melted against him, wrapped in warmth, love, and acceptance.

DAWN KIMBERLY JOHNSON is a native of West Virginia, where she earned a BA from the Marshall University W. Page Pitt School of Journalism and Mass Communications. She worked as a copy editor at the *Charleston Daily Mail* for eight years before quitting and driving alone across the country to settle in Oregon. After many adventures out West, she's back in her home state, doing the best she can. She enjoys writing just after waking, after her characters have strolled through her subconscious, chatting with one another, making love, arguing, figuring out how to live their lives and hold on to their lovers.

Blog: http://kimswritingagain.wordpress.com/
Twitter: https://twitter.com/Dawn_KJ
Facebook: https://www.facebook.com/DawnKimberlyJohnson
E-mail: KimsWritingAgain@yahoo.com

Audible

By Dawn Kimberly Johnson

Three years ago, cameraman Powell Perdue and quarterback Talbot Wojewódka called it quits, citing irreconcilable differences. Powell wanted to live honestly, while Talbot felt he couldn't and still succeed in professional football. One knee surgery and a trade later, Talbot finds himself back in town and quarterbacking for the Raptors, a struggling expansion team. Powell's also back, working as a cameraman for KJOC-TV, following two years in Amsterdam and a second failed relationship.

When an interview meant as a publicity play throws them into each other's path, they're forced to face a love that never quite died and wounds that never fully healed. For any hope at a win, they'll have to change up the game. Talbot must brave walking through his closet door and into Powell's arms, and Powell must risk his heart one more time by standing his ground and giving Talbot a second chance.

http://www.dreamspinnerpress.com

Broken

By Dawn Kimberly Johnson

Alec Sumner is fleeing yet another broken heart. By moving to London, he hopes to find peace and a fresh start. While shopping with a friend on a busy London street, he sees his chance, embodied in a mysterious young man with soulful blue eyes and a bad leg.

Eli Burke is broken in his own way, haunted by memories of his lover's murder and physically scarred from the same fatal assault. He, too, plans to run away—to Africa and a new life working with children. But when he meets Alec, his choice isn't so easy. He and Alec see the real possibility of new love and a brighter future, but they'll both have to face their fears of past pain and find a way to heal.

http://www.dreamspinnerpress.com

Home

By Dawn Kimberly Johnson

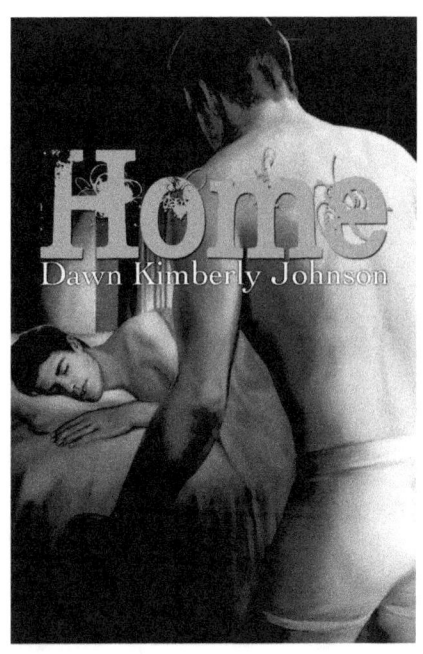

Eli Burke and Alec Sumner are finding out that falling in love isn't the happily-ever-after they expected. Their efforts to move forward as a couple and put their broken pasts behind them are made all the more difficult by new fears and old secrets.

There are other stressors too: disagreeing over where to live, dealing with other men intruding into their relationship, and deciding if they must abandon the families of their pasts to build one for the future.

It may hurt, but being honest about what they fear, what they've done, and what they want may be the only way to forge a happy home.

http://www.dreamspinnerpress.com

Button Down

By Dawn Kimberly Johnson

When he finds himself captivated by a movie-star handsome stranger he meets in a bar, lawyer Ford Reilly watches a simple one-night stand develop into a taste of what living honestly might bring him.

Out and proud Gus Hansen has built a small architectural firm from nothing, but could lose it all as he tries to break a contract he signed before knowing about the project's antigay ties.

After Ford discovers he spent a passionate night with the man on the other side of the dispute he's handling, he finds himself in more than one quandary. He can either maintain the status quo, enforcing the contract to the letter, or he can defy his overbearing father and break free of the closeted life he's built for himself in order to be with Gus.

Gus has his own choices to make. He knows the sting of loving a man who hides himself, but the longer he lingers in Ford's presence, the more difficult it becomes to deny their attraction.

http://www.dreamspinnerpress.com

Right on Time

By Dawn Kimberly Johnson

Throughout his life, successful artist Barnaby Rosenthal has been rescued repeatedly by his one constant, Charleston Meeks. But it's been seven tumultuous years since he's last seen the temporal agent outside of his dreams and paintings.

Recently retired from his father's Restore Point Program, Charleston's ready to approach Barnaby in their present year of 2020 and discover if the two of them can build a future on their harried past.

Standing between them is a conservative senator determined to erase the people saved by the RPP, and much of her rage is focused on Barnaby. For the senator, time travel goes against God's plan, so with the help of her hired guns, she intends to correct the program's meddling by any means necessary.

For the first time, Charleston may not be there to save Barnaby.

http://www.dreamspinnerpress.com

Plummet

By Dawn Kimberly Johnson

Dealing, or rather not dealing, with a recent breakup, Ari Melrose, CPA, nearly takes his car over a cliff. Instead, he is rescued by Brandt Steuben, a big, burly ex-firefighter who pulls him to safety and into his arms. Near-death experiences can make normally careful, rational people grab life by the horns, or men by the biceps, and hop on for a wild ride, so Ari figures what better way to get over his problems than to work them out with his super-hot savior? But a fateful afternoon soon leads to more than physical passion, and Ari finds he might not want to let go of Brandt.

http://www.dreamspinnerpress.com

What Happened to Larry Alan?

By Dawn Kimberly Johnson

Judson Heart, like all of us, has some regrets. Not his job: he writes for a daily newspaper. Maybe his introspection: he eats lunch alone. Definitely his timing: he hasn't had much luck in the love department. With his ten-year reunion approaching, those regrets intensify as he begins to recall a turbulent final year of high school. But with the help of three elderly, mystical strangers and a surprising assignment to interview a prison inmate, Jud may get the chance to make some changes. All he needs to do is find out what happened to Larry Alan.

http://www.dreamspinnerpress.com

Dirk Hunter

AFTER SCHOOL ACTIVITIES

http://www.dreamspinnerpress.com

GERRY'S LION

ashavan doyon

http://www.dreamspinnerpress.com

LINEMATES

D K DUNN

http://www.dreamspinnerpress.com

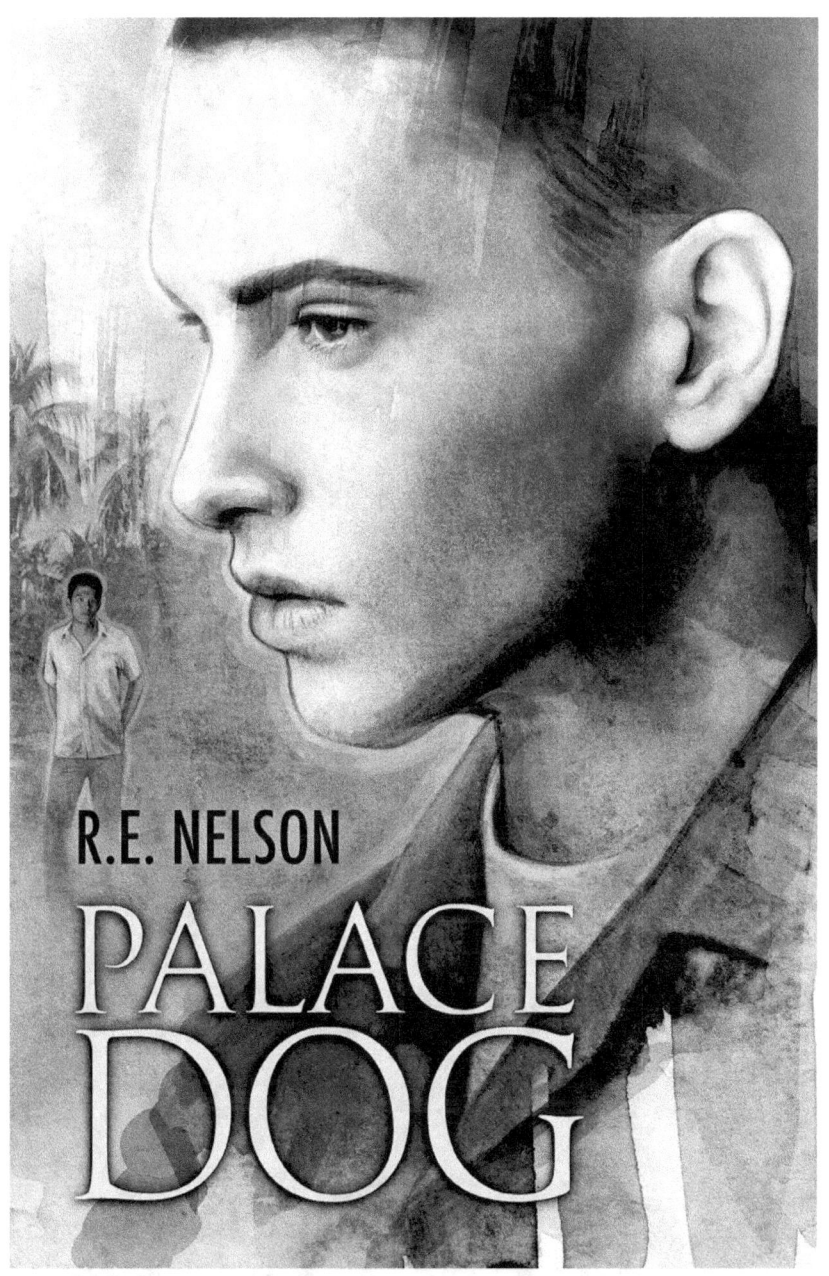

R.E. NELSON

PALACE
DOG

http://www.dreamspinnerpress.com

FOR **MORE** OF THE **BEST GAY ROMANCE**

DREAMSPINNER PRESS

dreamspinnerpress.com

www.ingramcontent.com/pod-product-compliance
Lightning Source LLC
Chambersburg PA
CBHW070117260626
47160CB00004B/1510